FROM THE AUTHOR

Writing **The Taming of a Scandal** was bittersweet for me. Phaedra Barrington has long been a favorite of readers and it took me longer than expected to craft a partner that was perfect for her. I hope I've done her justice.

And while Phaedra is technically the last of the Barringtons, **The Taming of a Scandal** is not the final book in *The Beautiful Barringtons*.

The Taming of a Scandal can be read as a stand-alone, but it does contain characters first introduced in **The Making of a Gentleman**. Enjoyment of this book will be greatly enhanced by starting at the beginning with **The Theory of Earls**.

THE TAMING OF A SCANDAL

KATHLEEN AYERS

Editing by Midnight Owl

Cover by Covers & Cupcakes

CONTENTS

From the Author   v

Prologue   1
Chapter 1   35
Chapter 2   52
Chapter 3   58
Chapter 4   68
Chapter 5   77
Chapter 6   82
Chapter 7   93
Chapter 8   100
Chapter 9   103
Chapter 10   118
Chapter 11   139
Chapter 12   151
Chapter 13   162
Chapter 14   166
Chapter 15   177
Chapter 16   185
Chapter 17   190
Chapter 18   206
Chapter 19   212
Chapter 20   221
Chapter 21   230
Chapter 22   236
Chapter 23   248
Chapter 24   254
Chapter 25   261
Chapter 26   266
Chapter 27   273
Epilogue   280

Author Notes   289

PROLOGUE

Hagerty's Boxing Establishment, London

L ady Phaedra Barrington skirted along the edges of the dusty interior of Hagerty's doing her best to avoid notice. Lord Torrington wasn't yet visible or near the roped off area which served as the boxing ring, but if Cousin Rosalind's husband saw Phaedra milling about, he was likely to toss her in a hack and send her home. She'd successfully managed to follow Torrington to Hagerty's on more than one occasion after noticing he often sported small injuries to his person which could only mean he either brawled or boxed.

Torrington didn't strike her as much of a brawler. He was far too elegant to be found fighting in a tavern, which meant fisticuffs. The gentlemanly sort.

And since Phaedra had an interest in such things, it seemed perfectly acceptable, at least to her, that she find out what Torrington was up to. But several weeks ago, during her last visit, Torrington had spotted her.

Phaedra paused for a moment as the toe of her half-boot

kicked at the remains of a rind of cheese hidden in the sawdust covering the floor.

Torrington had not been pleased. Even less happy to find that Phaedra had been frequenting Hagerty's and had made friends both with Boggins, who manned the boxing establishment's front door, as well as Mr. Hagerty himself.

A heated discussion had ensued. Phaedra had insisted she had every right to continue to venture to this seedy, dilapidated building in a run-down neighborhood. Boxing interested her. She carried a knife or a small rapier, depending on the situation. And, most importantly, her brother was the Duke of Averell. She was perfectly safe.

Torrington had vehemently disagreed. He'd threatened to inform Tony, her ducal brother, if she did not desist. The area was dangerous, and Phaedra was far from safe. Hagerty's boasted a cast of unsavory characters who didn't give a fig if she was a lady or that Tony was a duke. Phaedra could be hurt. Or worse. Torrington had taken her arm and dragged her unceremoniously outside to his carriage.

How will you explain that cut above your eye to Cousin Rosalind? Phaedra had sweetly countered, pleased when Torrington's mouth had thinned into a taut line and his footsteps had halted.

Rosalind, Phaedra's tart-baking cousin, was Lady Torrington. She wouldn't approve of her husband boxing and would be furious to know he was frequenting Hagerty's. Rosalind tended to be overprotective where Torrington was concerned. If she could put Torrington in a tiny bubble, where he couldn't so much as catch a cold, Rosalind would. She seemed to live in constant fear of Torrington being hurt or dropping dead while baking a soufflé.

Ridiculous, really. Torrington was in perfect health.

Détente had been the result of Phaedra's contentious conversation with Torrington.

A fragile truce.

She had promised Torrington that he wouldn't *see* her set foot in Hagerty's again. And Phaedra had kept that promise. There were many dark corners where she could hide in this large building which looked as if it might collapse at any moment. Torrington hadn't spotted her in some time. Phaedra observed the fights in peace while staying clear of her cousin's husband.

In future, Torrington should be careful in the wording of his demands. Phaedra was an expert at finding loopholes. She'd been outsmarting Tony for years.

Leo Murphy, her bastard half-brother, was far harder to deceive. Thankfully, he wasn't always in London.

Phaedra had become masterful at sneaking out of the Averell mansion unseen. She always took a hack to Hagerty's, one she hailed at some distance from her brother's home, careful not to be seen by any of the duke's servants, who would run straight to Pith, the Averell butler, with the news that Lady Phaedra was up to something. Pith had even placed a bounty on her. Imagine, paying the servants extra to tattle on her. She didn't think that the duty of a butler.

Nor did Phaedra possess any guilt over outmaneuvering Pith.

Buying the silence of Mr. Hagerty, however, had proved to be more difficult and required a month's worth of pin money. She couldn't have Mr. Hagerty mentioning her visits to Torrington—or anyone else. Completely worth the expense. Phaedra assured Mr. Hagerty the odds were incredibly slim that anyone would see or notice her.

Phaedra would know. She was an expert on odds. Nearly as good as Leo. He ran a gambling hell and could quote the laws of probability to anyone bored enough to listen. But calculating the odds in hazard wasn't considered very ladylike, though neither was boxing, fencing, or Phaedra's latest passion, knives.

Sidling along the wall, staying silent and drawing no attention, Phaedra concentrated on reaching the far corner, which had nothing to recommend it but a barrel. She'd had to accede to Mr. Hagerty's demands in order to continue her visits. No setting so much as a toe near the roped off area where the men fought. Do not be seen, and if she was, do not make eye contact or speak directly to anyone. No offering of her dubious opinion on matches—unfortunate because Phaedra thought her views enlightening. Absolutely no wagering. She was to stay hidden and out of sight. And under no circumstances was Phaedra to stray anywhere near the makeshift bar where Mr. Hagerty served gin to his patrons.

A pity because Phaedra had always wanted to try gin.

Mr. Hagerty, resigned to having Phaedra in his fine establishment, cautioned her that while he had a pistol stuck in his belt, it would do no good if some ruffian carried her off before he could use it. The men who frequented Hagerty's weren't the sort to be put off by a haughty manner or precise diction. Nor would they pause in their pursuit, even knowing she was a duke's sister. They were a collection of coarse men, their existence dependent on wagers, picking pockets, and stealing. All should be given wide berth.

Phaedra kept to her part of the bargain, staying as unobtrusive as possible so as not to draw attention, though a few curious patrons swilling gin outside Hagerty's had seen fit to address Phaedra as she'd snuck inside today. Boggins had snarled at one man, reminding him that the lady was not to be approached, but Phaedra had still felt eyes drilling into her back as she'd made her way inside.

Someday soon, Phaedra might need to bribe one of the Averell footmen to accompany her to Hagerty's. Probably Jonesy. He wasn't as afraid of Pith as the others.

Despite Mr. Hagerty's concerns—and Torrington's—she remained unafraid. The vast majority of Hagerty's patrons were merely stumbling about in gin-soaked euphoria, eager to see a bit of blood flying through the air during a fight. Not the least dangerous. And even if she'd been concerned, Phaedra had been taught early on that much like dogs, humans could smell one's panic and distress. Best not to give into it.

You are a daughter of the Duke of Averell. Me. Never let them see your fear or the wolves will pounce.

Papa's admonition, one made probably more on how to deal with the gossiping matrons of London society than the inhabitants of a place like Hagerty's, but the advice was still sound.

She stumbled at the thought of her father, but instantly righted herself.

Phaedra could still hear that rolling baritone, like a burst of thunder, demanding that she listen. How she missed the *sound* of Marcus Barrington. The scent of him, all worn leather and cheroot with a hint of smoke. The inherent arrogance that surrounded him like a cloak, so outrageously ducal and commanding, daring anyone to defy him. Phaedra had lived securely beneath that armor, confident nothing could ever touch her.

She blinked, not seeing Hagerty's for a moment but instead the pale shell of her father propped up in bed at Cherry Hill. His life ebbing away before Phaedra's very eyes. She hadn't learned odds from Leo, but Papa. He'd taught her to play whist and faro. Vingt-un. Just as he had Leo when her brother was no more than a child. How to bluff and read the tells of your opponents. She'd never beaten her father at cards until he was near the end.

The sting of longing for Papa struck hard, stretching over her heart. Always so sharp. Like teeth digging into her skin.

It had faded over time, but never completely went away. Phaedra often wondered how Mama survived it.

"She has," Phaedra said under her breath. "But not very well."

A large barrel awaited her, pushed into a darkened corner where whatever light managing to infiltrate Hagerty's didn't quite reach. She was farther from the fights in this part of the building, but if she climbed atop the old barrel and sat, Phaedra would be able to clearly see the ring. Several old crates surrounded her, along with an abandoned pile of bricks, but nothing else. Not even the mice cared for this spot.

Hopping up, Phaedra smoothed down her skirts, glancing about the immediate vicinity to ensure no one had noticed her. The weight of a small knife rested against one thigh, hidden in the pocket of her dress. Pockets in dresses and gowns were something Romy, her eldest sister and discreetly practicing modiste, insisted upon in her designs. Entirely useful. Romy reasoned that if men had pockets, why shouldn't ladies?

Clever Romy.

Phaedra's sister was brilliant, tackling every challenge with a confidence few possessed. Her only misstep had been in choosing the Duke of Granby as her husband. Why would anyone want to spend their life cuddled beside an enormous block of ice? Love, Phaedra supposed.

Her fingers, inside the hidden pocket, absently stroked the hilt of the blade. She only knew the basics in wielding the small weapon. Everyone she'd approached—three footmen, two grooms and eventually Pith—had refused to teach her. But someone was bound to relent eventually. Phaedra had a habit of wearing a person down until they gave in. The trait made her brilliant at negotiating with the wine merchant at Elysium.

Another thing I am no longer permitted to do.

She adored Leo, but sometimes she wished her brother had stayed in New York. Since his marriage to Georgina and having become a father, Leo seemed to think he was qualified to offer his opinion on Phaedra's behavior. Which was not welcome. At all.

Turning her attention to the match before her, Phaedra studied the two men as they circled each other, attempting to discern strengths and weaknesses. Had Torrington only relented, he and Phaedra could have had a spirited discussion on fisticuffs. She had several strong recommendations for him on his form.

"He wouldn't appreciate my suggestions at any rate," she said out loud.

The sound of fists thudding into flesh met her ears. Over and over. A slight coppery tang hovered in the air along with the smells of sawdust, sweat, and gin. The atmosphere, one of violence and unrestrained savagery, sent a surge of excitement down Phaedra's spine. Not the sort of entertainment a young lady of good breeding should enjoy.

A person's pedigree is overrated, Phaedra, Papa had often said. *We are not horses or dogs. Some of the worst human beings I've ever known, myself included, were notoriously well-bred.*

She placed a palm on her heart to still the returning sting before turning her attention once more to the fight.

The men inside the roped off area were evenly matched, something that didn't happen often at Hagerty's. Usually, one fighter had a physical advantage. Big fists. Prior experience. Gracefulness on their feet. While challengers often entered the ring at the urging of friends or by the lure of a large purse. Those fighters usually lost.

Several punches were thrown in succession. Droplets of blood sprayed upward into the air. One of the men went face down in the sawdust with a resounding plop.

Phaedra leaned forward to get a better view, watching as Hagerty, pencil and pad stuck in the brim of his hat, pressed through the crowd. He kept his wagers on that tiny pad of paper, his writing barely legible. While pressing her pin money into Hagerty's palm, Phaedra had attempted to convince him she would be an excellent asset to his business. Wagers, she'd insisted, were an area in which she had a great deal of experience, having been involved in the running of Elysium, the gaming establishment owned by her brothers.

Hagerty laughed. *This ain't no fine ducal pleasure palace, my lady.*

More gambling hell, she'd corrected automatically. It was an important distinction.

Nevertheless, Hagerty had refused her offer.

Hagerty's was not the sort of place where any gentleman, titled or otherwise, ordinarily engaged in fisticuffs. Torrington's patronage was an anomaly. Dozens of clubs in London were devoted to the sport. Pampered lords ventured to such places to slap and hurl insults at each other while their valets stood by to dab at a bloodied lip with a handkerchief. Lord Emberly, who had hoped to impress Phaedra with his manly form, had invited Phaedra to his own club so she could observe his prowess.

Needless to say, Phaedra could punch better than Emberly. The insults he'd used on his opponent, however, had been top notch.

Phaedra's lips pursed in annoyance. Emberly was exactly the sort of gentleman she was supposed to find appealing. He didn't even mind that she was a Barrington. But Emberly, though she liked him well enough, didn't interest her. Marcus Barrington had been an elegant, refined duke. Not the least rough in appearance. But when Papa had stepped into a room, he'd commanded with barely a word. His presence alone had been enough to force others to their knees. A man you would not wish as your enemy.

Emberly, bless him, had little in the way of presence and couldn't even throw a punch properly, which was a pity because Phaedra did enjoy his company. There was also Lord Hyde, whom Phaedra could outride even sidesaddle. And poor St. Clare. Had he any intelligence, it was well hidden. None of her potential suitors appealed to her at all.

Hagerty stepped inside the circle of ropes. Checked the man who'd fallen to the floor for a pulse, nodded, and had him carried away to be propped up in a corner until he opened his eyes. Hagerty made sure to have a glass of gin placed at the man's elbow for when he awoke. Phaedra thought that a nice touch.

A roar went up. The sounds of wagers won and lost, of coins slapped in palms, echoed through the sawdust choked air. Hagerty held up his pencil and pad, taking wagers for the next fight.

Hagerty's was a decent substitute for Elysium, but it *wasn't* Elysium.

Leo, upon his return from New York, had banned *his infant sister* from the gambling hell. Phaedra, he'd thundered, should be attending balls and being taken for carriage rides in the park. Paying calls and taking up embroidery.

Ugh and ugh.

Upon finding Phaedra seated calmly behind the massive desk in his office at Elysium, counting out markers and making notes in the ledger for Tony, a vein had popped out on Leo's forehead. Honestly, Phaedra had grown concerned Leo would have a fit of apoplexy and fall over onto the disgusting, blood-red settee he insisted on keeping in his office.

The settee was uncomfortable, possessed garish cushions, and belonged in a brothel.

Leo claimed the settee had sentimental value.

Needless to say, after a somewhat hostile, heated discussion between Leo and Tony, Phaedra was no longer permitted to count markers, negotiate with merchants on Elysium's behalf, or run odds at the hazard table. No matter how much she'd overseen Elysium's affairs for Tony in Leo's absence.

Completely unfair.

The management of Elysium was the only thing Phaedra was good at. Papa had taught her everything he knew about cards, odds, wagering and the like. She could run a faro table, not that she'd ever been allowed to. Spot someone cheating from across the gaming floor. Run numbers in the ledgers far faster than Tony and determine interest accrued on a debt in a trice. None of those skills were relevant, however, when one was a duke's daughter. Or even a Barrington.

Phaedra's sisters and Cousin Rosalind all possessed a particular skill. Talents practiced discreetly. Rosalind owned a bakery, for goodness's sake. Phaedra had tried to find something more acceptable than running a game of hazard or determining the value of a wager, but the only other interest Phaedra had besides Elysium and boxing was weaponry.

"I blame you, Marcus Barrington," she whispered while watching the two men across the building pummel each other. "All those bloodthirsty stories of Romans thrusting spears into the Celts." Papa had liked military history.

"Well, what have we here?"

Phaedra had been so absorbed in her utter despondency at having been barred from Elysium—and her obvious unsuitability for nearly everything else—that she'd failed to note the approach of a slightly shady looking gentleman...*no, two*... in the dim light.

The pair barely stood out from the broken crates and sawdust, looking nearly as worn and tawdry as their surroundings. She recognized them as the two who'd been warned off by Boggins outside earlier.

She glanced across the open space to the roped off area. Mr. Hagerty was on the other side of the room. He might hear her cry for help over the noise of the crowd. Or not.

The taller of the two sported a mop of dirty hair and a sore on his cheek, which, judging by the angry red color along the edges, was infected. The other man smiled, showing Phaedra a row of broken teeth, some missing all together. Both smelled like the inside of a dirty gin bottle found floating in the Thames.

The Thames. Lord Hallowick had wagered *one hundred pounds* in Elysium's Red Book that Phaedra would discard her clothing and go swimming in that filthy stretch of water. Why on earth would she do such a thing?

Hallowick was an idiot.

"You look a bit lonely, dove."

Phaedra pointedly ignored him, keeping her focus solely on the match taking place. Her hand slid into her pocket, fingers closing over the hilt of her knife.

"Too good to speak to me, are you?"

She continued to pay him no heed, even as he shuffled closer. *Boil*—she decided to name the man with the unfortunate sore on his cheek.

"Look, dove, I just want to share my gin with you. Have a swallow." Boil's breath was far worse than she'd expected. Like the rot one finds under a pile of mushrooms.

"No, thank you." Her icy dismissal was one guaranteed to send any gentleman fleeing in an instant. Except this was Hagerty's, and there were no gentlemen present. "I bid you good afternoon."

Boil shifted nervously at her haughty, confident tone, glancing in question at his friend.

He and the sore on his cheek were followers and wouldn't

act without someone leading them to do so. The other man, the one who hadn't so much as blinked at her tone, was the more dangerous of the two. Rabid in appearance. His ratty coat had a tear in the shoulder, and dung was caked over the tops of his boots. If he had ever been clean, it was a lifetime ago.

Ratty Coat.

Taking off his hat to reveal a matted head of tangled, greasy hair, Ratty Coat gave her a mocking bow. "A fancy lady like you must want to roll about in the dirt if you're at Hagerty's. Give yourself a bit of fun. Must get boring in Mayfair."

Phaedra didn't answer.

"I've seen you hanging about. Looking for amusement, are you?" He winked at her, full of false charm and reeking of gin, the sour smell nearly making her gag. "Lady who likes the fights is the kind I wish to know."

Boil took a swig from his own bottle of gin, nodding eagerly.

Ignoring them hadn't done any good. In fact, her silence had only seemed to encourage them. The knife in her pocket wasn't large, but Phaedra was reasonably sure she could stick Ratty Coat in the neck if he got too close. Screaming might bring Hagerty running—if he could hear her over the roar of the crowd. Torrington *was* here, but not where she could see him, and he would come running. But if Phaedra couldn't handle this problem herself, she would be forced to admit Torrington was correct and she shouldn't be here. Narrowing her eyes in distaste, she took in the two men. She'd been so bloody careful. Followed every rule Hagerty had set before her, though she was terrible at rules. And now these two filthy individuals were going to ruin things.

"Think you're too good for us, don't you, Miss Fancy Lace?"

Miss Fancy Lace. How eloquent. Truly a master of the English language.

"I heard you quite clearly," Phaedra retorted in a crisp tone. "But I do not care for gin. The smell puts me off. As do you." Her fingers tightened on the hilt of the knife. "My brother, the Duke of Averell," she said with authority, "wouldn't care for you bothering me."

Boil's eyes widened just slightly. "She's a duchess, Malloy."

"Don't care if she's the bloody queen."

Good grief. Well, she supposed *Debrett's Peerage* wasn't required reading material where Ratty Coat and Boil were from. The Duke of Averell was powerful, and the Barrington family, while eccentric, was one few would cross. Even Hagerty was afraid of Phaedra's brothers, particularly Leo, whose burly doormen at Elysium were usually fished from St. Giles and delighted in performing small errands for their employer. The more unsavory, the better.

A grimy hand touched her sleeve.

Phaedra made a sound of annoyance. Apparently Tony's title didn't matter in the least.

Boil took another swig of the gin, eyeing Phaedra warily. "Boggins said not to go near her. Hagerty don't want no trouble. Not with a duke."

"Boggins is at the door, and Hagerty's busy." Ratty Coat shrugged, eyes focused on Phaedra. "And I ain't afraid of a duke." He snorted. "She's probably lying anyway. I bet she's tupping Hagerty, the way she hangs about."

"I am not"—her lips tightened—"*tupping* Mr. Hagerty," Phaedra snapped. "And you *should* be afraid. Dukes are powerful beings. His Grace will see you hang for daring to touch me." She looked pointedly at his filthy hand.

"I don't see no duke about. Nor anyone else."

"Then you will have to deal with me." Phaedra pulled the knife out of her pocket, slashing at the back of Ratty Coat's hand, drawing a thin stream of blood. "Keep your hands to yourself."

"You little high-bred tart," Ratty Coat snarled, snatching back his hand.

"I am not a tart." Phaedra held the knife. "I am Lady Phaedra Barrington. Sister of the Duke of Averell." At this point, she cared little if they knew her identity, as long as they left her alone. "How dare you."

Ratty Coat pulled out his own blade, a long, wicked-looking thing that sent the first crackling whip of fear down Phaedra's spine. "Won't be so snooty if I carve you up a bit."

I'll stab him in the throat. It can't be terribly hard.

"Carving is for a decent roast." A raspy, cut-gravel sound came from just behind Phaedra, along with a whiff of something like apples and smoke mixing with the sawdust in the air. "Not for a young lady who is the sister of a duke." The unrounded vowels lingered, the flat, nasal quality assaulting her ears.

"Bugger off." Ratty Coat lowered the knife a fraction as he looked over Phaedra's shoulder. "This ain't your business. Me and the lady are friends."

A dark chuckle, like bubbling chocolate, erupted from the darkness to her left. "You should run off. Find another bottle of gin."

"Or what?" Ratty Coat's knife was still waving around in a threatening manner.

"Or I'll break each of your fingers one by one. Snap them like kindling," came the answer. "I imagine you won't be able to wield a knife then, will you?" The words were friendly. Matter-of-fact. "Or possibly I'll break both your wrists. Painful, from what I understand." But the menace was unmistakable. As was the accent. "I haven't decided yet."

American.

Phaedra recognized the lack of inflection. The flatness of

his vowels. He sounded very much like Georgina, Leo's wife, but without the upper-crust edge of Manhattan society.

The skin around Boil's sore paled as he took in the man standing behind Phaedra. He held up his hands. "Don't want no trouble." Scuttling back, he clutched at the bottle of gin. "Just having a bit of fun. The lady looked thirsty. Me and Malloy didn't mean no harm."

"Possibly you should find your amusements elsewhere," the American said in a pleasant growl, the threat much more noticeable.

Ratty Coat raised his knife again, refusing to back down. "I could cut up her pretty face."

"Yes, you've mentioned as much." A resigned sigh met Phaedra's ears. "But you won't. Good grief, you couldn't carve a pheasant with the way your arm trembles." The American finally stepped into Phaedra's view.

Every nerve in her body flared, like a torch lighting a line of oil or something equally combustible.

Big.

Muscled. Broad of chest like a bull or an ox. Tall, but with a stockiness that suggested layers of powerful muscle as he moved. The finely tailored clothing, all black with just a hint of crimson thread at the edges, barely contained the violence filling the small space as he stalked closer. He smiled at Ratty Coat with the delight of a predator, the sort who knows there isn't any other animal stupid enough or strong enough to offer the least bit of challenge.

He was dangerous, frightening, and frankly so bloody magnificent, all Phaedra could do was stare.

"I'll slice you up a bit," Ratty coat insisted bravely.

"Must we continue to debate your skill with a knife?" Eyes so pale they resembled tiny shards of ice regarded Ratty Coat. Those chips of frost were entirely devoid of any emotion. The muted light from the windows above streamed across his head, turning the strands of his hair to smoky topaz. "Malloy, is it?"

Ratty Coat spat into the sawdust at the man's feet. "What's it to you?"

"I wonder, Mr. Malloy, if you are familiar with piano wire." The big shoulders shrugged. "Or wire in general. Probably not, given your existence. Indulge me, won't you?" Reaching into his pocket, the American pulled out a compact spool, unrolling a length of wire with his fingers. "Piano wire. This is the thinnest, for higher notes. But exceptionally strong."

"Look, you bloody"

"Watch your tongue," the American interrupted. "Or I'll cut it out." A charming smile barely hid the cruelty hovering at his lips. "There is a lady present, in case you've forgotten. I won't remind you again. Now, back to this." He held up the spool. "What you may not know is that there are other uses for piano wire. Not many people consider them, I grant you. Which is why I want to educate you, Mr. Malloy." He pulled the wire tight between his hands. "You should reconsider coming at me with that knife because of this tiny bit of wire. I would find your efforts highly entertaining, but you would not." He snapped the wire taut drawing Ratty Coat's eye. "I promise," he purred, "I'm faster than you."

Phaedra found she couldn't look away from her murderous rescuer, fascinated with his threatening speech and the tiny bit of wire he held. Rather like watching Theseus, Cherry Hill's cat, toy with a mouse it had cornered. The dull thump of her heart reminded her to breathe.

Ratty Coat dropped the knife into the sawdust at his feet. His gaze never left the strand of piano wire. "I didn't hurt her. She's the one that cut me." He held up his bleeding hand.

The shards of ice softened into a pearly mist as the American turned to Phaedra, drawing over every inch of her, searching for any signs of harm, admiration lighting his features at the knife she held.

"Good girl," he whispered so quietly, Phaedra barely heard him. But her body did. Bits of pleasure lit along her skin at the sound of him.

"Now." He looked directly at Boil, who was still holding on to the bottle of gin like a talisman. "Tell your friends. The lady"—he jerked his chin at Phaedra—"is not to be bothered when she visits Hagerty's. Or *I* will come bother whoever is unwise enough to approach her. Give them a lesson in the uses of piano wire."

Boil made a sound of distress but nodded.

Ratty Coat picked up his knife once more. "You won't always be around." He glanced at Phaedra. "I'll see you again, dove. Maybe in Mayfair. I've always wanted to visit."

"I suppose I'll need to make an example of you, Mr. Malloy, if you persist. Now, run along." The American flicked his wrist before turning his back to Ratty Coat and dismissing him. He carefully rolled up the wire on the spool and tucked it away in a pocket.

Phaedra did not release her grip on the knife in her hand but drew in a slow, deep lungful of air. She'd never been in the presence of a man like the one before her. A man who could scatter any threat because he was the bigger one. He'd spoken so calmly of...*garroting* Ratty Coat without blinking an eye. His defense of her had left Phaedra...

Wobbly. As if she had a fever and could not think straight. Or her insides had suddenly gone mushy. She pressed her knees together to stifle the sudden flutter between her thighs.

Ratty Coat cast one more baleful glance in Phaedra's direction, raised the bottle of gin to his lips, and sauntered off.

"Did you really imagine you could protect yourself with

that tiny pigsticker?" His head tipped to the blade in her hand. "You're not even holding it correctly." Making an impatient sound, he took a step forward and adjusted her grip with his big, blunt fingers.

"Pigsticker?" She gasped at the unexpected touch. Rescuer or not, a gentleman did not simply touch a young lady with whom he wasn't acquainted. It wasn't done. Even Phaedra, with her disregard for so many rules, abided by that one.

"The knife. Your mouth is gaping open like a gutted fish." The moonlit eyes slid over her.

"We aren't acquainted," Phaedra stuttered, the sensation of his fingers along her hand sending a ripple up her arm and shoulder. The sensation finally quieted and settled between her breasts. She jerked her hand out of reach.

"You might be better with a pistol," he continued. "A small one. Or possibly not. I can see you stabbing someone with a hatpin, perhaps."

"A hatpin?" Phaedra choked out.

"You should have something besides the knife for protection, especially if you continue to come here unescorted, which," he said, shaking his head, "I'm sure you've been advised against. Your connections and status are weak protection in a place like this. I wouldn't make such an announcement again. You're sure to be robbed—or worse—if you aren't careful." He paused. "Though I did enjoy being the hero for a change." A low chuckle came from his chest. "That's a rarity."

"Hero? I believe you've read the situation incorrectly," she blurted out in a scathing, annoyed tone, struggling for composure while her insides twisted pleasurably in awareness of his larger form. That curious scent came to her nostrils again, coming from him. Like a warm fire at night in a dense forest. Smoky, but with a hint of apple.

"Oh, there she is," he murmured. "The well-bred young

lady. I haven't had a proper set-down in ages. Not since coming to London, if you can believe it."

"You are correct," she returned. "I cannot believe it. I can't imagine you entertaining a dance partner, for instance, with the uses of piano wire. Or that you dance at all."

"You'd be surprised. I find you entirely ungrateful for my timely intervention."

"I was in no need of your rescue. Despite what you might think." She held up the knife.

"Still not holding it properly. Should I have waited until he had your skirts up around your ears before stepping in?"

Phaedra's mouth popped open at his words before she composed herself. "Vulgarity is unnecessary. We are not even acquainted."

"So vulgarity is acceptable if we are acquainted?" He doffed his hat. "Morgan Stewart." The soft, raspy purr vibrated along Phaedra's arms. That woodsy scent, like a chilly autumn night, invaded her nostrils again, mixing with all that menace hovering about his shoulders.

"Lady Phaedra Barrington."

"Yes, I heard you brandishing your title about as if it were some sort of weapon that would protect you. I'm familiar with the name."

Unsurprising, of course. Anyone who spent an hour in London was inundated with gossip of *The Disastrous Barrington*. The one destined for horrific scandal, whose behavior would embarrass her family for centuries to come.

I shall exceed all their expectations.

"I disagree. Dukes are powerful. No one wishes to cross one."

A shrug of the broad shoulders was his only response. He didn't seem overly impressed, but he was American.

"I appreciate your efforts on my behalf, Mr. Stewart, no

matter how unnecessary. I was perfectly safe. Mr. Hagerty is just over there."

Mr. Stewart made an amused sound. "Ah, dismissal. A lady's finest weapon." He leaned back against the wall behind her, mere inches from her skirts, seemingly in no hurry to depart.

"One in which you fail to fall prey." Warmth crept along her spine from the big body so close to hers. A wise young lady might be compelled to flee, recognizing that she was in far more danger from Mr. Stewart than either Ratty Coat or Boil.

She sniffed the air, bringing that delicious scent to her nose once more.

A jagged scar curled over his chin, slicing through the close-cropped brush of hair lining his jaw, one she hadn't noticed until now. A small knot twisted at the bridge of his nose. She glanced down at his massive fists, the fingers blunt and powerful looking. He'd taken off his gloves without her noticing, as if expecting, at some point, that he would touch her again.

A shiver ran down her back. Not an entirely unpleasant thought.

"The American accent grates on the nerves," she said in her most aristocratic tone, hoping to dispel the sensation twisting about in her belly. "I can barely understand when you speak. Reminiscent of squawking waterfowl."

"A goose, is my understanding." The smirk widened, softening the cruel slant of his lips into a genuine smile. He was rather dazzling when not threatening others with piano wire. The chilly gaze trailed over her mouth, lingering much longer than was warranted.

"It is rude to stare at a lady in such a manner."

"What manner should I use? You'll need to instruct me. The English have a great many rules, far more than I anticipated. I can barely remember the correct form of address or to whom I should bow."

She sincerely doubted he ever bowed to anyone. "I can see you lack the most basic politeness, Mr. Stewart." Phaedra put her knife back in the pocket of her dress. He wasn't going to harm her. Possibly annoy her to death but little else.

"Among other things, Phaedra Barrington."

"*Lady* Phaedra."

"I don't think so. We fought a war over that. Your fancy tutors probably failed to mention it." Mr. Stewart leaned forward just an inch, enough so that Phaedra had the sense he was *inhaling* her, as if she were a pot of soup simmering above a fire. She immediately pulled back, glaring at him.

"You're quite something." His eyes held hers. "I like roses. The wilder, the better."

Phaedra froze at the reference to the scent she often wore. The delicate rose was more muted than others, crafted for her especially by a perfumer on Bond Street. The aroma did indeed come from a variety of roses, ones that vined with smaller buds, not found in a typical garden.

Her heart beat slightly out of rhythm.

And why shouldn't it? Today had been incredibly unsettling. First she'd been nearly accosted, and now she was engaged in a hostile *flirtation* with a brutish American who carried around piano wire in his pocket in case he had occasion to strangle someone.

Hop off the barrel this instant, Phaedra. Summon a hack and return home. Phaedra pushed aside the whisper of common sense, which oddly enough sounded like Pith. Always preaching caution. Restraint. She rarely ever listened to it.

Mr. Stewart's breath feathered over her cheek as his chin dipped towards her. "I wagered on the butcher, O'Leary." He nodded to the roped-off area where a mountain of a human being with ham-sized fists waited for the match to begin. "I understand he's fighting Lord Torrington today. Now, as a matter of fact."

Her cousin's husband jumped over the ring, confident and graceful, though he rarely ever won a round against O'Leary. Still, the crowd loved Torrington, whistling, and stomping their feet as he faced the Irishman. Another round of coins passed back and forth as wagers were made while O'Leary and Torrington circled each other.

"My money is on Torrington," she said, trying to ignore the sensation of Stewart's lips practically brushing her skin.

"I fear your loyalty is misplaced. O'Leary has the advantage of brute strength. He's younger. Heavier."

"But Torrington is quick on his feet," Phaedra replied defensively. "Graceful, even. And fast. I've seen him land several punches on O'Leary's jaw. I adore watching him."

The mist of his eyes hardened, solidifying into a flinty blue gray. "Is that why you're here at Hagerty's? For Torrington?"

"I enjoy watching him fight," she answered as Stewart leaned closer, bringing with him wood smoke. Apples. Leather. The warmth of a fire.

A healthy dollop of danger.

"*And* he's wed to my cousin," she felt the need to clarify, worrying momentarily over the future state of Torrington's health given the way Mr. Stewart's words had trailed off into a growl. "Not that it is any of your affair."

His harsh-cut features relaxed once more, the sharp edges disappearing. One blunt fingertip trailed purposefully down the fold of her skirts, right over her knee. "Torrington depends too heavily on his footwork. He'll lose the match."

Phaedra looked down at his fingers, watching as they returned to his side, hardly believing that he'd dared such an intimate gesture.

"Care to wager, Mr. Stewart?" she said, mostly to distract

herself from thinking of those same fingers trailing over her skin. O'Leary would win, but out of loyalty to Torrington, whom she liked very much because he adored Cousin Rosalind and made the most delicious cakes, Phaedra felt the need to support him. Besides, the idea of piano wire fascinated her. Was there a specific technique required? A lady might find such knowledge useful.

She could imagine carrying about a small spool in the pocket of her gown. No one would even notice.

A cheer went up as O'Leary threw the first punch, which Torrington neatly avoided.

"I do." The gravelly voice washed over her. "What do you wish to wager?"

Phaedra tapped her chin. "When I win"

"If." He cocked his head, a half-smile tilting at his lips.

"*When* I win, you will demonstrate how you use piano wire. Perhaps give up your tiny spool."

"Bloodthirsty little thing," he said, though Mr. Stewart didn't seem overly surprised by her request. "Why would you wish to know about that?"

"I have an interest in weaponry."

"What a strange hobby for a proper young lady." There was no censure in his words, only curiosity.

"I don't care for gardening or embroidery. Paying calls bores me. Dancing is exhausting. You find remembering a title or two tiresome." She gave him a sideways look. "Just think what I must go through every day."

The half-smile stretched across his features, the ice melting in an instant. "*Schatje*," he purred, sending a hum along her spine. "I agree to your terms."

Phaedra frowned. "I don't recognize that word." It didn't sound like French, which was the only other tongue she knew, and not well. "What does it mean?"

"Shouldn't you be more concerned with what I'll ask for when I win?" Stewart's gaze fell to her mouth once more.

The sound from the ring grew louder, but Phaedra barely heard anything except the blood pulsing beneath her skin. "Something improper?"

Stewart shrugged.

Run, Phaedra. This instant. Pith's voice inside her head urged her to be sensible.

Odd that it should be Pith's voice attempting to steer her from ruinous behavior. Not Mama's, for instance. Or Tony's.

"Very well. I agree."

Stewart made her feel as if she were...*melting* into a pool of honey. What other sensations might he inspire were he to kiss her? A bold, dangerous thought. She'd been kissed, of course. Not memorably. Wet lips. Trying to discern which way to turn so noses didn't bump. Awkward was the best word to describe her past experiences. But she hadn't been kissed by a man such as Stewart. And wouldn't it benefit her to learn the best use of piano wire?

You should flee immediately, Pith's voice insisted.

"Now, look." Stewart pointed. "See how Torrington dances around The Butcher? He is graceful. Fast. Your observations are correct. But O'Leary's arms are longer and thus his reach greater. Lack of stamina for a long fight is one of O'Leary's weaknesses, though, so Torrington's strategy is to wear him out and land a punch there."

Phaedra turned towards the ring, intent on O'Leary as he danced around, forgetting all about the melting sensation lingering in her mid-section. "You mean just inside his ribs? Why?"

"If you are smaller than your opponent, not as strong"— he looked pointedly down at her—"you should always aim for the liver. Or perhaps the kidneys." O'Leary had turned, and Stewart pointed at the larger man's lower back. "Just there. It will cause the most pain, if the punch is well-placed, possibly injure your opponent enough so he'll cough up blood."

Fascinated, Phaedra watched as Torrington attempted to land a punch in those areas. "You know quite a bit about fisticuffs. Do you fight at Hagerty's?" She nodded towards the roped off area. "Is that why you're here, Mr. Stewart?"

"I've been known to enjoy a round of fists, but not for amusement's sake. I have an old friend who does fight for entertainment. On occasion. I'd heard he planned to visit London. I thought I might see him."

"That's not the least mysterious," she ventured. "I'll assume he is also American?" Phaedra bit her lip. "Forgive me for prying, Mr. Stewart, but your accent is much like that of my brother's wife, Georgina. She's from New York."

Stewart didn't bother to respond to her carefully worded inquiry one way or another.

"Do you see how O'Leary feints to the right before he uses his left fist?" He directed her attention back to the Irish butcher. "That is a tell, of sorts."

"Such as when one is playing cards?"

A pleased look came over his face. "Exactly."

Phaedra turned towards Torrington and O'Leary once more, proud she'd managed to impress him with her acumen at cards, if not her ducal lineage.

"Torrington," Stewart continued, "should make note of that tell. It may help him win, though I think it unlikely. O'Leary won't be beat, even though he isn't trying to harm Torrington. Do you see how careful he is with his punches?"

Phaedra turned her attention back to the Irishman in the ring, studying him.

"O'Leary isn't trying to hurt Torrington. Not really."

"He isn't?" She tilted her chin, surprised to find the tip of Stewart's nose nearly trailing along her cheek. The scar could be clearly seen from this angle, a thin line of raised white flesh neatly bisecting his chin. Faded at the edges. Old. She had the urge to trace the tip of her finger along that jagged path before trailing over his bottom lip.

She jerked her gaze back to the fight.

Never once had she had the inclination to stroke Emberly's chin, and he was one of the most sought-after gentlemen in London, his lack of ability in punching notwithstanding. Before she'd watched him prance about and slap at his opponent during the fight at his club, Phaedra *had* honestly considered having him court her. Given she was *The Disastrous Barrington*, there were only a handful of gentlemen brave enough to do so.

"If O'Leary meant to hurt Torrington," Stewart continued, "the match would already be over. He isn't even aiming for Torrington's face. Only the line of his jaw or the ribs. Or his hip. He's had three chances to break Torrington's nose but hasn't taken any of them. Every so often he'll catch him in the lip, but just enough to make things look good."

Watching for a few more minutes, Phaedra could see Stewart was right. O'Leary wasn't trying to hurt Torrington, only rough him up a bit.

"I saw O'Leary fight in earnest just the other day," Stewart said. "When he wants to hurt his opponent, he does. The only reason Torrington survives these matches with his face intact is that O'Leary doesn't want to get into trouble by breaking the nose or cracking the skull of a peer." He held up a broad palm. "Though I grant you, Torrington does fight well. Better than most."

Phaedra stared at the knot in Mr. Stewart's nose, wondering how he'd gotten it. A fight, she decided, though she didn't think a polite one. "Thank you for explaining such things to me, Mr. Stewart. Not even Torrington appreciates my interest in boxing."

"That's a pity. You've got good instincts."

Phaedra felt a burst of pride. "I've always wanted to learn to throw a punch. I fence, but it isn't at all the same."

"I imagine not. Make a fist." He leaned over, the silver of his eyes was once more a misty gray, not the least cold.

Phaedra curled her fingers.

Stewart shook his head. "No, *schatje*, like this." Gently he pried her fingers apart and tucked her thumb outside while Phaedra's heart skipped about at his touch. "Never put your thumb inside. You'll break it."

"What does that mean? Shot"

"*Schatje*. It means..." He hesitated. "Troublesome."

"Humph." Phaedra didn't care for that explanation at all. She wasn't troublesome, only curious about many things—and because she was female, wasn't supposed to be. Looking down at his hands next to hers, a delicious tingle trailed down Phaedra's arm. In comparison to Stewart, Phaedra was positively diminutive. Those large hands were powerful and brutal-looking, the knuckles scarred in places, yet gentle where they touched her.

Another twist of her insides.

"Now, imagine I am Lord Ashley, who nearly lost the right to sire an heir after escorting you to the terrace at the Upton ball."

Phaedra raised her eyes to his. "How on earth do you know about that?"

"I listen, particularly in London where everyone likes to pretend they can't understand me. You've quite a reputation." His thumb rubbed lightly over her knuckles.

Lord Ashley had not only attempted to take liberties, but he'd also had the audacity to wager on his ability to do so. Phaedra had seen proof of Ashley's arrogance in Elysium's Red Book after the altercation at the Upton ball.

Lady Phaedra will allow liberties with a young lord on the terrace at the Upton ball. L. Ashley. Two hundred pounds.

Were she able to go back in time, he wouldn't have only received a well-placed knee to the bollocks, but also the sting of her rapier. Ashley had pretended interest in her to win a wager. And he had not been the first to do so.

She glanced at Mr. Stewart. Nor would Ashley be the last.

"Three hundred pounds for teaching *The Disastrous Barrington* how to box. Does that sound like a proper wager, Mr. Stewart?"

He raised a brow at her.

"Allow me to advise you, sir." Phaedra's tone grew haughtier. "There are at least four wagers about me witnessing fisticuffs or visiting a boxing establishment." She paused and tapped her chin. "Wait, no, there are only three. The fourth is that *I* will engage in fisticuffs. Plenty has already been said about my habit of going about without escort, if that is your next gambit. Two wagers state I'll be kidnapped, but only one assumes I'll be held for ransom. New to London you may be, but I'm sure you are not ignorant of Elysium's Red Book, nor my place in it. Lord Ashley certainly was not." She glared at him. "He did not win his wager."

That large finger trailed over the fold in her skirt once more before retreating. "Perhaps I should show Lord Ashley the uses of piano wire."

"He's an earl," Phaedra said needlessly.

"Even so."

"That is oddly protective of you, Mr. Stewart, given our short acquaintance. And slightly murderous, I might add."

"Duly noted, Phaedra."

She drew in a slow breath. "*Lady* Phaedra."

"I don't think so," he whispered, sending sparks down her spine.

The crowd in the middle of the room erupted in cheers. Hagerty held O'Leary's hand up in the air, declaring him the winner, while Torrington staggered over to sit in a hastily procured chair. But he was grinning at O'Leary.

"I don't usually make wagers," Stewart breathed along the curve of her ear. "Not unless I am absolutely certain of the outcome. You've lost."

"What is it you'll ask for?" she didn't move or turn her head.

"For you to stay still."

Warm lips hovered over the skin of Phaedra's neck, barely grazing the surface, to settle at a sensitive spot just below her ear. She jumped at the graze of his teeth, anticipating the sting of a bite.

"I won't leave a mark," he murmured. "Not yet."

All the air left Phaedra's lungs so quickly, she became dizzy. His delicious aroma settled along her shoulders, adding to the sense of intoxication.

A sound came from him. Slightly feral. A predator about to pounce.

"Shall we make another wager, Phaedra? Or should I say—are you prepared to lose again?" His mouth stayed mere inches from her own, the words spoken against her lips with just enough pressure to not be accidental but still far less than a kiss.

"If you like." The words in her mouth felt unsteady.

"Agreed. The same terms." Stewart pulled back.

The next match was between a lean, wiry little man named Jones and someone Hagerty referred to as Figglestaff. Figglestaff was larger. Meatier.

Phaedra chose him.

Jones won.

She stayed still once more as her forfeit was paid, struggling not to arch her back as the heat of his fingers stroked up and down her spine. He explored the edges of her shoulder blades, trailing along the curve of her bones, his palm stretching along her back in a painfully drawn-out, sensual manner. The buds of her nipples tightened sharply, begging for his hands.

"Again?" Stewart asked as he ceased his torture of her person.

"Yes. The same terms," was Phaedra's bold reply.

An hour passed, their conversation constrained to fisticuffs, brawling with knives, and how a well-placed lady's hatpin could injure an unwelcome assailant by hitting a specific vein in the neck. Nothing at all about piano wire because she hadn't yet won any of their wagers. The small area of skin exposed by her neckline was explored by the tip of his once broken nose. Her waist delicately outlined with his blunt fingertips. A palm extended over one thigh dangerously close to the ache which had taken root between her thighs.

Phaedra didn't want to win any of the wagers. What she wanted was for Stewart to kiss her.

Every inch of her felt raw. Sensitive. Aching for something she couldn't name. The place between her thighs became damp and warm. Phaedra was usually nonchalant when considering physical relations, the result of a mother who was incredibly progressive and had given an exceptionally detailed description of what it meant to be bedded.

You really should return home, Pith murmured in the recesses of her mind.

"What is it, exactly, you do in America, Mr. Stewart?" she asked, pushing her knees tightly together, though it did nothing to stanch the sensation.

"Railroads, primarily. Railways, here. But I seek diversification. I've recently been apprised of an opportunity in London, one which interests me greatly." Something dark moved about in his eyes. "Enterprises work best when complementing each other."

30

Phaedra thought for a moment. Rosalind had formed an agreement with Elysium, for instance, to provide pastries. Granby had given her sister Romy a silk ribbon factory in Coventry for her last birthday. Which made perfect sense, given the amount of fripperies Romy used in designing gowns.

"If you have hundreds of sheep, you should also own a textile mill. Then possibly the draper where you sell the fabric. So you control and own it all. That is what you mean, isn't it?"

A low groan left him. Barely heard. A sort of appreciation. Or longing.

Phaedra's heart became unsteady once more.

"Exactly like that. The railroad in which I hold the majority interest in America runs along the Erie Canal. Once, building the tracks was mocked. Who could compete with the barges for moving people and cargo? But now, there are nearly as many passengers on my railroad as there are barrels of grain. Now, imagine, if all that grain was people. Maybe they wish to go to Chicago. When they arrive, won't some of them need a place to stay? Shouldn't I perhaps own a hotel nearby? Or a restaurant. Or the coal which fuels the train's engine?"

Phaedra nodded, seeing what he meant. "You own—or at least own part of—every link in the chain. Which benefits you the most, I think."

Stewart laughed, a deep sound that reminded Phaedra of the thickest, creamiest chocolate she'd ever tasted. "So clever." The tip of his forefinger gently brushed along her lower lip.

The last match was being fought before them, but neither she nor Stewart seemed terribly interested. He was likely to win again, at any rate. The man Phaedra had chosen was already wobbling on his feet.

I don't want to win.

She dared a glance up at the windows, noting with a tiny wisp of panic that the hour was growing late and if she didn't return home soon, her absence will have been noted, even with the multitude of precautions she'd taken. Her reluctance at leaving was due to Mr. Stewart, perhaps the first person who'd actually spoken to her as an equal since the death of her father. Not even Tony was so patient with her.

The match ended when Phaedra's fighter fell face down into the sawdust.

"It seems I've chosen incorrectly once more. You win, Mr. Stewart. I'll have to find a book on the uses of piano wire or venture into the Rookery, perhaps."

"You'll do no such thing."

She hopped off the barrel and smiled up at him, unsurprised to see the top of her head barely came to his chin. "You're hardly in a position to stop me. As delightful as this afternoon has been, I fear I must return home. Enjoy your time in London, Mr. Stewart."

He looked down on her, eyes soft like mist. "What sort of story will you spin to explain your long absence, I wonder?"

"A charitable endeavor." Would he ask to call upon her? Or at least suggest Phaedra meet him again at Hagerty's? "My mother thinks I assist in teaching music to orphans."

"Do you even play an instrument?"

Phaedra thought of the violin she'd tried to master. The looks of relief on the faces of her family when she had given it up. "Not well, I'm afraid. I'm a duke's sister. My mere presence is meant to inspire others."

Another dark bubble of laughter came from him before he said, "Now, as to my winning, Phaedra."

"*Lady* Phaedra," she corrected him. He deliberately refused to address her properly.

A big hand reached out to cup the side of her cheek, stroking the soft skin, weakening her knees.

"Have you ever been kissed?" He leaned in, lips whispering at the edge of her mouth.

"Yes, but not by you."

"Ferocious little creature." Stewart's mouth closed firmly over hers, quieting any response she might have made. There was a laziness to his kiss. No urgency. All loose and languid. As if Phaedra were a small snifter of brandy he meant to sip and enjoy for hours. One arm skimmed her hip before clasping her bottom firmly with one broad hand.

A whimper crawled up her throat. A hitch of her breath. A desperate sort of madness.

Teeth nipped and grazed, urging her to part her lips to allow him entry, which she did without a qualm. A tremble ran through her, shocked as she was at the intimate feel of his tongue twisting around her own. The gentleness ended, morphing into urgent hunger. Every bit of it for Phaedra.

Her body molded along the hard lines of his massive form, wanting to be closer as their breaths mingled. Back arching, her fingers crawled up his broad chest, feeling the powerful muscles moving subtly beneath his coat. Images floated before her, of being naked and twisted up in sheets with this man. Of his mouth and tongue. That larger body dominating hers as she willingly submitted.

And Phaedra did nothing willingly.

"*Schatje*," he whispered, pulling away, the ache in that one word doing terrible, wonderful things to her heart. The intensity of his gaze, the awe and muted surprise, nearly sent Phaedra to her knees. He inhaled abruptly, as if he'd been holding his breath. "Damn," he said softly, more to himself than to her.

"I..." she stuttered, unable to form a coherent thought,

feeling the impending loss of him far more keenly than she should have. "But..."

One thing was apparent. Lord Ashley had no idea how to kiss. Or Lord Emberly.

I feel as if I've drunk an entire bottle of champagne.

"How unexpected you are, Phaedra Barrington. In every possible way."

"*Lady* Phaedra," she barely choked out.

His thumb trailed over her bottom lip once more before retreating.

"Stay here until I am gone." Stewart's words were low. Scratchy. "I'll have a hack waiting for you just outside the door. You aren't to go into the street by yourself." He took her hand in his.

Phaedra bristled. "I arrived here perfectly well on my own, and I can—"

"Allow me to do this. Ferocious creature," he murmured, pressing an open-mouthed kiss to her wrist. "Try to behave." His tongue flicked across her wildly beating pulse. "Or not."

Cherry Hill, a few weeks later

Phaedra did not take Mr. Stewart's advice.

Nor was she sure about seeing him ever again. Not after the disastrous events of the last week.

Since meeting her murderous American, Phaedra had thought of little else, though there were plenty of issues that required her immediate attention. Olivia, Phaedra's foster sister and ward of the dowager duchess of Averell, had been her primary concern. Olivia had reconciled, much to every Barrington's dismay, with her maternal grandfather, from whom she'd been estranged for years. The dreaded Lord Daring. Phaedra should have guessed he was an appropriate harbinger of doom. He meant to wed Olivia to Mr. Peter Thomlinson, tedious heir to his earldom and who possessed an overly large head. Marriage to Mr. Thomlinson would doom Olivia to a life of boredom surrounded by children with enormous noggins.

Phaedra had to do something to shake some sense into her.

A visit to Elysium was long overdue. That was certain to jostle the sensibilities of any young lady.

But the tour of the gambling hell hadn't gone exactly as planned. Having been caught by Peckham, the gambling hell's faithful floor manager, Phaedra had been escorted out while Olivia had been forced to take refuge in one of the rooms on the second floor. The pleasure rooms. When Phaedra had returned for Olivia, she'd been surprised to see her sister with swollen lips, reddened cheeks, and enveloped in a piney scent that reminded Phaedra of some primal forest.

Highly suspicious.

But Phaedra hadn't guessed, not then, what had happened. She'd been too distressed by the fact that Olivia had seemed more determined than ever to wed Tedious Thomlinson.

Since she thought better when sitting atop a horse, Phaedra had taken a ride through the park, never once considering a sidesaddle would be more appropriate than riding astride. Unfortunately, the entire episode had been witnessed by the incredibly proper Lady Wentworth, who had promptly called upon the Dowager Duchess of Averell to inform Her Grace that the youngest Barrington daughter was running wild.

Not that anyone in London should have been surprised. Mama especially. She'd fed Lady Wentworth a few biscuits then tactfully had Pith show her out. A lecture had followed on discretion while Phaedra had pretended to listen.

Ignoring her mother's admonitions to stay out of trouble, Phaedra had decided to visit Hagerty's once more, surprised upon her arrival to find that every patron of the boxing establishment, including Mr. Hagerty, had shied away from her as if she had the pox. Even O'Leary, whom she'd thought of as a friend, wouldn't look her in the eye. Not even Boggins had greeted her. There had been no sign of her murderous

American or his piano wire, at any rate, nor had Torrington been boxing that day. Phaedra had left early, somewhat deflated.

The following evening, Maggie, Tony's duchess, had decided to host a family dinner to welcome Georgina's cousin to London. The entire family was to dine together. Tony and Leo would spend most of it lobbing insults at either Haven, husband of Phaedra's sister Theo, or the Duke of Granby, Romy's spouse. Neither brother bothered to insult Torrington, as he always brought dessert, which kept him out of the line of fire. Mr. Thomlinson had been invited, much to her dismay.

But the highlight of the meal was Phaedra's dinner companion.

Mr. Benjamin Cooke of New York. Georgina's cousin.

Cooke, savagely handsome and reeking of menace, possessed the same sharp, ruthless edge as Mr. Stewart but with a bit more charm. He defiantly flirted with Tony's duchess, which in turn, gave Tony fits. Pith didn't like Cooke, as evidenced by the tiny burnt bits of dinner placed on his plate. But what surprised Phaedra the most was the way Cooke eyed Olivia over the mushroom soup, nearly leaping across the table at her like some rabid dog—*and* the fact that his shaving soap smelled of something piney. The two were obviously well-acquainted.

"I knew she'd had liberties taken," Phaedra muttered aloud as she left the main house and marched outside to the lawn, rapier in hand.

Unsurprisingly, given that Cooke had the appearance of someone who used his fists, he also knew Torrington—but pretended not to. Hagerty's seemed the obvious explanation.

At any rate, she much preferred Mr. Cooke to the bland Thomlinson, who practically faded into the paneled walls of the dining room. Even though Cooke had compared Phaedra to the Mohawk, a tribe from the Americas. She found it less insulting than he'd intended.

Phaedra blew out a breath at the memory of that night, the impetus for everything that had come after. Her eyes took in the splendor of Cherry Hill, the Duke of Averell's estate, wishing, as she often did, that her father would simply step out of the woods at the edge of the sweep of perfectly manicured grass and ask if she wanted to go fishing. He'd know what to do about this mess.

"I've mucked it all up," she bit out into the breeze.

Her efforts to gently push Olivia in Benjamin Cooke's direction had led them all here, to the countryside. Olivia was a short distance away at Halloway Park, Daring's estate, floating about his gardens and waiting to wed Tedious Thomlinson while Phaedra and Mama cooled their heels at Cherry Hill, hoping she'd change her mind.

Clutching her rapier, uncaring if she slashed the fabric of her skirts, Phaedra sliced at the grass. "Olivia might already be wed to Thomlinson, and I won't even know because she refuses to speak to me."

She and Olivia fought often. Sometimes loudly. Sisters often did. But they'd never been separated. Never not spoken.

The silence was due to Phaedra having taken Olivia to Hagerty's.

Partially because she'd been hoping to see Mr. Stewart again, but mainly so Olivia would see Cooke and realize— well, *something*. Enough to keep her from Thomlinson. After bribing Hagerty with yet more of her pin money, he'd finally admitted that a gentleman from America named Cooke would be sparring that day. Phaedra had hoped sparks would fly between Olivia and Cooke.

"Oh." A swing of the rapier and a daisy was instantly decapitated. "Sparks most certainly did fly about. In a most spectacular, horrible way."

A tiny scream of frustration bubbled from Phaedra's lips, startling a small flock of wrens in the tree above her. She, who did not believe in coincidences and considered herself to be highly intuitive, had *completely missed* the absurdity of meeting two Americans, both from New York, each cut from the same menacing bolt of cloth, within such a short time. The pair were connected, as surely as she and Olivia.

Another slash of the rapier and bits of bluebells flew into the air.

Stewart's old friend, the one he'd claimed to have been looking for at Hagerty's, was Benjamin Cooke, and the two men were the farthest thing from chummy. The visit to the boxing establishment had started well enough, with Olivia completely enthralled at watching Cooke spin about and take on O'Leary with his fists.

Then Morgan Stewart had appeared.

At the sight of him, Phaedra's entire being had come to a halt, as if she'd been placed under a spell, completely transfixed. She had nearly flung herself into his arms, which, considering what had come next, would have been a terrible idea.

The seething animosity between Cooke and Stewart had seeped out, poisoning the air around them. Threats had been hurled. Snarling like two dogs about to fight over a bone, they had spoken of boundaries, every word hinting at a deep and ancient dislike.

Quite honestly, Phaedra had thought the two might kill each other.

She paused and took a deep, shaking breath, seeing Stewart's face that day. The rough, attractive features contorted into hatred, eyes like bits of flint frozen in ice.

Spinning about, Phaedra forced her body into a lunge, pretending to parry at an invisible opponent.

The shock at Stewart's sudden appearance, snapping and

growling at everyone *but* her, had struck Phaedra speechless. No easy feat, as she nearly always had an opinion. But it was the delicious pull at her skin, as if he were summoning her to his side, that had left Phaedra trembling.

But not with fear.

She spun about once more, neatly taking off a twig from the small tree before her with a leap.

Wagers, Stewart had spat at Cooke. *I'm here to remind someone of a wager.*

At first, Phaedra had thought Stewart meant the wagers at Hagerty's they'd made the day they'd met. Silly, seductive gambits which had led to the most delicious liberties.

But that wasn't what Stewart had been talking about at all.

"Bloody page seventy-eight of Elysium's Red Book," she yelled out at the trees.

In that instant, her menacing American had become like every other gentleman in London. He'd put a wager on her, in the Red Book. Used her. She could only imagine how he'd worded his wager. The sum he'd placed on her. How foolish Phaedra had been, sharing so much of herself with a complete stranger simply because he set her skin on fire.

An anguished sound came from her before Phaedra firmly clamped her lips shut.

Do not be a coward. You are a daughter of the Duke of Averell.

She'd been so...unsettled by Stewart's appearance that when Cooke had finally chased him away, Phaedra had followed. Breathless and angrier than she'd ever been in her life, she had reached the alley beside Hagerty's in time to see Stewart's carriage pull away. Pacing over those bloody cobblestones, Phaedra had berated herself until a furious Cooke had found her, lecturing Phaedra on her lack of common sense for wandering off in such a neighborhood.

Phaedra had never considered she might be in danger.

Miscreants had littered the streets and alleys surrounding Hagerty's, but not one of them had even glanced in her direction.

Now, as she stomped across the grass in the direction of a half-dead maple, her target for today, Phaedra tried to force Morgan Stewart from her thoughts and out of that tiny portion of her heart he'd somehow managed to conquer. Undoubtedly, he had gone back to America by now, cackling about his wager on *The Disastrous Barrington*. London was full of amusements. Picadilly. Hyde Park. Wagering on Phaedra.

"I would slice his cravat." *Whack. Whack.* Bits of rotted wood flew up in the air as she wielded her rapier. "Then his coat. Add another scar to his chin."

"Such a little savage," a soft growl came from behind her. "Your propensity for violence is highly arousing."

Phaedra stilled, chest heaving from her exertions, but did not turn. Her imagination, always vivid, was playing tricks on her. After all, her conscience sounded exactly like Pith. The wind could sound like Morgan Stewart.

"Phaedra," he murmured.

How could Stewart be at Cherry Hill? She blinked several times, focused on the poor, now slightly tattered, stump of the maple before her. This was the English countryside. She was meant to be safe from savage Americans, though Benjamin Cooke was currently in residence at Cherry Hill, mooning over an absent Olivia while teaching Phaedra to throw knives. The only bright spot in this entire mess.

She whirled about and pointed the end of the rapier at him, close enough to pierce his chest if she chose. "You."

"Yes, me."

Stewart didn't try to evade her attack. Didn't move. His manner was that of a gentleman who had happened upon her while taking a stroll. Blandly cold expression. Dressed in yet another expensive coat, although now

Phaedra had an inkling of what really lay beneath all that fine wool. She took in the cut of his trousers, so sharp she could make out the lines of muscle defining his thighs.

Fashionable and menacing. Splendid.

No hat. If he had one, it was not in evidence. The breeze ruffled the smoky topaz of his hair, bits of gold shining in the strands. He calmly took off his gloves and placed them in his pocket while the tip of her rapier threatened the buttons of his coat.

"My deadly creature." Stewart's lips held the ghost of a smile.

"I'm not your anything."

He inhaled softly, leaning forward as if scenting her like some sort of animal. "I beg to differ. You're angry."

"How observant of you, Mr. Stewart." The slow hum started along her collarbone, dipping down her shoulders, striking along the curves of her body no matter how she tried to stop it. "If you are here to challenge Mr. Cooke to a duel of sorts, he isn't here."

"Not at present. I knew he'd follow Miss Nelson to the country and beg a room at Cherry Hill." Stewart raised his chin, taking in the stunning parkland surrounding them. "Not a cherry tree in sight." The big shoulders rolled. "At any rate, I know exactly where he is." Morgan regarded her with a solemn look. "He's just sold me a piece of property."

"If that is the case, there isn't any reason for your presence." The rapier trailed farther down, suggesting she might slash at the edges of his coat. Stab out the crimson thread at the hem or take one of his silver buttons.

"Goodness, Phaedra. You *are* out of sorts today." Stewart took a step closer, pushing away the rapier with a brush of one broad palm. "Isn't it the polite thing to do to ask me for tea?" Stewart glanced towards the massive house in the distance. "I understand Cherry Hill is notable for its lavish but understated elegance."

"Why aren't you gone? From England? Don't you have matters which require your attention in New York or wherever it is you haunt? I imagine your home to resemble St. Giles or Saffron Hill."

The tiniest twitch of his left forefinger against one upper thigh drew her eye. The remark annoyed him.

Stewart had a tell.

"More Five Points," he replied smoothly. "I doubt you're familiar. Even your most squalid neighborhoods are well-mannered and far too polite. I found St. Giles rather tame." Bitter cold held his features. "But highly entertaining." A bark of laughter came from him. "I was nearly robbed. Twice."

"I should run you straight through."

"Honestly, you probably should. You are distressed that Cooke and I are acquainted. My appearance at Hagerty's and the confrontation that followed." His brow furrowed. "Unfortunate. I lost my temper. But..." His words lowered to a dangerous purr that caught against her skin. "I suspect what *you* are most furious about, my little savage, is the wager on page seventy-eight of Elysium's Red Book."

Warmth crept over her cheeks. Another weakness of her body she couldn't stop, much like the delicate flutter between her thighs the moment he'd stepped out of the line of trees.

"You blush so beautifully. I wonder if that lovely color extends across the rest of you."

"There's that charm from Hagerty's," she managed to choke out, startled by the sudden intensity of his gaze. Phaedra knew she wasn't unattractive, though she thought herself far less beautiful than her siblings. Even as *The Disastrous Barrington*, Phaedra still drew a gentleman's attention. But this was not admiration but a deliberately sexual perusal.

Her pulse waffled madly.

"Did you look at it? The wager?" The flintiness of his eyes glowed like tiny bits of frost.

Phaedra lowered the rapier. In truth, she had not consulted the Red Book. The knowledge that their time at Hagerty's had been nothing more than an attempt on his part to win a lump sum from Elysium and not...whatever this unsettling attraction was between them had kept her from doing so. The wager made Stewart akin to Ashley, or any number of the idiots populating London who thought eccentric, reckless Phaedra Barrington to be worth no more than a fistful of banknotes. Like she was a bloody horse at Newmarket. She couldn't bear to see what he'd wagered.

"You didn't," he said in surprise. "You never looked." Stewart loomed closer. "I wagered ten *thousand* pounds."

Phaedra sucked in a breath at the astronomical sum. It was the sort of wager that, if won, might bankrupt Elysium. Or at the very least put Leo in dire straits. Especially since he was now building his grand hotel in New York.

"You must have been certain of winning when you made it." She circled away from him. "Was it compromising me in a boxing establishment? You nearly succeeded." Her voice hardened.

"No." The ice in his eyes took on the sheen of freshwater pearls. "That you would run away with an American."

The punch of his words, the sheer audacity, had Phaedra nearly dropping the rapier. "No." She shook her head.

"Yes," he assured her. "I intend to win it."

"You will not."

"I disagree." Stewart shot her a bemused look, longing flickering across those savagely beautiful features before disappearing.

Phaedra's heart skipped about inside her chest, even as a tremble twisted down her spine. Not fear that Stewart meant to hurt *her*. Though she suspected him capable of a great many questionable things.

"You are entirely serious."

"Absolutely," he assured her.

"The wager, if won, could bankrupt Elysium," she breathed. "*If* you succeed, which I assure you..." She lifted up the rapier once more. "You will not. I would never allow you to destroy Elysium and in the process, my brother."

"Even though he allows others to wager on you? Poor of him, I think."

Phaedra flinched. That was a sore spot for her. Leo's casual disregard for the wagers made on her in the Red Book. She wondered if he paid them any attention or merely allowed Peckham to handle everything. Tony, Phaedra knew, rarely gave the book more than a passing glance. The Red Book was full of ridiculous, ill-conceived bets, the products of overindulged gentlemen seeking to be as outlandish as possible. There were wagers on the color of a woman's undergarments, for instance. Whether a duke would perish by Christmas. How many times a notorious widow might forgive her lover.

And what *The Disastrous Barrington* might do to cause a scandal.

"My family's affairs aren't your concern, Mr. Stewart," Phaedra said in a firm tone. "One afternoon at Hagerty's does not give you leave to offer your opinion, nor does it make us friends."

"I never said we were *friends*, Phaedra." Unmistakable lust filtered across his face, far more ravenous than before. "I don't usually want to fuck my friends."

Phaedra's body flamed at the vulgarity. As if she'd been dipped in pitch and lit up like some bloody torch. The word wasn't unknown to her. Leo had uttered it any number of times.

Tony less so. The employees at Elysium with far greater frequency. She pursed her lips, determined to give him a scathing rebuke, but a host of images flooded her mind. Naked flesh, his and her own, that hard muscled body pressing Phaedra beneath him. The act of physical relations wasn't something she had contemplated overmuch in the past, but when in Stewart's presence, Phaedra found she could think of little else.

"So at odds with the world, aren't you? Sensual yet innocent. Full of well-mannered ferocity. A brilliant mind trapped in skirts."

There was nothing mocking in Stewart's words, only admiration. Pride. No one ever expressed appreciation for her somewhat challenging personality.

Highly suspicious.

He is dangerous. You should run. Pith's voice again. Instructing her to be wise.

"If this is your attempt at seduction, Mr. Stewart, it leaves much to be desired. As does your charm. You should accept the loss of your ten thousand pounds and retreat across the ocean. Now. Before I begin to scream and bring every one of my brother's footmen to rescue me."

"You are magnificent when you are outraged. And lying."

"You are *detestable*." Phaedra was shaking from the anger searing across her skin, mixing with her overpowering attraction to him.

"As it happens, I *am* returning to New York." Producing a package wrapped in paper from his coat pocket, he held it out to her. "For you. So you won't miss me overmuch."

"I don't want it." Phaedra pressed her lips together.

The smallest bit of annoyance bled into his features, tightening the granite line of his jaw. "You do."

She approached warily, that insistent pull in his direction making it impossible for her to simply walk away. The insidious hum at his nearness increased the closer she got to his

46

larger form. How could Stewart possibly think she would simply run off with him? Bankrupt Leo. Allow him to *win*?

"Fine." Curiosity got the best of her. She took the package, feeling the deliberate press of his fingers along hers before releasing the small bundle to her. Untying the twine, the paper fell away to reveal a long, wooden box. "I don't care much for jewelry, Mr. Stewart."

"Don't insult me. I've been alone with you twice, and even I know that."

The hum picked up once again. The desire to press her head against his chest.

She jerked back and lifted the lid from the box.

Inside, lying on a bed of red satin, was a beautifully made knife crafted of the finest silver. The edge of the blade glinted in the sunlight. Wild roses were etched into the silver, the vines twisting around the hilt, ending in Phaedra's initials.

She stared at the beautiful weapon, at once terrified and pleased he saw her so clearly.

"Lighter. Balanced for your hand. You are decent with Cooke's knives, but your aim will improve with this one. Keep practicing. If anyone asks, you purchased the knife with your pin money."

"You've been watching us, haven't you?" Cooke had been teaching her to throw near this very spot. She plucked the knife out of the box, feeling the reassuring weight of it in her hand. No one else would have ever bought her such an exquisite gift. Not even her father.

Stewart did *know* her.

"I should stab you straight through your heart."

Phaedra caught a glimpse of that raw hunger again, moving in the paleness of his eyes.

"Not much of a thank you." He lowered his gaze and looked away. Taking a deep breath, he turned once more in her direction, features again covered in ice, impenetrable. "A weakness is a terrible thing, don't you think?" he said under his breath. Before Phaedra could answer, a long arm snaked out to wrap around her waist. Leaning in, Stewart licked a small drop of sweat trailing down her cheek, one caused by her previous exertions, before pressing his lips to the same spot.

Like sinking into a warm bath scented with woodsmoke and apple.

That's what it felt like to be caught in Stewart's embrace. Solid. Comforting. Her entire form melting into his. The most wonderful sort of drowning.

The voice of Pith, ever her sense of reason, demanded that she slap Stewart for taking such a liberty. Push him aside or possibly slash at him with her newly acquired knife.

"Now," he said, the flat, nasal tone soft, "would be an excellent time to stab me. Right beneath the ribs." Then his mouth fell against hers, hungry and insistent, as if he couldn't bear to be apart from her another moment. Big hands ran over the curves of her body, brushing along the edges of her waist and hips with a proprietary touch.

Phaedra whimpered. Grabbed at his shoulders, nearly dropping the knife. This was far better than she remembered, this insatiable craving pulsing between their lips. Stewart had her back arching as he lifted her. Grabbing at her bottom to angle her more closely to his hips before his mouth gentled.

Absorbed.

Phaedra had difficulty describing the sensation of his lips on hers.

Inhaled.

Like a glass of the finest French brandy. A lifetime of longing was spilling into her, wrapping itself around her very soul.

Stewart slowly pulled his mouth from hers, the breath from his lips ragged and uncontrolled. He carefully pressed their foreheads together, those pale eyes holding Phaedra in place, swirling with an entire host of emotions that terrified her.

"Phaedra," he whispered.

My God.

She sucked in a lungful of air, horrified at having almost been swept away. No wonder Stewart thought he could win his wager. Surrendering to him came so easily. People were not meant to come together with such ferocity.

She pulled away, or as far as he allowed, to put some distance between them.

How quickly he could destroy Leo. Or Cooke, whom she knew without a doubt Olivia loved.

Pushing hard at the line of his chest, she forced herself out of his grasp.

"I hope *you* can stand to lose ten thousand pounds."

"I can afford to." Stewart tucked a loose strand of Phaedra's hair behind her ear. "Such a beautiful color," he whispered. "Like a glass of Kentucky bourbon." His eyes raised to hers. "But I won't lose."

"So arrogant," Phaedra hissed, mortified that he could possibly be right. He'd sought her out deliberately at Hagerty's, she could see that clearly. For what reasons, Phaedra had no idea. Possibly he wanted Elysium. To ruin Leo and his hotel. Or possibly he meant to use her to get close to Cooke. "What is it you are really after, Mr. Stewart?"

Stewart leaned in, brushing the warmth of his lips along her cheek, refusing to let her go completely.

Lifting her chin, Phaedra looked him right in the eye. "Answer me, you well-dressed thug."

A smile ghosted his lips. "There's my girl." His hands floated away from her, fingers retreating to curl at his sides.

"I am many things, but not yours," she stuttered, unable

to think clearly after such a declaration because Phaedra was afraid it might be true.

"I think I've just proven you wrong."

Phaedra turned the knife over in her hand. "You *will not* harm Benjamin Cooke."

"Careful." He glared at her, frozen and cold, like the worst blizzard in one hundred years, not so much as a hint of emotion lingering over his features. Stewart was not a man to whom anyone dictated.

"I don't care what you two have been fighting over for decades. Cooke is a member of my extended family. If you hurt him *or* any Barrington, I will *never* forgive you, Morgan." She deliberately used his name.

"Not even the name I was born with." Shards of ice fluttered around him. She had to struggle not to shiver in the sunlight spilling through the trees. "But I applaud your negotiation strategy. Don't make a habit of it." His eyes drew over her one last time before he turned and walked back towards the tree line.

Phaedra's fingers stayed steady as she took up the gift he'd given her, the steel cool against her hand. She twisted as Cooke had shown her and threw the knife. It whizzed dreadfully close to Morgan's ear before embedding itself in a tree mere inches from him.

"*Boundaries*, Morgan." She used the same word Cooke had, knowing it must have some meaning between the two of them.

"Fair enough," he growled, over his shoulder. "But not where you are concerned. That, I fear, is a non-negotiable point. You'll appreciate my gift"—he nodded at the knife now sticking in the tree before him—"when you arrive in New York."

New York.

Phaedra's entire family was traveling across the Atlantic

to witness the grand opening of Leo's hotel, The Barrington. Her brother's modern marvel, built in the middle of Manhattan. The trip had been planned for months. Phaedra showed no surprise Morgan knew she was going to America. Her future had suddenly become quite uncertain now that she'd garnered this man's attention.

And he'd garnered hers.

"Handy to carry a blade," he continued. "The city is filled with unsavory people."

"I'm sure it is," she called after him as he disappeared into the thick wood surrounding Cherry Hill. "You being the worst."

✥ 2 ✥

Manhattan, *New York*

   Phaedra strolled out of her family's apartments atop Leo's magnificent hotel, admiring the delicately papered walls with their wainscoting and the honey-colored wood floors beneath her feet. There were rugs, of course. Dozens. Wonderful creations Leo had had shipped from England, all procured by Benjamin Cooke. There was little clarity on exactly where Cooke had found such magnificent floor coverings, the best of which were inside the family's private rooms. A great deal of the side tables, knickknacks, and even an Egyptian vase looked far too expensive to have been sold without thought to an American seeking to furnish a hotel in New York. Phaedra's mother, the dowager duchess, had exclaimed just yesterday that the large urn in the lobby looked remarkably like one owned by the Earl of Rathburn.

   Phaedra was certain the vase *was* Rathburn's. Just as she recognized the painting hanging inside the lobby as a landscape which had once graced the drawing room of Lord Maxwell, a viscount hellbent on impoverishing the title he'd inherited. She'd asked Leo how Georgina's cousin had happened upon such treasures, but her brother had waved her off, and she hadn't asked again.

What Phaedra should have inquired about was Mr. Morgan Stewart, his grudges and wagers.

She had surmised Leo did not know about page seventy-eight in the Red Book else she might never have been allowed to set foot in New York. And Phaedra wasn't about to tell him. Besides, the entire family was too busy worrying over Mr. Cooke.

Especially Olivia.

Olivia had refused the suit of Mr. Thomlinson, which was splendid as Thomlinson didn't want to wed Olivia either. He had since happily married a young lady by the name of Miss Armwood, ignoring Lord Daring's threats to disinherit him. The Barringtons had given a collective sigh of relief that Thomlinson would not be a fixture at family dinners. Olivia had then proceeded to inform Lord Daring of her future intentions, which seemed to revolve around Mr. Cooke.

But best of all, Olivia and Phaedra were once more firmly fixed together, as they had been all their lives. A great relief because she'd missed Olivia terribly, though Phaedra would never admit to it.

Still, she was reluctant to disclose her relationship with Morgan Stewart to her sister or anyone else.

Pausing at the top of the stairs, she tapped a finger against her lips in consideration.

Could it rightfully be termed a relationship if one of the parties was dishonest, perhaps intent on murdering a future family member—certain as she was that Cooke meant to wed Olivia—as well as making wagers that might result in Leo's destruction for undisclosed reasons?

"Probably not," she said under her breath, though her pulse kicked up at merely the thought of Morgan.

"Stop that," she hissed to her heart, startling one of the maids.

The poor girl widened her eyes and ran off before Phaedra could explain.

Phaedra shrugged and turned back to the stairs, resolving to compliment the maid on her dusting when next they met.

But back to Morgan.

She really should confide in someone. Olivia, for instance, though not at present. Her sister was far too busy agonizing over Cooke and designing Leo's English garden. She'd exclaimed in pleasure, jumping up and down at the thought of transforming a patch of dirt, trees, and weeds into a space more fitting for a manor house in Surrey than a deserted plot of land in the middle of the city. Olivia had forced Phaedra into service just yesterday, instructing her to trail behind and take notes while she dictated the names of various plants she'd be placing in the overall design.

In Latin.

Acting as Olivia's reluctant secretary, Phaedra had struggled to spell out plant names and finally given up, eschewing the Latin names Olivia rattled off and substituting 'small shrub of some sort.' Latin, combined with her sister's moping about Cooke, had been enough to send Phaedra back inside, but *someone* had switched the salt for sugar in the kitchen, spoiling the platter of eggs at breakfast that morning and sending Leo's temperamental chef into a frenzy.

Proof Olivia had regained some of her spirit and was not wallowing in melancholy.

Jacob Rutherford, Georgina's father and Cooke's uncle, had informed them all that his nephew was merely in Boston on business, declining to say little else other than to mention the name of the hotel where Cooke was staying. Georgina had already dashed off a note to her cousin, but not before exchanging a meaningful glance with Olivia.

Phaedra didn't understand their worry. She'd already assured Olivia that Morgan wouldn't harm Cooke, and according to Rutherford, his nephew was perfectly well. At least her menacing American had kept his word. And he'd apparently lost interest in Phaedra, as evidenced by the fact she hadn't seen him since her arrival.

Which was a profound relief. Truly.

"Drat."

A sharp twist to her mid-section said differently. A sense of loss Phaedra didn't want to feel.

Morgan was to be avoided. The wager could not be won if he wasn't in the vicinity, meaning Elysium would not teeter at the edge of bankruptcy. Morgan's absence was to be applauded, not just for Leo's sake, but her own. He was far too *overwhelming* to Phaedra's senses. The possessive way he'd held her, the claiming of her mouth and—

"Bloody hell," she said quietly, not wishing to alarm the two stewards she passed on her way to the lobby. The entire staff knew her as Leo's eccentric, reckless younger sister, Lady Phaedra. But there wasn't any reason for her to prove the point further by being caught whispering vulgarities.

Things all came down to page seventy-eight in Elysium's Red Book, which Phaedra had viewed, finally, in the weeks before the journey to America. Cracking open the large red leather tome, she'd seen the wager, recorded in Peckham's careful handwriting and dutifully witnessed by him, pages away from all the other nonsensical bets on *The Disastrous Barrington.*

So easy to overlook. Hidden, almost.

Ten *thousand* pounds. Neither Leo nor Tony could have possibly seen or known about the wager and failed to comment on it.

Ten thousand bloody pounds. *For her.*

Phaedra toyed with the idea of nudging Peckham with a

few carefully placed words to inform Leo of the staggering sum, but it would mean admitting she had gone to Elysium. And then there was the matter of her acquaintance with Morgan, which would be difficult to explain. Better to handle matters on her own. There wouldn't be any winning of any wager.

"I won't allow it." Phaedra smoothed her skirts.

"What won't you allow, dearest?" Her mother, the Dowager Duchess of Averell, stood just to the side of the stairs, resplendent in steel gray silk decorated with tiny seed pearls. A small tiara had been woven into the faded copper of her hair, and diamonds dripped from her ears and throat. She was slightly overdressed but every inch a commanding duchess, which Phaedra assumed was the point.

"To be late, Your Grace. Mrs. Rutherford expects it, I think. But we shouldn't allow it." Phaedra spun about, the green silk swirling around her ankles. The gown was a design of Romy's, with vines stitched along the skirt.

Mama nodded. "Lovely, Lady Phaedra." She winked at her. "Your sister is clever with a needle." Her lips pursed. "I can depend on you to behave this evening, can I not?"

That was the problem with being disastrous. No one assumed anything else. "Of course, Your Grace."

The entire family, save Rosalind who wasn't feeling well and would stay behind with Torrington, had been invited to a dinner party hosted by Jacob and Cordelia Rutherford. Sure to be an overblown affair. Mrs. Rutherford was one of the reigning doyennes of Manhattan society. She was a chilly, ambitious woman who had nothing of Georgina's warmth about her. Tonight's dinner was more about Cordelia reaffirming her connections to a ducal family than anything else.

Phaedra had relished setting foot in America, hoping to be free of the constraints of London, though Georgina had warned her things were very much the same. Everyone here walked about with confidence, flattening their vowels and speaking of money. A tad crass, but Phaedra adored such brashness. New York was bold. Big. She'd been prepared to embrace the city.

So, imagine the disappointment to find Georgina correct. Society on this side of the Atlantic functioned in a similar manner to London. Even the disapproval with which Mrs. Rutherford eyed Phaedra felt remarkably similar.

"I'm sure," Georgina said, stunning in blue-patterned silk as she took Mama's arm. "My mother would relish a bit of scandalous behavior for the sake of her guests. No doubt half the city has been apprised of the Beautiful Barringtons."

"Georgina," Mama admonished. "Such a silly name you've given us. I had hoped it wouldn't follow us from London."

A dark blonde curl fell over Georgina's cheek, and she brushed it away before leading Mama out the doors of The Barrington with Phaedra trailing behind.

"I've already apologized to Maggie." Georgina nodded at the other carriage pulling away from the hotel. "My mother will likely ask her to play for us all tonight. My parents do own a decently tuned piano, though not one of us Rutherfords can play. If Tony joins his duchess in a duet, my mother might faint."

Mama laughed. "You sound rather hopeful."

"Oh, I am, Your Grace." Georgina turned and winked at Phaedra.

Leo's wife liked to make a bit of trouble. "I'll be discreetly outlandish. Will that suffice, Georgina?"

"Perfectly," her sister-in-law answered.

"I fear Phaedra needs little encouragement. Come along, dearest." Mama waved her forward. "We don't want to be too late."

Phaedra dutifully followed, already wishing the evening was over.

3

Once the overly lengthy dinner came to a close and the gentlemen had been left to their brandy, Phaedra and Olivia wandered through the cavernous lavish drawing room of the Rutherford mansion with the other female guests. The talk over the excellent roast duck had all focused on The Barrington. The grand opening. Leo's vague plans for expansion, at which he hinted but refused to discuss further, while Rutherford presided over the table with a smug smile. The description of The Barrington's rooftop garden drew gasps of awe. Not to be confused with the *English* garden adjacent to The Barrington which Olivia was supervising, much to everyone's surprise. Mrs. Rutherford assured her guests that both gardens were true marvels of horticulture and stunning creations. There was nothing in Manhattan like either. She dropped a well-placed hint that the Ladies Social Society had already reserved the English garden to hold their monthly gatherings, which of course had the other ladies in attendance plying Leo with questions as to how they might reserve the space for their own use.

Mrs. Rutherford basked in their envy. She was the chair-woman of the Ladies Social Society.

And just as Georgina had suspected, Mrs. Rutherford was busy coaxing Maggie into playing the piano to entertain her guests, which of course brought the conversation to a discussion of music led by the dowager duchess. Mama and Maggie were immediately surrounded by a group of fawning ladies.

Phaedra rolled her eyes. "Good grief."

"I feel as if we should rescue Her Grace," Olivia murmured.

Her sister was the very epitome of English ladyhood. Coolly sedate in a gown of soft rose, hands clasped loosely before her as she floated about Mrs. Rutherford's drawing room, her posture absolutely perfect. Phaedra could have placed a dozen books on Olivia's head and not been concerned about them toppling off.

"Which one?" Phaedra stubbed her toe on a side table, stifled the curse on her lips, and continued to wander in the direction of a pair of ladies who spoke in hushed tones, dropping names and gossip with abandon. "You know as well as I that Maggie will relish any excuse to play the piano, and I'm certain Mrs. Rutherford is no match for Mama."

"I tend to agree. There is already music set atop the piano, however. I suppose it would be quite the coup for Mrs. Rutherford to have a duchess play."

"She appeared unimpressed with titles upon our initial introduction, but I suppose that was only pretense."

"Of course, it was," Olivia answered. "She's quite ambitious."

"I think the word you mean is ruthless. Stop being so polite about it. Didn't you notice you were introduced as the granddaughter of the Earl of Daring? Mrs. Rutherford would put a pirate captain to shame, and tonight, she is plundering the Barringtons."

Olivia gave a soft giggle. "I did note her introduction."

"Once Mr. Cooke finally returns from Boston, which he is bound to do any day"—Phaedra took Olivia's fingers and squeezed—"you'll be stuck with the Rutherfords as family."

"They are already my family, given Leo is wed to Georgina." A wrinkle took up residence between Olivia's dark brows. "I'm not sure *what* will happen upon Mr. Cooke's return."

What rubbish. "Olivia—"

"I'll return in a moment. I need to refresh myself." Olivia stopped her with a weak smile. She turned and gracefully wove through the other ladies present before exiting the drawing room, probably to mope about in private before composing herself once more.

Phaedra moved to stand before one of the tall windows overlooking Lafayette Square. There wasn't much to see, not with the light having faded. But the moon was out. And she was feeling unsettled. She inclined her head as she passed the two women seated on a settee, each sipping a glass of sherry, ignoring the way their eyes narrowed on her. Two of Manhattan's premiere matrons, doubtless both descended from the old Dutch families who'd settled New York and who continued to run things. According to Georgina.

An entire ocean separated those two women from London, yet they would have been at home at the Upton ball. All they required was a pair of fans to snap while they whispered about everyone in attendance. Phaedra struggled to recall their names, having been introduced earlier, but failed. Just as well. She was not interested at furthering their acquaintance.

She ran her finger along the sill of the window, hoping to catch their conversation without appearing too obvious. While she was firmly resolved to keep her distance from Morgan Stewart should they cross paths, Phaedra could not help her curiosity about him. Morgan's name had come up at the dinner table over the third course—from the flintiness of Mr. Rutherford's gaze, a topic not to his liking.

"She'll hold this little dinner over our heads for the next year. Our Cordelia has become such a mercenary. But I suppose that is what happens when you wed someone like Jacob Rutherford. I understand Acadia Van Matre still refuses to call upon Cordelia. It's been twenty years, and they're cousins."

One of the women tittered.

"Rutherford's father probably brought mine the brandy Papa liked to indulge in every evening. Hauling it up the Hudson on that barge. Barely literate, from what I understand. At least Rutherford isn't a sot like his father. I suppose that's something. But he's rabble, through and through. The sort you can't ignore."

Her companion paused and made a *tsk*ing sound before continuing.

"I'm only surprised Rutherford is here to dine this evening instead of in Baltimore."

Both women made sounds of amusement before sipping their sherry.

Phaedra hadn't any idea why it was so entertaining that Georgina's father liked to dine in Baltimore. Perhaps the restaurants were better.

"Did you see his face when Mr. Cuthbert mentioned Stewart? Cordelia barely raised a brow, ever composed. Surely, she knows about...Gertrude, though it's been a long time. Cuthbert certainly does."

"She's dead now. What does it matter?"

Phaedra pretended complete absorption in the view, her heart kicking around at the mention of Morgan. She could see both women clearly reflected in the glass of the window, their heads together, cackling like a pair of geese.

"Speaking of which, I saw Stewart at the opera the other night in

the company of another gentleman. Guests of Mr. and Mrs. Beekman."

A small gasp sounded. *"Aren't they distantly related to—"*

"They are." Her friend cut her off. *"Keep your voice down. I was as shocked as you to see them together, but Beekman is a shareholder of Mohawk & Hudson. And there are rumors he's allowing Stewart to court his daughter Iris."*

Phaedra's fingers bit into the wood of the windowsill. Iris Beekman?

Her stomach pitched just a bit. Probably from the cream sauce at dinner. It could not be the news of Morgan's involvement with another woman, which was a profound relief. He would no longer be interested in her—or the wager. Wonderful news.

"I can't fathom that Beekman would give him Iris. He's wealthy, of course. Has his hands in every pie, Mr. Abernathy says."

Mrs. Abernathy. That was the woman's name, the one speaking.

"And he did manage to wiggle himself free of that business with Gertrude, though he's clearly guilty, even if the matter was swept aside long ago. I'm not sure how he managed it." A pause. *"He's like a mongrel off his leash. Any one of us might be taken in, as Beekman surely has been".*

"Gertrude knew well what might happen." Mrs. Abernathy's friend, whose name Phaedra could still not recall, raised her chin and surveyed the room, checking to make sure no one was paying attention to their conversation. *"She had such a big heart, though I fear she was misguided in her affection for Stewart. Pity things ended so poorly. Let us not speak of this further. I wouldn't put it past Rutherford to ask us to leave, as I'm sure he did Cuthbert for mentioning Stewart."*

Phaedra lingered at her place by the window, hoping Mrs. Abernathy and her friend would say more, but they moved on to other topics, specifically when or if Georgina's sister,

Lilian, would ever be coaxed to wed again. From their conversation, it seemed as if Morgan had been involved with this Gertrude and things had ended on a sour note. But why would that matter to Mrs. Rutherford?

A willowy blonde, far too thin in Phaedra's opinion, strolled in her direction, a knowing glint in her eye. "Goodness, my lady." Georgina's sister, Lilian, took the spot beside Phaedra, sparing a glance for the two women on the settee. "Are they talking about me once more? And to think I used to be envious that Georgina garnered so much attention."

"Indeed, they are," Phaedra assured her with a smile. "I'm waiting for them to make a wager on your marital prospects."

The widowed Lilian Rutherford Harrison reminded Phaedra of a piece of fine Belgium lace. Delicate and wispy. Features so finely spun, she often didn't look real, more like a carefully crafted porcelain doll come to life. But for all her beauty, sadness clung to Lilian, no matter how she smiled and laughed. Shadows often lingered in her eyes. She had none of Georgina's robust, rebellious personality or her sister's generous curves. Only the hint of steel in her spine was identical to Georgina's.

"Apparently you're to wed a senator at some point," Phaedra informed her. "He's older, but he will make you an excellent husband. They are curious why Mr. Rutherford has not yet pushed you to wed him."

"Jacob wouldn't dare." An edge, hard and brittle, shone in Lilian's eye. "Besides, Senator Howell is his choice, not mine. My father is better at choosing a winning horse, not husbands."

Lilian's previous marriage had ended abruptly. Tragically, her husband had died, and she'd lost the child she'd carried. Leo had explained only the bare minimum of what had occurred that winter day in Brooklyn. Georgina refused to speak of it at all.

"Well." Phaedra shot her a look. "It isn't only *your* marital prospects Mrs. Abernathy is concerned over, but those of Iris Beekman."

Lilian raised a brow. "Iris Beekman? Oh, yes. I recall her. She's lovely. Wealthy. Prestigious family. I can't fathom what their concern would be."

"Apparently, Miss Beekman's father is allowing her to be courted by a gentleman named Morgan Stewart. I'm not familiar with the name," Phaedra lied smoothly.

"There's no reason for you to be." Lilian's voice thinned. "Stewart is a man of business. Not considered respectable for —various reasons. He and my cousin, Ben, don't get along. Some sort of business rivalry, which means Jacob doesn't care for Stewart either. Nor does anyone else. The mere mention of his name angers my father to no end." A short, bitter laugh came from her. "Stewart won in a business deal, I'm sure. Jacob hates to lose."

The animosity Phaedra had witnessed between Cooke and Morgan was far greater than a simple disagreement over a business matter. More personal in nature.

"Stewart is the primary shareholder of Mohawk & Hudson. My father is in shipping. I suppose they consider themselves competitors."

"Mohawk & Hudson?"

"The tracks that run along the Erie Canal. Still contested in some quarters. Stewart builds railroads."

The railroad in which I hold the majority interest in America runs along the Erie Canal.

Phaedra could clearly hear Morgan's words from their first meeting at Hagerty's, though he hadn't given any more information. Or even a name. But now she had one.

"There wasn't anyone in New York who thought to challenge those running the Erie Canal, but Stewart did. The tracks along the canal were considered to be a fool's gambit, never to be permitted. But Stewart managed to accomplish the impossible. I'm sure not everyone agrees with his negotiation tactics, but the tracks were laid. Made him wealthier than..." Lilian hesitated and pursed her lips.

"Than what?"

"*Before*. But even so, I doubt Beekman would hand over Iris, though I did see her flirting shamelessly with Stewart at an event I attended some time ago. His origins leave something to be desired. He makes being the son of a drunken barge owner seem almost tame in comparison." Lilian gave her a wry look. "My grandfather."

"So I've heard." Phaedra nodded in the direction of Mrs. Abernathy and her friend. "I wonder that they were invited, given their opinion of Mr. Rutherford."

Lilian waved a hand. "My mother's way of putting others in their place while reminding them of her influence despite my father."

Phaedra thought carefully about how to phrase her next words. "Perhaps Miss Beekman has a rival for Stewart's affections. A Gertrude was mentioned," she said casually. "Though by the sound of it, things did not end well."

"You could say that. Why are you so interested in Mr. Stewart? Have you made his acquaintance?" Lilian's dark eyes were shrewd.

"Merely idle curiosity." Phaedra gave her a brilliant smile, the one she used often enough on Peckham to know it worked. "At any rate, those two"—she tilted her chin at the pair of women still sipping sherry—"seemed overly concerned about him and poor Miss Beekman. I confess I was curious. Also, if I'm being honest, I'm a bit bored. The gossip was at least interesting."

This time Lilian's laughter was genuine. "I'm sorry to inform you, my lady, that this evening will not come to a quick end. My mother is putting her newest possessions on display tonight."

"Us?" Phaedra raised a brow.

"Well, yes. She chose an exclusive list for tonight's dinner. In her own way, my mother's ambition rivals that of my father. You should have seen the way Cordelia trotted out Leo when he and Georgina were first married."

Phaedra nodded, not really caring about Mrs. Rutherford or her tactics. She was thinking of Morgan, whom everyone disliked. Well, having made his acquaintance, she could see why. He had a displeasing personality.

A tingle of warmth bled over her skin, calling out her lie.

Fine. She *was* curious about Iris Beekman. And the mysterious Gertrude, who evidently was dead. Had Morgan been embroiled in a scandalous affair with her? Then there was the matter of Five Points, which, even after she'd strolled about the city with Georgina, had not been mentioned. She had the impression it was a place no one dared to speak about.

Lilian would know, but Phaedra didn't want to ask.

A beautiful haunting melody suddenly filled the drawing room, and Phaedra turned, unsurprised to see the Duchess of Averell, Maggie, sitting before the piano. Her small form swayed back and forth atop the bench as her fingers flew over the keys.

The door to the drawing room opened, and a collective sigh went up among every female present. Mrs. Abernathy placed a hand on her throat. Her companion batted her eyelashes as if she were half-blind.

"I thought I heard you playing, Your Grace," said the stunningly beautiful man as he entered and stopped in place, probably so each lady in attendance could admire him for a moment, before going to the piano.

"Ugh." Phaedra said under her breath.

Lilian laughed softly.

"May I join you, Your Grace?" The rumbling baritone of Phaedra's brother, Tony, echoed through the room, blending with the music coming from the piano.

Maggie slid across the bench and patted the empty spot beside her. "I should want nothing else, duke."

Mrs. Abernathy looked about to swoon. "He's quite splendid," she said to her friend. "Notoriously faithful." She regarded Tony with a not so polite leer. "A pity."

Phaedra made a face. How on earth Maggie tolerated such nonsense was beyond her understanding. *Yes,* Tony was rather magnificent. As was Leo. But there wasn't any reason to faint at the sight of them. Good lord, it was embarrassing, having your brother mooned over in such a public manner.

She tapped her foot rather impatiently and looked over at the large clock above the fireplace, wishing the evening to come to a more rapid close.

4

Morgan Stewart made his way around Lafayette Square, cheroot in hand, blowing smoke rings, after he and Lewis Armwood had left the Beekman home. Dinner had been a sumptuous affair because Beekman wanted to impress Morgan, though Mrs. Beekman looked as if she'd have been happier had Morgan and Lew declined the invitation.

Iris, the Beekman's daughter, had sat across from Morgan during the entire meal, as flirtatious as her modesty and decorum would allow. She was a lovely girl, beautiful and well-mannered.

Unfortunately for Iris, Morgan preferred a bit of savagery in a young lady.

It was Beekman who had first broached the idea, months ago, of a match between his daughter and Morgan. At the time, the match had made a great deal of sense. Iris would make a good wife. Excellent pedigree from one of the oldest Dutch families, though the Beekman fortune wasn't as robust as it once had been.

"These invitations from Beekman are becoming quite regular. He might be kicked out of the Upper Tens if he continues furthering his association with you. They won't welcome you happily into their fold either." Lew lit a cheroot with the flick of one wrist.

"You mean if I wed Iris?" Morgan wasn't the most desirable of dinner companions, but as a son-in-law, his company would perhaps become more tolerable among Manhattan society. Beekman owned a ten percent share in Mohawk & Hudson and wanted more, given the state of his finances. Dangling Iris, and the respectability she would bring Morgan, was an inspired move.

He appreciated the strategy.

"If? I thought you'd decided it would be good for business —and your reputation."

"There isn't any saving my reputation, Lew. I think we both know that."

Morgan could wed the Queen of England and it would do little to change society's opinion of him. Some would say he needed to return to the filth of the streets that spawned him. Others, that he should hang for murder.

"Well, thank goodness one of us has a pedigree."

Morgan snorted. Lewis Armwood's family did hold some prestige, but otherwise, his friend and business partner had a personality far closer to Morgan's own. Save the more murderous aspects.

"Not impressive, I grant you, but entirely acceptable. Also, I'm English, which guarantees me a place at anyone's table in New York. Oh, and I'm related to a future earl, that is, if Lord Daring ever forgives poor Thomlinson for wedding my sister and not his granddaughter, Miss Nelson."

"Just as well. I'm fairly certain Miss Nelson is already spoken for." Morgan gave him a sideways look.

Miss Nelson was involved with Morgan's old friend from Canal Street, Twist, though Twist hadn't used the name in years. Everyone in Manhattan now knew him as Benjamin Cooke, nephew and heir to Jacob Rutherford, never assuming Cooke had come from the same vile part of the city as Morgan. Such was the power of Rutherford.

His fingers curled tightly around the cheroot.

"Thomlinson inferred as much. Is that why you haven't tossed Cooke into the East River yet? For Miss Nelson's sake?"

"Among other reasons."

The most important being a promise, reluctantly given, to one ferocious little creature not to harm any member of her family. Which Morgan supposed also included winning a wager in Elysium's Red Book that would bankrupt Leo Murphy.

Damn.

He paused before Rutherford's mansion, alit with lights, letting all the loathing he had for the man sear his skin. Mrs. Beekman had mentioned that the Rutherfords were hosting a duke at their table tonight, and Morgan didn't need to guess it was Averell. Carriages were stacked along the street. The sounds of laughter and piano music floated outside. The duke and his duchess were both known for their skills at the piano.

Morgan would bet his entire fortune that Phaedra was inside, tormenting Manhattan society.

I hope she is exceeding their expectations of poor behavior.

A smile tugged at his lips at the thought of Phaedra challenging the likes of Cordelia Rutherford.

"What's so amusing?" Lew said. "You almost look as if you're about to smile. Did you have too much of Beekman's brandy?"

Morgan was thinking what a scene it would cause, were he

to storm the Rutherford mansion and steal Phaedra out from under all those disapproving twits. The duke and Murphy would be sure to object. Benjamin Cooke was not in town at present, but Rutherford might shoot Morgan in his nephew's absence.

Worth it.

"So if threatening to expose Benjamin Cooke's true identity didn't rouse Rutherford——"

"He's known for years," Morgan interrupted.

"And you aren't going to kill his precious nephew, I'm not sure what else you can do to gain his attention."

Attention. He had wanted Rutherford's for quite a long time. Or a confession. They were one and the same.

"I am considering several options."

The simplest would be to continue with his current scheme. Seduce Phaedra. Run off with her. Win the wager in Elysium's Red Book. Murphy had overextended himself with the building of his grand hotel, and the sum Morgan had wagered would put Elysium in a precarious position. The threat would be withdrawn, however, in return for the truth from Rutherford. In any case, Morgan planned on keeping Phaedra.

He thought of her spinning about, nearly taking his ear off at Cherry Hill with the knife he'd just gifted her. Morgan had never been so aroused in his entire life.

"You mean the property in London? The plot of land Murphy has been eyeing for his London version of The Barrington? I like tossing Cooke in the river better."

Morgan raised a brow. "He'll toss you in the river if you don't stop following his cousin Lilian about. You should be more careful."

Lew paused and cleared his throat. "I helped Mrs. Harrison out of a potentially unwelcome situation."

"For which I'm sure she's grateful. Cooke will not be. He's overly protective of his cousins, *especially* Lilian. There's a gentleman or two in Manhattan sporting a bruised windpipe. And the last dandy who attempted liberties with the lovely widow disappeared entirely."

Lew made a disgruntled sound. "I'm good with a pistol—and my fists."

"Yes, but not with knives. Not like Cooke is. There is a reason he was nicknamed Twist when we were children."

"Even so. I can handle Cooke."

Cooke, who had once been Twist, the companion of another boy called Nubbs. Raised in a brothel together like brothers. And for all Morgan knew, they might well have been. Ragged and starved. Forced to earn their keep by picking pockets and petty thieving to earn a place at Sister Bridget's.

Morgan absently rubbed his wrist where the mark Sister Bridget had put there still burned his skin. That bitch still haunted him, even though he was no longer a child under her control.

On that chilly day, he and Twist had been drawn to an alley off Canal Street by a horrible smell. A dead body, which usually meant clothing or shoes. Possibly coin. But they'd only left with a coat. Or at least, one of them had.

That damned coat.

Had Morgan, who had once been the scrawny, sickly child Nubbs, entered that alley a few minutes before Twist, the dying madwoman hunched in the corner might have placed the coat on Morgan's shoulders. Not Twist's.

He could have become Benjamin Cooke, Rutherford's nephew and heir.

Instead, his friend had left Morgan to the muck and filth, not to mention the tender care of Sister Bridget. He'd become more of an animal than ever before once he'd lost his best friend and protector. Paid for the sin dearly.

Until Gertrude Van Rhys.

"Don't be too sure you can deal with Cooke, Lew. I'd prefer not to have a dead partner. I've quite a bit invested in you."

His friend laughed into the night air.

Morgan's gaze was drawn once more to the brightly lit windows of the house before him, where Jacob Rutherford was likely sipping an expensive brandy, scheming about how to use everyone in his drawing room for his own purposes. Did he ever think of Gertie? Or was she only a distant memory to him?

"Morgan," Lew said quietly. "Rutherford is unlikely to give you the answers you seek about Gertrude's death. He's avoided doing so for years."

"I'm going to make sure he can't ignore me any longer."

Gertrude Van Rhys, Morgan's adoptive mother, had been Jacob Rutherford's lover. No one had known about their affair, certainly not Cordelia, Rutherford's wife. Morgan had been away at school when their relationship had started but had grown accustomed to seeing Rutherford when he'd visited during breaks. Back then, Rutherford had been kind to Morgan.

"You've tried every trap. Spun your webs."

Lew had no idea.

"Maybe there isn't anything to tell you about that night. Even if he was Gertrude's lover, that doesn't make Rutherford guilty of anything."

"Then why not simply speak to me?" He turned to Lew. "There isn't a soul in Manhattan who doesn't assume I murdered the woman who saved me," Morgan replied in a chilly tone. The one person in all the world who had *loved* him.

Gertrude Van Rhys, opinionated spinster and brilliant businesswoman, could have had Morgan imprisoned for attempting to steal her reticule, but instead she'd embraced him. "I've been hounded for years, Lew. Spat at. Eyed as if I might suddenly go mad and use my teeth to destroy those around me."

"Maybe Rutherford doesn't know what happened."

"He behaves as a guilty man would. Refusing to speak to me. Going out of his way to avoid the pretense of even having known me. Do you really expect me to leave Gertrude unavenged?"

Lew looked away. "No, of course not."

The death of Gertrude Van Rhys had devastated him. Morgan had found her, lying on the floor in her bedroom next to the desk she used for correspondence. Blood had pooled around her head like a halo, her skin already cold. Morgan had buried his head against her chest, begging her to *please* not be dead.

Gertie's lady's maid, a sour-faced woman named Boyd, had found him beside the body and sent word to Gertie's brother.

When Martin Van Rhys had arrived, he brought the authorities, and immediately accused Morgan of killing Gertie without even asking what happened. Assumed guilty because everyone knew where Morgan had come from. That he was some sort of animal. He'd spoken not a word in his own defense. What had it mattered? Gertie was gone.

He'd sat in a jail cell, listening to Martin's vile accusations, that Morgan had bedded Gertrude. Murdered her. Honestly, Morgan hadn't cared at that point what happened to him. He'd been cast adrift once more after having lost his anchor. But somehow, he had been released. Set free the following day. Gertie's death ruled accidental.

Didn't matter. It still didn't. Martin had tried to have him arrested again, but the only other person who had been there that night was Boyd, Gertie's maid, and she'd disappeared.

There wasn't a soul in all New York who thought him innocent of the murder of Gertrude Van Rhys.

Except for Jacob Rutherford, of course. Because he had killed her.

Morgan tossed his cheroot to the ground, grinding the end beneath one heel, thinking of Rutherford. "He was there the night Gertie died. They argued. Rutherford has a temper. It makes sense that he could have hurt her. I want his confession. So, yes. I've found a way to force him to speak to me."

Or at least he'd found leverage. Only now, that scheme was in jeopardy.

"But if you can't use Cooke— " Lew regarded him with a wide stare. "Leo Murphy."

Morgan looked away from Rutherford's home.

"Rutherford's son-in-law. *He's* your leverage. The bastard Barrington, with his grand hotel—and Rutherford is undoubtedly a partner. You put your thumb on Murphy, threaten him, and it sets off a slew of reactions in Cooke, Georgina, and, lastly, Jacob Rutherford." Lew shook his head. "How utterly complicated."

"A bit."

More so now because of a small, hostile creature Morgan wanted with every fiber of his being.

"How will you get a hold on Murphy?"

Morgan glanced back up at one of Rutherford's drawing room windows just in time to see a slender silhouette pass before the curtains—and felt his pulse pick up.

"Murphy's plan to expand The Barrington," he said to Lew. "Find out everything you can about it. There's bound to be an investment opportunity in his enterprise, especially from a fellow Englishman. No mention of me."

Lew nodded slowly. "Consider it done."

Morgan's original plan, to threaten Elysium with bankruptcy over a wager, no longer held the appeal it once had, though he had not yet let it go. Possibly controlling enough of Murphy's hotel might be enough to make a statement.

Ruthless and cruel he might be, but Morgan didn't think he could bear to hurt Phaedra. Or use her.

Not even for Gertie.

5

The day after the Rutherford's dinner party, Phaedra came down the stairs dressed for the family outing Georgina had planned. She had learned nothing more about Morgan and instead spent the remainder of the evening at the Rutherford home trying not to doze off in one of the overstuffed chairs sitting before the fire. Phaedra had learned that Iris Beekman was lauded as a great beauty and a modest young lady, neither of which improved her mood.

She drummed her fingers along the banister, polished to a vibrant shine and smelling of beeswax.

A short time ago, she had taken the opportunity to ask one of the maids, a lovely Irish girl named Molly, about Five Points. Better than going to either Georgina or Lilian, and she didn't dare ask Leo.

Why would you want to know about such a terrible place, my lady? Babies die in the street and the dogs gnaw on their bones. Filth everywhere. You'd get your throat slit afore you could say your name. Nothing good comes from there.

Well, that didn't sound at all pleasant, but it did sound rather perfect for Morgan Stewart. She still hadn't figured out how Morgan and Cooke could have been childhood friends if that were the case, however. Yet another mystery to be solved. Maybe Morgan had lied about that.

She recalled Cooke's face when Morgan had called him Twist.

No. I don't think he was lying.

Which meant—well, she wasn't ready to draw such a conclusion about Cooke.

But none of her assumptions truly mattered, considering Phaedra meant not to set eyes on Morgan Stewart again. She couldn't risk him winning the wager. Their brief acquaintance was at an end. Upon her return to London, Phaedra meant to tear page seventy-eight from the Red Book as if it had never existed. Leo would never have to know of her stupidity and her involvement with Morgan. Or that Elysium had been threatened because of it.

Phaedra lifted her chin. Nodded to herself. Morgan did not merit further introspection. Who cared where he came from or if he wed Iris Beekman?

A tug at her heart had her sucking in a breath.

She cared. And wished she did not.

Georgina had planned an entire day of sightseeing for the family. They had all been working so hard on the grand opening of The Barrington that a pleasant day out of doors—with a picnic—was required. Rosalind and Torrington were busy in the kitchens arguing with Leo's temperamental chef but would try to join them after ensuring the kitchens were in order. The servants who had traveled with the family from London had been given the day off to explore on their own.

Oddly, the only one exempted from Georgina's plans was Olivia. The English garden was coming along, but a delivery of manure was expected today, and Georgina had insisted only Olivia could properly instruct the laborers on how to disperse it.

Rubbish. Or manure, as the case may be.

Georgina obviously had reasons for excluding Olivia, and Phaedra suspected they had something to do with Benjamin Cooke. A smug, knowing smile sat on Georgina's lips as they left The Barrington. She seemed terribly pleased with herself.

IMMEDIATELY AFTER THEIR RETURN TO THE HOTEL LATER that day, the entire family was made aware that Benjamin Cooke was in good health. And back in Manhattan. Phaedra could vouch for him being uninjured. As could the rest of the Barringtons.

At least that was the assumption after having seen him naked and lounging in Olivia's bed.

Cooke hadn't seemed as bothered by his unclothed state nearly as much as everyone else.

Phaedra really did like Ben—she was no longer addressing him as Mr. Cooke after having seen so much of him— far more than Thomlinson.

After an overly exhausting day of seeing the sights, a ferry ride, *and* a picnic which, in Phaedra's opinion had taken far too long, the small herd of Barringtons had only been anticipating hot baths. Not scandal.

Leo roared at the sight of Georgina's cousin's naked form wrapped around Olivia. The vein in his head stuck out in a startling manner.

Tony snarled, looking entirely too ducal. And furious.

Georgina appeared wholly satisfied at her cousin's appearance, though she did instruct Ben to cover up.

Mama, to her credit, barely batted an eye at Olivia's ruination. And after a family meeting, which Phaedra had not been permitted to attend, a wedding was planned.

Today, as it happened. This very morning. In Leo's

English garden, where the very air smelled of manure, owing to Olivia's determination to properly fertilize every shrub. A perfect spot since Olivia had been sneaking out to the garden every night to meet Ben after assuming Phaedra was asleep.

Phaedra rolled her eyes at such needless subterfuge.

Did Olivia imagine the back door of The Barrington propped itself open?

She straightened her shoulders, looking out at her family, solemnly standing in the morning sunshine, knocking a clod of dirt off the heel of her slipper, as Ben and Olivia stood smiling before the minister. They made a perfectly lovely couple. Leo was still grumbling, but that was to be expected.

Phaedra's neck prickled softly as she listened to the ceremony, as if a broad palm first caressed her skin then drew down the length of her spine, blotting out the minister's words. A wholly unsettling, yet delicious sensation. And only one person could be responsible.

Discreetly, she snuck a look at the thick shrubbery surrounding the edges of the garden. Beyond the shrubs stood a line of trees before a stone wall circled the entire area to keep passersby from having a view in. Her eyes caught a flicker of movement in the greenery. Far too large to be a squirrel. Smoky topaz glittered among the leaves.

A much bigger animal was stalking her.

Another ripple of sensation floated over her shoulders and back.

Morgan.

Phaedra's heart whispered his name before she could stop it, thumping loudly against the confines of her chest. The minister's voice dulled and faded. The joyful weeping of her mother grew softer. Phaedra's eyes fluttered shut, knowing he was there but unseen, bathing in his presence, and instantly comforted.

He hadn't forgotten Phaedra after all.

The remainder of the ceremony, she searched for him beneath the brush of her lashes, the longing for him fierce and unexpected. Had she any sense at all, Phaedra would have alerted Leo's staff that an intruder had been spotted.

But she did no such thing.

Phaedra thought about Morgan all during the wedding breakfast that followed the ceremony, glancing through the large windows to the garden just outside the dining room, but if Morgan still hid in the shrubbery, she couldn't find him.

Anticipation filled her. A violent, willful passion that pushed aside all common sense. Wrong, all of it. Yet the feeling lingered. Grew. Kept her from enjoying the delicious desserts placed on the table, which Rosalind proclaimed inferior, particularly the cherry tart. A debate ensued, about whether it had been wise to fire the combative Monsieur Mardeux when it was his pastry chef, Bartu, who couldn't make a decent tart.

Honestly, a tart was a bloody tart. Phaedra couldn't tell if the crust was flaking properly or not.

The worst part of all, besides watching Leo growl at Ben over the poached chicken, was that no matter how Phaedra listed Morgan Stewart's faults, starting with his affinity for piano wire and ending with his wager on her, it did nothing whatsoever to dissuade her heart.

6

Phaedra smoothed down the silk skirts of her gown as she stood in the lobby of The Barrington, unsurprised to see Rosalind and Torrington marching to the kitchens like two generals intent on marshaling the troops. And with good reason. Now that Monsieur Mardeux had been dismissed and the kitchens put under Torrington's supervision, a small revolt was brewing, led by Bartu, the pastry chef.

Phaedra scanned the lobby, already bustling with activity. Leo's employees scurried about, most casting nervous glances in the direction of the kitchen. Torrington's raised voice echoed down the hall, snarling at Bartu in flawless French.

Pity she hadn't paid more attention to learning the language better because Phaedra was certain Torrington was uttering the most vile curses at Bartu and it would be useful to have an arsenal of vulgarities in several languages. Torrington was generally considered the calmest family member, so whatever was happening in the kitchens must be truly terrible.

"There you are, Phaedra." The dowager's cool tone met her ears. "Finally."

"Where else would I be, Mama? I promised Leo I would greet all his patrons personally, like Pith ushering in guests for a ball, except I'm not expected to announce any of them."

"No, you are not." Mama raised a brow at her flippant remark.

"And it isn't as if I'm going to run off and be ruined," she continued in an innocent tone. "Not like Olivia. You must be sorely disappointed."

"Not in the least. Olivia has made a love match." Mama's tone grew wistful. "What I've always wished. Nor will her children have overly large heads."

Possibly they would come out holding knives or some other weapon, but Phaedra decided it best not to mention that point.

"Very true. Strange how Mr. Thomlinson has such an oversized skull, isn't it? Not really noticeable until one points it out. I liken him to a sunflower, bending on a thin stalk beneath the weight. His neck being the stalk."

"I understood your metaphor, dearest."

"I think Mr. Cooke the better choice, even considering the scandal. I'm sure that's why they changed their plans to leave today. Avoidance."

"There is no scandal, Phaedra." Mama gave her a pointed look. "I daresay we are still waiting for one to envelop us all."

For only a moment, Phaedra imagined her mother had seen Morgan Stewart's wager in Elysium's Red Book. But the Dowager Duchess of Averell would never set foot in Elysium —at least, Phaedra didn't think she would.

"I take offense, Your Grace. I've been rather perfect on this visit to New York." Phaedra lifted her chin. "I wish to bring that to your attention."

"We haven't been in residence at The Barrington for

long," Mama countered, amethysts and diamonds glittering in her copper hair. "I'm sure only time is needed." She shook out her skirts, making the pale purple silk, a shade darker than lavender, flutter about her ankles. The color was nearly as awful as gray but not as detestable as black. Phaedra was rather glad her mother had moved on to something lighter. Finally.

When Marcus Barrington was alive, Mama had worn pale yellow, looking like a fairy princess caught up in buttercups. Or sea-foam green. Papa had adored her in green.

Phaedra doubted Mama would ever wear either color again.

Grief plowed into her. Still so sharp. Probably because she had dreamt of her father last night.

He'd been handsome and whole, sitting atop his grave at Cherry Hill, eating the wild strawberries that never failed to grow there. Eyes, so like her own, glinted back at her with a hint of mischief.

I always wanted to see America, Phaedra.

She hadn't known that. Papa had never mentioned wanting to travel across the sea, but there were likely dozens of things Phaedra hadn't known about Marcus Barrington. Then he had gestured towards the stand of trees growing just behind his grave, where a dark, broad-shouldered form was taking shape in the shadows. Phaedra knew it could only be Morgan. The pale slivers of his eyes glowed at her from the darkness. She'd kissed her father and run into those shadows.

Schatje.

She had jerked awake, panting as if she'd actually been running across the small hill where her father's grave sat.

"Phaedra?" Mama touched her arm with a concerned look. "What is it?"

She blinked away the unsettling dream. Mentioning Papa would only upset her mother.

"I was only considering the state of the kitchens, Your Grace. I think Torrington is about to engage in a round of fisticuffs with the pompous Bartu. He of the unflaky tarts." Phaedra put up her fists and pretended to punch at something. "While Ros hits him over the head with a skillet. Bartu, not Torrington. I'm sure the curses are terrible." She gave her mother an expectant look.

Mama spoke fluent French.

"Hmm. What do you know of fisticuffs, Phaedra?" Her mother asked. "You speak with familiarity."

"Well, yes, I'm familiar. Don't you recall the afternoon Lord Emberly invited me to watch him at his club? You accompanied me. I learned quite a bit."

"I do." Mama still looked suspicious. "Well, I suppose we are fortunate to have Torrington step in. He's a far better cook, at any rate, than Mardeux, and his tarts are always perfect. And as far as Emberly..." A tiny smile pulled at her mother's lips. "I found his manly display quite riveting."

Good grief. Emberly had slapped his opponent at one point.

"I was pleased," her mother continued, "to see you show some interest in such a lovely gentleman."

Why were they discussing Emberly? Phaedra had barely given him a second thought, even when he'd called upon her the day before the family departed London. She couldn't even remember what they'd talked about.

Very unlike Morgan. She could recall every breath he'd taken in her presence. The way he smelled, like apples and a warm fire.

A rush of heat blew up beneath her skirts, dragging fingers along her legs.

Bollocks.

"I didn't mean to embarrass you, dearest. After such a display by Emberly, it is only natural for you to find him more

85

physically appealing." The copper brows drew together, her smile widening. "If we need to have another discussion on courtship and physical relations—"

"We do not, Your Grace." Her mother considered herself to be progressive in her views. And her desire to prepare Phaedra for the inevitable had resulted in more than a few awkward conversations. Further education on the subject was not required. Having savage, delicious liberties taken with her person after having been gifted a knife had imbued Phaedra with a fairly good idea of what to expect.

Though she was not going to speak to Morgan again. She could not. Despite his having lurked about the gardens during Olivia's wedding and her own complicated feelings for him.

"Might I then express my opinion of Lord Ashley?" Mama clasped her hands. "Your behavior towards him was a bit... extreme. I've been meaning to bring it to your attention, especially since tonight we must all be on our best behavior for Leo's sake."

Did her family think Phaedra was completely lacking in decorum?

Yes, they do.

"Ashley was a unique situation, Your Grace. He made a wager on me. That *I would* grant him liberties. He put it in Elysium's Red Book. If you're upset with anyone, it should be Leo, who permits the gentlemen of London to place bets on his sister. Frankly, doing so encourages outlandish behavior."

"I *should* speak to Leo about that." The dowager duchess tapped her chin with an elegant finger, not overly concerned, but then she had a soft spot for both her boys. *Especially* Leo. "It's rather unseemly. I did not realize the situation had gotten so out of hand."

"Speak to me about what?" Leo interrupted as he came forward, radiant and shining like some bloody jewel, looking very much like their father, Marcus Barrington. The same careless masculine beauty, the arrogance guiding his speech. Exactly like Tony. The two looked shockingly alike, considering Tony and Leo had different mothers.

"The Red Book at Elysium where you allow wagers to be made on your *infant* sister," Phaedra said, plucking at the edges of her gloves.

Leo made a dismissive wave as if it was of no import that half of London was betting on her. "Well, I know you aren't actually going to *do* any of those things. Challenge Lord Winslow to a duel with pistols? Take up with a footman?" He made a piffling sound. "Pith would never allow it. Besides, Elysium always wins the wager because they are so outrageous. Frivolous. Never to be collected upon. It only makes good business sense."

She thought of Stewart's wager, sitting on page seventy-eight. If he knew—well, Leo wouldn't think it so frivolous then, would he?

"Yes, but it isn't right," Phaedra insisted. "When was the last time you really looked at the Red Book?"

"Peckham handles the wagers. And I can't tell gentlemen what they can and cannot bet on, Phaedra. I've no control over that. Once you're wed to"—his eyes looked to the ceiling as if for divine assistance—"*someone*, all that will go away. Perhaps Emberly. He's shown a great deal of interest."

"You are unbelievable."

"Stop pouting. Wagers in the Red Book aren't your concern. You shouldn't be running the account ledgers at Elysium either. Or counting markers. Period." He looked at her mother for confirmation.

"No, she should not," Mama said firmly.

Leo had finally confessed everything to the dowager duchess. The wretch.

"I'm not sure if Tony was merely in his cups," her brother continued, "when he allowed you to —"

"I wasn't." Tony interjected as he joined them, splendid in his formal wear, his hair perfectly windswept as if he'd just come from riding across the moors. Or stepped out of a painting. Too magnificent to be real. "In my cups. I was quite sane at the time, though bloody overwhelmed having to handle everything in London while *you* were here."

Two of the maids arranging flowers in a vase at the far side of the hall stopped to stare at Tony with rapt adoration. A rose dropped to the floor and was ignored.

So annoying.

"Anthony." Mama chastised him and looked at Phaedra. "Do not speak so in front of your sister. No cursing."

"Madam, I assure you *Demon* has heard far worse."

"That is not at all comforting, Anthony." Mama's lips pursed. "Please do not call her by that horrid nickname in public. Bad enough that you do so in private. She is a young lady. A duke's daughter. Not some wild urchin."

Dear God.

"Apologies, madam. But *Phaedra* is good with figures and can calculate the odds nearly as well as Leo." Tony winked at her, thinking he was helping the situation when, in fact, he was making it worse. "I needed the assistance." He shot an apologetic look at her mother. "I should have told you sooner, but I was drowning."

"My *infant* sister," Leo bit out. "Running *my* gambling hell. So you could be a duke. And don't toss about drowning in such a casual manner."

Leo had a deep and intense fear of water, having nearly once drowned while fishing with Tony when they were children. That had been the best part about the voyage to New York—watching Leo turn green.

"Well, yes." Tony flicked a piece of lint from his sleeve. "I was born to be a duke. It isn't easy, you know. And as for the other, it was a rather unfortunate choice of words."

Infant sister. As if she were still in need of a nursemaid.

Phaedra took the opportunity to stomp on Leo's foot with the heel of her slipper. It probably wouldn't hurt nearly as much as she wished it to, but it did make her point.

"Ouch." Leo gave her a resigned look. "Childish tantrums are not helping your case."

"I'm good at it. Managing Elysium." Phaedra's chest hurt at the dismissal of her talents. The only ones she possessed outside of knife throwing, which she'd gotten quite good at, but as a skill, it had little practical use. The knife Stewart had gifted her—*a soft wave, like someone tickling her calves ran up her skirts once more*—was tucked away in her dresser drawer upstairs. She ought to retrieve it. Iris Beekman was on tonight's guest list.

What an unwarranted savage thought, Pith's voice intoned in her head. *Where is your decorum?*

"I daresay," Phaedra continued, ignoring the voice of Pith, "the only reason for your distress, Leo, is because I might be better at managing Elysium than you."

"Doubtful. I've been doing so for years without your help," Leo returned.

"I think she might be correct." Tony gave a shrug. "*Dem*—Phaedra doesn't embroider or garden. Music is out of the question. I think we can all appreciate the lack of violin playing, though it resulted in her taking up fencing."

A collective sigh of relief came from her brothers and Mama.

"I did my best. At the violin," Phaedra muttered, though no one cared in the least. She detested when this happened. Speaking *around* her and *about* her, but not *to* her.

"I don't see," Tony insisted, "why she couldn't continue to assist me discreetly."

Leo's face reddened. He might punch Tony. Wouldn't be the first time. "Because she's—"

89

"My sons." The dowager duchess purred in a soothing tone, placing a hand on each of their arms. "I must remind you again—we have no privacy at present, and tonight is about The Barrington. No squabbling." She gave a gentle nod to the maids, who had finally stopped swooning over Tony. The floral arrangement looked as if a blind man had done it. Even Phaedra could tell the ferns were all wrong. Thank goodness Olivia and Ben had already left the city. Her sister would have had fits at seeing such a poorly done vase of flowers.

"We can discuss all this at a later time."

Mama always referred to Tony and Leo as her sons, especially when in public, though she was far too young to have given birth to either of them. A united Barrington front and all that. The Duke of Averell and his family against the world —or at least London. There was a reason Phaedra had grown up mostly at Cherry Hill.

Leo inclined his head. "Your Grace, you look stunning in that gown. The color suits you."

"Splendid, madam," Tony added in the same charming tone. "I hope I shall not have to spend most of the evening protecting your virtue."

Mama laughed gaily. "Now you both border on the ridiculous. But I accept your admiration." She held out her cheek, which each dutifully kissed.

Phaedra's mother, Amanda, was the iron spine of the Barringtons. Lest anyone be foolish enough to think her nothing but an elegantly coiffured dowager, they would only have to witness her bringing both Tony and Leo to heel. Even during their terrible estrangement from Marcus Barrington, one which Phaedra still didn't think her brothers were totally absolved, both had deferred to Mama.

"Now, shall you two escort me inside?" Mama motioned towards the double doors leading into the dining room, which was also serving as the area for tonight's reception and the dancing that would follow.

"It would be my pleasure." Leo took her arm. "Phaedra, as discussed, you will greet our guests as they arrive, but with only Mr. Chipplewit, I'm afraid. Rosalind and Torrington are sorely needed in the kitchens at present but will join us later."

Another roar of French cursing filtered down the hall.

"And Olivia has already departed."

Originally, Phaedra, Olivia, Rosalind, *and* Torrington had all been meant to form a greeting line of sorts.

"Yes, due to her ruination," Phaedra felt the need to add.

"Her *marriage*," Leo growled. It had taken him two days to speak to Ben once more. Georgina had threatened to make him sleep in the lobby if he didn't relent.

"It is my understanding Bartu has staged a rebellion," Tony murmured, least anyone hear. "Bold for a pastry chef."

"Probably under Mardeux's direction. Apparently that pompous frog was incensed I didn't beg him to return to his position after he quit. Torrington is going to sack Bartu as a favor to me and continue to direct the kitchens for the time being." He frowned, eyeing Phaedra. "I suppose I could send out Georgie to help you, but I wanted her inside the dining room with me. Maybe—"

"I'm capable of greeting your guests, Leo." Phaedra glanced at Chipplewit, Leo's manager of The Barrington, who stood near the door directing Leo's staff. "And I'll have Chipplewit."

"It's only for a short time," Leo continued. "An hour at most. Please don't regale anyone about your acumen with a rapier or discuss the benefits of riding astride. And for good-ness's sake, don't speak of your talent at running a faro table."

Phaedra did not care for Leo at present. Not in the least. Had he been closer, she would have stomped on his foot once more. When had he become such an arbiter of morals and upstanding behavior? He did, after all, own a gambling hell.

"I'm anxious to introduce you to Mr. Armwood when he arrives," Leo said to Mama and Tony as they drifted away. "He does business in both London and New York and wants to make a proposal to me."

Phaedra stared at Leo's back, the question on her lips, though it wouldn't be a good idea to simply yell it across the lobby. Mr. Thomlinson had wed a girl whose last name was Armwood.

"My lady." Mr. Chipplewit made a sweeping bow. "I'll be here the entire time. We'll do quite well, I think, without Lord and Lady Torrington."

Chipplewit was a thin, spare gentleman, with a pair of striking green eyes that missed little of what went on around him. Though his physical appearance belied it, Phaedra had the sense Mr. Chipplewit was quite capable, if the small lump in his pocket was any indication. She suspected it was a pistol.

"Thank you, Mr. Chipplewit," she replied. "I haven't any doubt."

7

Morgan surveyed the monstrosity that Leo Murphy had built on a corner of Broadway in Manhattan, counting the windows until he landed on the one that belonged to Phaedra. He'd had an insane urge to climb the building or dangle over the roof by rope to drop inside her rooms since her arrival in New York, but he had restrained himself. Just as he'd stopped short of rushing inside Rutherford's mansion the other night to carry her away. Or merely grabbing her during this morning's wedding. He would have made it over the stone wall before Murphy or Averell knew what was happening.

Such a weakness, his *schatje*.

Until today, when he'd seen her squinting into the shrubs, somehow knowing he was there, Phaedra might have wrongly assumed Morgan had forgotten about her.

Never.

Morgan had known the minute her small half-boots had stepped onto American soil. She had never been out of reach. Not at the Rutherford's overblown dinner party, nor during

Miss Nelson's marriage this morning to Cooke in what Murphy kept touting as his English garden.

Pompous ass.

He had never met such a pampered bastard before. It would have been a pleasure to bankrupt Elysium, though Morgan could no longer do so. His complicated plans would now have to be revised, thanks to his tiny rapier-wielding savage.

In the garden this morning, Morgan had been unable to take his eyes from Phaedra, his gaze tracing every line of her stubborn, ferocious little form. A small curl, like a splash of bourbon, had fallen over her nose, the strands of copper in her hair glinting in the morning sun. Crossing her eyes, she'd studied the errant strand for a moment before pursing her lips and puffing the bit of hair away.

Morgan had had to bite his lip to keep from groaning at the sight of that perfect mouth which would have given away the fact he was hiding among the trees and shrubs.

Lust. Possession. *Longing.*

Things he never thought to feel for another human being overwhelmed his senses before Morgan could once more encase himself in ice. When Phaedra's knife, poorly wielded, had slashed the hand of that filthy cur at Hagerty's, Morgan had known she would be his undoing. His heart had fluttered at the sight of her.

Fluttered. As if he were some lovesick boy writing an ode to a woman's eyelashes.

Ambition, avenging Gertie, hounding Rutherford. Those had been the only things Morgan had considered for years until Phaedra. She was a rogue wave in the ocean, with startling blue eyes and wearing half-boots, threatening to pull him under.

Gertie would have laughed that Morgan had been caught in a web of his own making.

His adopted mother had often cautioned Morgan on overly complicated schemes. How every plan was doomed to face a setback or two and sometimes must be abandoned entirely. No matter his careful planning and multiple layers to hide his involvement. Using Murphy had been an inspired choice and far too tempting to ignore—after all, he'd been considering a way to do so for some time. And once Morgan had found out about *The Disastrous Barrington?*

She isn't the least bit disastrous.

His heart fluttered gently again, an altogether unsettling sensation.

Morgan had listened to the gossip about Phaedra in London and, without considering further, decided to place the wager in Elysium's Red Book. How difficult could it be to seduce one innocent English girl? He'd expected Leo Murphy's sister to be an overly privileged, pampered nitwit, considered scandalous because she liked to ride astride. Not —well, not *Phaedra.*

Morgan sucked in a breath and glanced at The Barrington once more.

You cannot control everything, Morgan. Not the dictates of your heart.

He'd blithely informed Gertie, after that little speech made so long ago, that *his* heart would never dictate his actions. Nothing and no one would ever control him again. Morgan's emotions were firmly iced over, except when it came to Gertie.

A bitterness filled his chest. An emptiness that was still there, years after her death.

He owed Gertrude Van Rhys his life. The least Morgan could do was find out what had happened to her. If it had truly been an accident, so be it. But if Rutherford had murdered her...

Morgan positioned himself farther inside the shadows

across from the hotel to watch the Upper Tens of Manhattan in their sleek, expensive carriages and glittering jewels, garbed in the finest silks, enter through the front door. Were he still picking pockets for Sister Bridget, he would have lifted enough purses at the front door to never have to do so again.

But there were no footpads surrounding The Barrington looking for an easy mark. Nor any lingering at all along the street in either direction. Cooke had made sure a group of the boys he used from the Bowery were set up in a perimeter to protect Murphy's guests. Coarse, rough looking men who hid in the bushes and shadows, much like Morgan was doing.

Grooms wearing the hotel's uniform hurried back and forth, helping the elite out of their lavish carriages and through the front door, to be greeted by Lady Phaedra Barrington.

Murphy was nothing if not a showman. Knowing his guests would be impressed at being ushered inside by his titled sister was smart. But it still annoyed Morgan to no end.

Weren't the wagers in the Red Book enough?

The rush of protectiveness for Phaedra made him want to punch Leo Murphy right in his arrogant nose.

After greeting each guest with her crisp, aristocratic accent, Lady Phaedra would submit to being fawned over before directing them inside. Chipplewit would then snap his fingers, and champagne would be offered as each guest was escorted to the enormous dining room, which was set up with a buffet, musicians, and dozens of round tables. Dancing would come later, after much champagne. This event might even rival the overblown opening of Cordelia Rutherford's opera house.

Rutherford and his well-bred wife had arrived earlier, heads held high, sailing inside the hotel as if they were royalty coming to bless the endeavor of their son-in-law.

Morgan wanted to wrap piano wire around Rutherford's neck. For Gertie's sake.

The Beekmans sauntered into the hotel as Morgan lit a cheroot. Iris Beekman was resplendent in pale blue, catching the eye of every male in the vicinity—save his. Pity he couldn't wed her because in addition to the match making sense, from a business standpoint, it would have also pissed off every old Dutch family in New York. A taint in the bloodline, so to speak. But marrying Iris simply wasn't possible.

After London, once Morgan had seen Phaedra—touched her, felt the beat of her heart in rhythm with his own—his interest in any other woman had evaporated. His cock agreed, not even bothering to be aroused at the sight of Morgan's mistress, naked and sprawled across his bed to greet him when he'd returned from England.

He'd sent Corrine on her way with a generous settlement.

"Damn it to hell," Morgan said under his breath. He pressed the palm of his free hand to his chest, feeling Phaedra inside his heart and unable to force her out. Or maybe he was simply unwilling. If he closed his eyes, Morgan could almost feel the silky strands of her hair against his nose and smell the scent of wild roses emanating from her skin.

He meant to see her tonight. Nothing on earth would stop him.

Lewis Armwood appeared, hopping out of his carriage to make his way inside, casually glancing Morgan's way. Lew had gently wormed his way into Murphy's graces, all without anyone knowing he was in league with Morgan. Cooke, who might have suspected, was otherwise occupied, having taken his new bride for an extended stay at the old Rutherford estate up the Hudson. Earlier than intended. According to Chipplewit.

Chipplewit was an endless source of information. It was

Murphy's manager who had informed Morgan where Phaedra's room was located, the time of Cooke's wedding to Miss Nelson, and other less pertinent facts such as the specific spot in the English garden that would give one the best view of a party taking place inside tonight. But then, Chipplewit was as much in Morgan's employ as The Barrington's.

Another carriage pulled up,

Martin Van Rhys stepped out, pausing only to smooth down his coat before making his way inside.

Morgan's fingers tightened, curling into fists. He should have expected Martin would be here tonight. Gertrude's social-climbing younger brother lived on influence and connections. He used events such as these to continue to spread his accusations that Morgan had murdered his sister. That poor Gertrude had been coerced into signing the Van Rhys family home over to the criminal she'd taken in, a particularly sore point for Martin.

But what he was really upset about was Mohawk & Hudson.

Martin had sold Gertie his own shares in the railroad years ago when he was in desperate need of funds, but since her death, he had never stopped demanding Morgan return them. He insisted the shares were meant to stay in the Van Rhys family, not squandered away on some street ruffian his sister had taken a liking to.

Never mind that the value of those shares had quadrupled.

Morgan waited, impatiently, for Martin to disappear inside. That entitled little prick wasn't going to dissuade him from this evening's event. Or from seeing Phaedra.

Might be best, though, if he entered this fine event from somewhere other than the front door. Chipplewit would wave him in without an invitation, but he didn't want to cause a scene if Martin saw him. He might be too tempted just to snap his neck.

Tossing his cheroot to the ground, Morgan turned and made his way down the opposite side of the street to the gate which would let him into Murphy's English garden.

8

However annoyed she was with Leo, Phaedra could not fault her brother's ability to plan a grand event, one guaranteed to be spoken of for months to come. No expense had been spared. The buffet to be served at midnight alone, with delicacies such as clams, oysters, and crab sitting on giant platters of ice, had cost a fortune. Leo's staff, a small army in starched uniforms, circulated around the guests, their arms heavy with trays of champagne and the finest French wines.

Phaedra smiled at a gentleman and his wife, directing them with a wave of her arm to the main dining room where Leo stood at the door, greeting each guest personally. Chipplewit was in charge of taking the invitations as people arrived, leaving Phaedra to smile, say a few polite words, and send them in Leo's direction. Easy enough.

She smoothed the skirts of her peacock-blue gown as the trickle of guests started to finally thin. Several of the older women had cast gazes of disapproval in Phaedra's direction upon seeing the color of her gown. Pink or pale blue silk, perhaps, covered with an assortment of frills and laces, would have been far more appropriate for a young lady. Instead, Phaedra's silk skirts were patterned with thin stripes of silver amid the blue, the gown free of adornment. There wasn't even any lace to be found edging the bodice, only silver thread.

Georgina had taken one look at the peacock-blue and silver striped fabric, pressed a kiss to Phaedra's cheek, and said, "Splendid shot over the bow. You'll make my mother's forehead wrinkle. Thank you for that."

Phaedra turned her attention back to the door, trying to ignore her disappointment that Morgan wasn't one of the guests, even knowing that he hadn't been invited. But after his presence in the garden earlier today...well, she'd thought—

I don't want to see him. Nor have him stalking about.

That wasn't even remotely true.

Forcing another polite smile to her lips, she took in the last guest waiting at the door. "Good evening," she greeted the handsome older gentleman standing before her.

"Martin Van Rhys." He bowed and took her hand, producing the invitation from his coat. "Lady Phaedra, I presume. Mr. Murphy has mentioned you quite fondly."

"Mr. Van Rhys, a pleasure."

He stood for a moment, neck craning about, studying the interior of the lobby with a practiced eye. "I must say, Murphy's done wonders since the last time I was here. Barely more than plaster then." White teeth flashed as he grinned at her. "I was one of the first to insist on membership for the private club at The Barrington."

The look of him, a combination of wealth and privilege, said as much. "Were you? A wise decision. The waiting list is now nearly a year."

Van Rhys's gaze ran discreetly over Phaedra. He was a bit older than Tony, with just a hint of silver at his temples. Expensively dressed. Accustomed to charming females.

"If I may be so bold, my lady"—Van Rhys held out his arm—"there doesn't seem to be any further reason for you to greet guests at the door. I believe I'm the last one. Would you care for escort inside?"

"I should be delighted." She took the arm of Mr. Van Rhys. "Mr. Chipplewit, can you manage any stragglers without me?"

"I believe I can do so, my lady." Chipplewit's gaze passed over Van Rhys with careful politeness. He bowed to her. "Enjoy your evening."

"Let us hope the captain of this venture"—Phaedra nodded her head in Leo's direction—"doesn't court-martial me for abandoning my post."

"I'll say you did so under duress, my lady." Van Rhys gave her a flirtatious look and led her to the dining room.

9

If Morgan hadn't already detested Martin Van Rhys, seeing Phaedra dangling from the man's arm would have done it. He reconsidered his idea to snap Martin's neck.

Moving around to the back of The Barrington, Morgan slipped through the gardens. A good place to observe the proceedings inside without being seen, at least until he decided to make his presence known to Phaedra. The shadows hid him well enough.

Lew Armwood stood off to the side, a glass of champagne in one hand, his gaze riveted on something to the left. He was barely listening to the older man beside him. Morgan turned to see what had caught his friend's eye.

Lilian Rutherford Harrison.

The widowed and tragically beautiful Lilian stood in a simple gown of pale green silk, the skirt decorated with what looked like daisies. The color set off her magnificent bone structure and willowy figure. Fragile. Like fine blown glass. A good gust of wind might snap her in half. Completely unlike the generously curved Georgina, with her slightly bawdy laugh and brazen nature.

How fortunate for Armwood that Cooke had already left Manhattan.

A choking sound came from the shrub to his left, along with a small sob, drawing his attention away from the windows.

A young woman stood still in the near darkness, hand on her mid-section. She wobbled a bit, and fearing she would faint, Morgan rushed to her side, hearing the soft gasp of surprise as he caught her before she stumbled. Taking her arm, he led her over to a bench hidden in one corner and helped her sit.

Another sound left her, like that of a distressed mouse.

"It helps if you lower your head. Between your knees," he said quietly. "Breathe through your nose."

She gave him an odd look but did as he suggested. After a few deep breaths, her trembling subsided. "Do you often rescue swooning women during grand openings, Mr. ...?" Her voice was slightly muffled by her skirts.

"You are the first in some time. But you appeared close to fainting." Morgan could make out the faint sheen of sweat on her forehead as she straightened. "Slowly, Lady Torrington." He'd recognized Phaedra's cousin the moment she'd stumbled into him. The baker and discreet owner of Pennyfoil's. She was a lovely thing, all plump and curved, smelling of sugar.

"How do you know who I am?" She gave him a suspicious look.

"I've been to Pennyfoil's," he returned. "Your lemon tart is one I still dream of, my lady."

"Odd. You don't look like a gentleman who enjoys tarts."

"I assure you, I *do*."

She inhaled sharply at the veiled innuendo in his tone, tried to stand, and promptly sat once more. Then she laughed. "Clever."

Morgan took out a handkerchief and held it out to her.

"Thank you." She gave him a sideways glance. "I'm not the least offended at your little play on words. I'm"—another sob—"not feeling well. The dining room," she said, gesturing to the guests eating oysters and dancing inside, "grew overly warm, so I came out for a bit of fresh air."

"Morgan Stewart," he murmured. "I am pleased to make your acquaintance since I'm already familiar with your tarts. Where is your husband, my lady?"

"Busy, at present. I didn't want to disturb him. He's in the kitchens. Or possibly he's made it to the party by now."

Lady Torrington was obviously with child, whether she was aware of the fact or not. Growing up in a brothel, Morgan had seen more than his fair share of women in such a state. Given how small and sickly he'd once been, when Morgan couldn't go out to work the streets with the other pickpockets and petty thieves, Sister Bridget had had him care for her stable of 'girls.' Fetch them water. Food. Linens. Hold the chamber pot when they became ill. Mop their foreheads. He hadn't minded. Those poor women had nearly always been grateful for his help. Softly stroking his hair and perhaps handing him a sweet. Or an extra roll at dinner.

"Shall I fetch Lord Torrington for you?"

"I don't wish to disturb him. Things are rather chaotic at present."

"You won't be disturbing him. I will. Keep the handkerchief. I'll return in a moment," he said gently.

"I think it's the oysters, Mr. Stewart. The smell alone—the briny scent—that's why I left the kitchens. And then there they were at the party—"

"Don't think of them." Morgan stood. "Breathe in the aroma of the garden." He took her hand. "If you feel you might become ill, there is a convenient rhododendron just behind you."

VAN RHYS TOOK UP YET ANOTHER OYSTER, GLANCING WITH surprise at the face Phaedra made. "You don't care for oysters?"

"Not in the least," Phaedra assured him with a laugh.

After having been greeted by Leo and exchanged pleasantries with him, Mr. Van Rhys stayed close to Phaedra's side, trying to entice her with oysters and conversation. It helped take her mind from Iris Beekman, who waltzed by more than once. What on earth could Morgan possibly see in her aside from flawless beauty, decorum, and a delicate, swan-like neck?

"You're frowning. At the oysters. Is it the texture?"

"I beg your pardon?" Phaedra pulled her eyes from Miss Beekman, annoyed she even gave a fig.

"It is the texture of the oyster, not the taste that you object to. Am I correct, Lady Phaedra?"

Considering his question, she nodded. "Slimy. Like the underside of a rock covered in moss which has been sitting in a pond."

Van Rhys grinned, showing a line of even white teeth and a dimple in his cheek. "Very descriptive, my lady. You have given this some thought."

"I have," Phaedra assured him, scanning the room. Even knowing Stewart had not been on the guest list, she imagined him popping up somewhere. Perhaps near Miss Beekman. Glaring once more at the glamorous girl who twirled and giggled across the dance floor, Phaedra's lips drew tight.

Well, I'm certainly no Iris Beekman, am I?

"My sister has the same problem with mushrooms," Phaedra forced her attention back to Van Rhys. "She regards mushrooms to be little better than snails absent their shells." She gave the oysters a pained look. "The same holds true of oysters."

"I don't care for mushrooms either, as it happens. Too earthy in taste. But honestly, there is very little to an oyster. The trick is to allow it to slide down your throat before you can think too much about the texture." He dabbed a small bit of horseradish the waiter had provided onto the oyster and then tipped the shell against his mouth before swallowing. "I barely let it wiggle about." He smiled at Phaedra. "That's how to do it. Swallow before your brain can advise you of what is in your mouth." Van Rhys made the same blissful face. "Delicious."

Phaedra laughed softly. Van Rhys was an amusing companion. Handsome and attentive. "I think all you taste is the horseradish."

"Perhaps."

Torrington slid into the dining room, smoothing down his coat and frowning at a small stain on the lapel. He'd obviously only just left the kitchens and would probably return after making an appearance. Walking about in a semi-circle, he appeared to be looking for Rosalind.

Phaedra could have sworn she'd caught sight of her cousin only a moment ago. She looked about the room, but Rosalind was nowhere to be found.

"Something wrong, my lady?" Van Rhys's brow wrinkled.

"No, I—" The back of her neck prickled, that sensation, of being submerged into warm water, the same as she'd had this morning in the garden, returned. Her back arched, as if fingers stroked along her spine and she caught sight of a large, brutishly handsome gentleman. He strolled into the room, ignoring the surprised looks on the faces of the other guests, while the light of the chandelier caught on the gold in his hair.

Morgan.

Uninvited or not, he seemed to approach Iris Beekman with a great deal of determination.

Phaedra's chest actually hummed at the sight of him, which was rather embarrassing, given Morgan hadn't once looked in her direction. Her muscles tightened, fingers curling at her sides.

"Wonder how he got in here." Van Rhys shot a look of dislike at Morgan. "Miss Beekman must have invited him." He inclined his head in Iris's direction. "Have you become acquainted with Miss Beekman? Lovely girl."

"I have not." *I doubt she can throw a knife properly.*

Another ripple of awareness tickled Phaedra's skin as she took in Morgan's dark evening coat stretched taut over his massive shoulders and broad chest. No matter that the clothing created an elegant, expensive foil for his golden coloring, he still looked out of place. A wolf wearing sheep-skin. The rough, brutal edges of his handsome features were so unlike the cultured attractiveness of say...Van Rhys. Quite a few of the ladies present, regardless of their feelings towards Morgan glanced at him from beneath their lashes in admiration.

A slight quiver of awareness shot down her spine.

When one plucked the strings of a violin, the vibration could be felt inside the instrument, reverberating against the fingertips. That's what Morgan felt like to Phaedra. A vibra-tion. A constant echo. No matter his dishonesty and murderous inclinations.

Miss Beekman's lips curved in a tiny, flirtatious smile. She gazed unabashedly at Morgan's approach, thrusting out her grotesque bosom in an improper manner.

Phaedra gave a sigh.

Fine. Not grotesque in the least. Miss Beekman's neckline was modest. But her bosom was certainly on display given the proportions of her—Phaedra looked down at her own assets. Paltry, though she had much more in the way of curves than her sister, Olivia. The knowledge had never bothered her until now.

Her foot tapped in agitation, wishing she had brought her knife. At this distance, she could slice one of Miss Beekman's curls clean off.

Morgan didn't stop and greet Miss Beekman as Phaedra had expected. Rather, he ignored her completely. It was the gentleman standing *behind* Miss Beekman who had his attention.

Torrington.

Morgan leaned over, ignoring the whispers of those in the ballroom who obviously didn't care to have him here. He said something to Torrington, who immediately straightened, panic stamped on his handsome features as he rushed out of the crowd with Morgan at his heels.

"Excuse me, Mr. Van Rhys," Phaedra said, her eyes on Morgan as he disappeared behind Torrington. Something had happened to Cousin Rosalind. Because only a fire in the kitchens or Rosalind would cause such a look on Torrington's face. "I need to check on something."

Van Rhys's lips pulled into a thin smile, his eyes trailing Morgan. "No need to inform Mr. Murphy that an unwelcome guest has invaded his party, my lady. I'll handle the matter and have him escorted out."

"I don't believe that's necessary." Phaedra's feet were already moving towards the exit.

"Oh, I believe it is." Loathing dripped from his words. "Usurper."

Usurper?

Morgan didn't seem to have many friends in Manhattan, given the general dislike he invoked in others.

She hurried out of the room, only to be stopped by one of the guests who wanted to ask how she was enjoying her stay in New York. Phaedra answered all his questions as politely as possible, trying to see over his shoulder to find out where Morgan and Torrington had gone.

"Mr. Adamson," she said, fairly certain that was his name. "I do apologize. But I am on an errand for my brother. Please excuse me."

Phaedra hurried down the hall and looked in both directions, but the area was empty. One door led into the gardens, the other to the kitchens. She sidestepped two waiters as she tried to determine where they'd gone.

The gardens.

The cooler night air slid along her arms as she stepped outside. Phaedra's slippers crunched on the gravel of the path, one that wove behind the large windows of the dining room. Anyone standing in the nearly completed garden would clearly see the entire party from this spot. Such as a gentleman who hadn't been invited to Leo's grand opening. A murderous suitor who wasn't looking for Miss Beekman—

Phaedra placed a palm over her heart, which wanted to leap from her chest.

She shouldn't want Morgan lurking about, spying on her, threatening Leo, but yet the tripping of her pulse said differently.

Page seventy-eight of Elysium's Red Book. Pith's disappointed tone filled her mind.

A concerned whisper met her ears, followed by her cousin's subdued voice.

Peering around the edge of the fountain she caught sight of Rosalind, barely upright on a bench, her husband's head bent towards her as Morgan's large shadow loomed over them both. Even in the muted light spilling from the dining room windows, Phaedra could see the pale, almost green cast to Rosalind's skin.

Morgan tilted his head, turning his chin in Phaedra's direction. The glimmer of his eyes, pale slices of silver moonlight, took her in, completely unsurprised to see her hiding behind a shrub. Or a small tree. Could have been a rose bush, for all she knew. Plants didn't interest her in the least.

He gave a small nod. A silent instruction not to reveal herself.

Phaedra didn't make a sound. Not because Morgan had demanded she stay quiet but because Rosalind might be embarrassed to be found in such a state.

Torrington gently helped Rosalind to her feet, murmuring to her in a soothing tone. As he led her away, Rosalind paused before Morgan, lightly touching his arm, a soft smile on her pale features. When the door shut behind them, Morgan looked at her through the branches of the shrub.

"You'd make a terrible assassin, *schatje*. A wounded bull is quieter."

"Untrue." Phaedra stepped forward. Of all the things she'd thought they might say to each other after so many months apart and her confusion over, well, nearly *everything*, Morgan's criticism of her ability to be quiet while potentially stalking someone for ill intent hadn't been considered. He was so terribly attractive in the soft light coming through the windows. All sleek gold power with a dusting of menace. She had the urge to either slice him to bits or, conversely, throw herself into his arms. Both sounded appropriate.

"I beg to differ." The side of his mouth tugged into a half-smile. "And I would know, wouldn't I?"

"I suppose so, since you're the one sneaking about without an invitation."

"Guilty. Though I'm hardly sneaking about."

"And"—Phaedra pointed to the windows where she could see Van Rhys speaking to Leo—"there's quite a few of the guests inside who don't care for you. Mr. Cooke isn't alone in his dislike."

"I'm an acquired taste, Phaedra."

"*Lady* Phaedra."

The smile deepened. "I don't think so." He stepped closer, and the awareness of him had Phaedra's entire body flaring. Violently. As if all her nerves were set aflame at once.

She abruptly turned her chin to view the party inside. Even after so much time had passed since their last meeting at Cherry Hill, the effect he had on her hadn't lessened. Phaedra wasn't sure if she was happy or horrified to see him. Probably a mix of both.

Inside, Cordelia Rutherford's elegant form spun effortlessly about in Tony's arms. Of course she would make sure everyone in Manhattan saw her dancing with a duke, including her husband. Jacob Rutherford stood off to the side, eyes narrowed, thin lips curled into something resembling a smile, though the calculating look in his eyes ruined the effect.

"I will give you the benefit of the doubt and assume you were assisting Lady Torrington and not—"

"Did you think I was threatening her for a tart recipe?" A bark of laughter came from him. "Perhaps I'm contemplating a takeover of Pennyfoil's."

"Not amusing."

"Lady Torrington was unwell. I merely offered to find her husband." There was a softness to his words. A gentleness Phaedra hadn't expected from Morgan.

"I thank you for your kindness to my cousin," she said in her stiffest, most haughty tone. "Good evening, Mr. Stewart."

"Does dismissing a gentleman ever work, Phaedra?"

"*Lady* Phaedra," she hissed back. "And yes, in general, a man of good breeding would take the hint."

Morgan's grin widened, and he placed a hand over his heart. "Alas, I am not one."

"My mistake." Phaedra thought again of her knife hidden upstairs. The weapon hadn't really gone with the gown, but then, she'd thought she might only have to face Miss Beekman. Though Morgan might find her wielding the knife to be encouragement of sorts.

"I think..." He circled around her, sending that enticing woodsy aroma mixed with apple into her nostrils. "You are angry that I haven't sought you out before now. Possibly you are concerned I've forgotten all about you. Fourth floor," the timbre of his voice lowered. "Second window from the right."

Phaedra swayed. That was her set of rooms. Her bedroom. She tamped down the pleasure at knowing he might have scaled The Barrington for her.

"On the contrary, I had hoped you'd forgotten all about me. Miss Beekman is inside. I'm sure she would welcome your attentions."

The dark, rich sound of his amusement lingered in the air. "I fear my affections are already firmly fixed." He leaned forward, the tip of his nose just brushing the hair above her left ear. "I am not interested in Miss Beekman." He breathed her in, sending a tremor down her arms. "You may stand down, *schatje*."

Phaedra swatted at him as if he were an annoying insect. "I'll have you escorted out."

"You won't," he murmured. "Didn't you miss me?"

Desperately. Shamefully.

Something she hadn't realized until his warmth was brushing against her bosom.

Voices sounded on the other side of the garden, farther down along the path. A burst of laughter followed by the crunch of boots and the smell of a cheroot. She peeked around the bush. Or tree. Whatever was the proper name of this greenery surrounding her. It was in her best interests to go back inside. Let Morgan stay out here cloaked in darkness like some villain in a novel.

Her feet refused to move.

Morgan's fingertips bushed lightly at the tip of her shoulder, then trailed down the length of her arm in a lazy fashion, searing every bit of skin he touched.

Phaedra's lips parted, but no gasp of outrage came from her throat. Just a mewling sound. A whimper.

Morgan quickly covered her mouth with one broad hand, half-dragging her farther into the shadows of the garden. "Don't make a sound." The words and his lips brushed along her ear.

She didn't even try to struggle. Made no effort to defend her person. Heat stirred between her thighs, spreading upward and out across her limbs, tightening the buds of her nipples.

Morgan held her tight, her spine trapped against his muscled chest. Warmth and sensation pooled at every spot their bodies touched.

"Release me," her muffled voice said behind his fingers.

"I can't understand you." His hips pushed more firmly into the crease of her bottom, the hardness between his thighs unmistakable. "You should make your demands clearer."

Dizzying. Drunk on something Phaedra couldn't name. What little indignation she could muster was rapidly evaporating. On impulse, Phaedra nipped at the fingers covering her mouth. A needy sound emanated from her throat.

A groan left Morgan. His free hand moved from her waist to one hip, pushing her more tightly to him. "You are a dangerous creature," he breathed along her collarbone. The large fingers slowly slid from her mouth, dragging along the plump contours of her bottom lip.

Run, Phaedra.

She didn't listen to that careful, cautious whisper in Pith's voice. Besides, her legs were trembling, barely capable of holding her upright. Running seemed highly unlikely.

Morgan brought her mouth to his, pulling Phaedra up to her toes. The air caught in her lungs as his lips fell on hers, devouring every objection she might have had. Squeezing her harder, he deepened the kiss until Phaedra's other senses dulled. Nothing mattered but his mouth on hers. They melted together in the darkness as Morgan's hand moved to palm her breast, teasing at the edge of her nipple lying beneath the silk of the gown.

Phaedra tried to fix her mouth more firmly to his.

His fingers dipped abruptly, a growl coming from his chest as one big hand lowered to cup possessively at her sex.

The ache there intensified, though it was muted through layers of cotton and silk. She tilted her hips, wanting him to rub and stroke her. Truly mortifying behavior.

"You smell of wild roses," he whispered, his lips at the corner of her mouth. "The sort with thorns and vines that twist about a man and pierce his skin." Fingers squeezed over her mound before sliding back and forth along the silk. "One day," he whispered. "I'll savor the way you taste. Put my mouth on you." Stewart pressed the heel of his hand more firmly. "No matter how your thorns might mark me."

A low moan crept up her throat. Yes. She wanted that. For his mouth to press along every inch of her body. Lick her skin. Phaedra placed her hand over his, lacing their fingers together, hips moving in unison.

"I'm sorely tempted to lift your skirts. Take you right here in your brother's garden."

Why don't you?

The thought roared for an instant in her head, hammering

along with her heart. How easy she was making it for Morgan to win his wager.

The wager.

Phaedra stomped on his foot, which was akin to kicking a piece of marble. The heel nearly broke off her slipper. She tore her mouth from his. "Release me. This instant."

"I will never." Morgan turned her around, hands roaming up her arms to finally cup her face between his broad palms. "Still so angry. So hostile. So mine."

"I am not yours." But there was no conviction in her words.

Morgan pressed a kiss to her forehead. "Perhaps, then, you don't want the surprise I have planned for you tomorrow."

Phaedra stilled. "I want nothing from you."

"You'll like it," he whispered along the corner of her mouth. "I promise." His arms retreated, leaving Phaedra cold without his warmth. "But if you'd rather not, I understand. Would be too much of a challenge for you to leave the safety of The Barrington without being seen. You aren't quiet in the least. Not a hint of stealth. I understand."

"Perhaps it is only that I don't like you." He was goading her. But she *was* curious. Which Morgan counted on. "That seems to be the prevailing opinion in Manhattan."

"I'll be outside in the alley." Morgan tipped his head to the narrow street running behind The Barrington. "Eleven o'clock. But I doubt you'll manage to slip away." He shrugged those muscled shoulders. "In fact, I *wager* that you will not." The pale slices of his eyes gleamed at her. "I will win, of course."

Damn him.

Phaedra wrenched free. She was perfectly capable of leaving The Barrington without notice. She had nothing to prove to Morgan. Whatever his 'surprise,' Phaedra doubted it would be anything of interest. And meeting him, unchaper-oned and alone, would be reckless. Dangerous, even.

"Good evening, Mr. Stewart." Phaedra inclined her head politely, mouth still tingling—as well as other key parts of her body. "I believe I'll return to the party. Do not follow."

"Try to behave," he murmured, reaching out to take her wrist. "Or not." He pressed a kiss to her palm. "*Schatje.*"

10

Phaedra pulled up the gardening trousers she'd borrowed from Olivia, grateful to have found a pair without manure still clinging to the knees. The trousers were longer than she'd expected, but then Olivia was a few inches taller. The boots she'd stolen from behind the kitchen door probably belonged to one of the lads who ran errands for The Barrington. He would be most distressed to find them missing, but she'd return them as soon as possible, though they fit reasonably well and she considered keeping them. One of Tony's shirts, thrown into a pile for mending, helped complete her outfit. Oh, and the hat. Some ancient thing she'd found discarded behind the hotel, left behind by one of the masons who'd recently finished the wall around the garden.

Not one person looked at Phaedra as she made her way out of The Barrington. The staff completely ignored her. This was far easier than trying to outwit Pith to leave the Averell mansion in London.

Phaedra whistled a ribald tune, one Papa had taught her, though she couldn't recall the words, and made her way down to the end of the alley where a small carriage waited. Little more than a gig one uses in the country. The vehicle rocked as the occupant inside moved at catching sight of her.

She took a deep breath. She could still turn around. She'd proved her point.

Morgan leaned out of the gig so she could see him.

There was a very good chance, she surmised, that he might simply kidnap her and this was all a ruse. He'd easily win the wager, bankrupt Leo, and—well, she wasn't sure what he meant to actually do with her.

The ache between her thighs took up residence once more.

Phaedra could hazard a guess.

But while Morgan could easily abscond with her person for parts unknown, Phaedra sensed he wanted her surrender.

Which I have no intention of giving.

Brave words indeed.

After she'd left Morgan in the gardens, Phaedra had deliberately danced the remainder of the night. Not because she'd wanted to. Dancing was, at best, tedious. The conversation, tiring. Limited to mundane topics such as the weather. Or a comparison of the night's event with those glittering balls she'd attended in London. Van Rhys had suggested a carriage ride to view something called The Battery, with the dowager duchess as chaperone. She'd nodded absently, her eyes firmly fixed on the windows.

Phaedra had assumed Stewart watched, and there was a point to be made.

She'd spent an inordinate amount of time glancing out the windows, trying to discern any sign of a large shadow in the garden. Not one of the gentlemen who had twirled her about appealed to Phaedra in the least. Not even Van Rhys, whom she'd decided she liked.

The evening had ended late but been deemed a complete

success. Leo was certainly pleased. Phaedra had gone to her rooms, which felt deserted now that Olivia had wed Ben, feet aching and mind refusing to let go of Morgan. What sort of surprise could he possibly have for her? It had taken some time, but she'd finally fallen asleep.

And dreamt of her father.

Papa sat atop his grave once more, brilliant in the sunlight, so perfect and healthy it hurt to look at him. He popped a strawberry into his mouth but didn't offer her one.

This must stop, Phaedra. I am dead.

May I have a strawberry?

No, you greedy chit. You may not. And stop waffling about. That bloody wager is very much like The Iliad. *Or the Broadwood. I don't know why you can't see it.*

What does Tony's piano have to do with anything? Or Mama's favorite book?

Papa only shook his head.

Phaedra had tried to hold on to the dream, or at least her father, but she'd awoken, face wet with tears, missing Papa terribly. When he'd died, Phaedra had felt unmoored. Bereft, without her anchor. Irrationally, she was often furious with Papa for having left her, though she knew he'd had little say in the matter. And while Phaedra adored Tony and Leo, both were poor substitutes for Marcus Barrington.

Ringing for her maid, Phaedra had made the decision, possibly a poor one, that Morgan's challenge could not go unanswered. He'd known that. Damn him.

"I am a daughter of the Duke of Averell," Phaedra said under her breath as she approached the gig waiting for her. "It is not in my nature to show fear, and I will not do so now."

"You did very well." The breeze ruffled the short strands of Morgan's hair. "As adept as you are with a blade, I should have realized how you would take to pistols. Your aim is excellent."

Morgan's surprise had been rather splendid. Not a sedate carriage ride. Or attempted abduction.

Pistols.

Phaedra walked towards him, pausing only to hitch up the trousers, not missing the way Morgan's eyes lingered over the swell of her hips. His eyes, the exact color always so difficult to discern, had gone the hue of a worn piece of slate. The broad chest rose and fell with a small hitch as he studied her.

"Your choice of attire today is one of which I approve. I like the trousers. Where did you get them?" The question was casual but tinged with something dark.

Phaedra had trouble deciding whether Morgan was aroused by her wearing trousers or merely contemplating strangling the owner of the trousers, whom he would assume to be male.

Both, she thought.

"They belong to Olivia. She wears these while spreading manure in the gardens. So there isn't any need to go around threatening the staff at The Barrington. Or murdering any of the grooms. A boy dressed as such and running errands for the hotel goes unnoticed."

"Clever. I admire your creativity." The side of his mouth twitched. "I'd no idea Miss Nelson liked to muck about, though considering her choice of husband, I should have guessed. I assumed all she did was snip at roses and peonies while floating sedately above the grass, directing the gardeners."

"Olivia does float about dreadfully well. Like a swan." Phaedra had never been able to master such a skill.

"I find her tone of dismissal is far better than yours. And

I'd forgotten about the graceful floating about. She's quite well-bred."

"I'm a duke's daughter," Phaedra said defensively.

Morgan's lips twitched. "I don't think that a guarantee of anything."

She sighed, resigned to his teasing. "I suppose not."

The afternoon had been spent in comfortable companionship with Morgan. He hadn't tried to touch her, save for helping her in and out of the gig. They'd ridden out of the city, traversing a road running along marshy waters until the buildings and people became nonexistent. Turning down another road, this one leading into an area thick with trees and bramble, they'd passed not one other soul until Morgan had halted the gig before a narrow trail. Leaving the gig behind, he'd led Phaedra further into the canopy of the trees, explaining that the marshland surrounding them was his, as was the abandoned shanty they'd passed, windows full of broken glass.

"Olivia has always been impossibly prim," Phaedra continued. "We are very different. She's an expert at polite conversation, pouring tea, *and* designing gardens."

"Garden design?"

"Had she been born male, Olivia would be a master gardener. She creates diagrams of each bed and makes notes on which plants will work better than others to achieve maximum color and coverage throughout any season. Sometimes I am forced to assist her. She purposefully gives me the names of all her beloved plants in Latin." Phaedra sniffed. "Which is incredibly snobbish."

"Incredibly," Morgan agreed. "Gardens serve a purpose. A very *well-bred* one." This time, a tiny smile broached his lips.

Phaedra snorted.

Morgan sported no black today. Instead he wore a coat of deep caramel a shade or two darker than his hair. The scar along his chin gleamed in the sunlight, slicing perfectly through the close-cropped beard lining his jaw. Her heart stopped beating for a moment, drinking in Morgan, who became more beautiful to Phaedra at each encounter.

"When you grow up surrounded by unpleasant aromas," he said. "You learn to appreciate the scent of flowers. The softness of a rosebud." He waved one hand. "Or simply the smell of the trees and grass."

There were dozens of small cracks in Morgan, fissures, allowing Phaedra to see inside the ice with which he surrounded himself like a suit of armor. She held on to each one, determined to examine them later.

"My sisters all possess a singular talent. Olivia included," Phaedra said lightly. "She might be adopted, but she's a Barrington. Romy, the Duchess of Granby, is a discreetly practicing modiste who would be horrified by my attire today. She does, however, insist on putting pockets in the gowns she designs."

"Pockets are useful."

"Indeed. Theo, Marchioness of Haven, paints. Exclusively miniatures for a time, but now she's gone the opposite direction. Murals are her passion. Clients for her work abound. Discreetly, of course. You can't announce at a ball that the mural gracing your drawing room was done by a marchioness."

"Of course not." The rough edges of his features had softened, making him appear younger and not quite so menacing.

"You are familiar with Lady Torrington, given you were intent on threatening her for a lemon tart recipe last night." She grinned at him. How kind Morgan had been to Rosalind. When Phaedra had checked on her cousin later that night, Rosalind had been so deeply grateful for his care and assistance. This brutal, savage beast of a man. Her murderous suitor. Who'd kept Rosalind from fainting and lent her his handkerchief.

That, as much as anything, had propelled her out the door of The Barrington.

"Pennyfoil's is rather famous. And I adore lemon."

"Alas, I possess no such talent. No one gives a fig for my interest in weaponry. They are only pleased that some poor footman hasn't lost an eye while fencing with me. I attempted the violin with limited success. My playing was compared to the screeching of a tortured cat."

"I believe you've mentioned before you do not possess an ear for music. But I would consider running Elysium to be a talent." There was a gentle note to his words.

"Completely useless skills, given I'm a female from a ducal family. No one wants me negotiating with wine merchants or running a hazard table." Had she ever mentioned the running of Elysium to Morgan? Phaedra didn't think so, but neither was she surprised that he knew.

"Or calculating the interest due on someone's markers? Balancing the account books? Managing a staff, and a duke, all without anyone knowing, is proof of your skill in business if nothing else. Such acumen cannot be taught."

Phaedra studied him carefully, looking for any hint of condescension, but found none. Pride crept along her chest, warming her from the inside out. "You are one of the few who appreciate such things. I blame my father's overindulgence."

"Marcus Barrington, Duke of Averell."

Morgan knew her father's name, something else that shouldn't surprise her. She nodded slowly, trying not to allow the prick of grief stab so deeply into her.

"My father was once a rake. A terrible one. He regretted his treatment of the fairer sex, especially after having four females plus my mother bestowed upon him in his later years.

Her Grace believes in embracing that which brings you joy, regardless of what society thinks. That women have talents beyond bearing children and overseeing a dinner menu. Her ideas rubbed off on Papa. He adored her. Spoiled her." Phaedra's voice grew thick. "As he did all of us."

"Especially you."

Phaedra supposed that was true. She had been closest to him, though he'd doted on all of them.

"London mocked Papa for his devotion to my mother. But he became a better man because of her. And he did not die the selfish, haughty duke he'd once been, but a good man, cherished and adored by his family." Phaedra admired that about her father. His ability to admit to his mistakes. To change. Be better. "At any rate," she said, giving Morgan a weak smile, "my mother rubbed off on him. Papa came around to the idea that a woman shouldn't be restricted to riding sidesaddle, bearing children, and floating about looking ornamental."

"What a pity for Miss Nelson."

"A daughter of the Duke of Averell would not be forced to marry for wealth or property. No arranged matches. He wanted us to all have a choice. Granted, all three of my sisters were ruined, but even so, had they not loved the men doing the ruining, my brother wouldn't have insisted they wed."

"A curious stance for a titled gentleman."

"My father was a most unusual duke. He taught me to play cards. How to calculate odds." She glanced at him. "How to bluff and pretend confidence when you have none. My father could charm you out of your entire purse, and you'd thank him for it. I suppose that's where Leo gets it."

"And your enjoyment of weaponry?" Morgan's eyes had gone a soft, misty gray.

"Well, he certainly didn't discourage it." He'd been proud of her skill with a rapier, making Phaedra practice in his rooms while he lay dying at Cherry Hill. "My father enjoyed military history, primarily that of the Romans. And the Ottoman Empire. Cnut's conquest of England was some of his favorite reading." She gave him a wry look. "He was a Viking."

"I'm aware. They educate we American mongrels properly now. Even the ones like me."

Phaedra plucked at a loose thread on the trousers, thinking of her father and wondering why she dreamt of him, always eating strawberries and dispensing useless advice.

"When he...couldn't see the words in his favorite books anymore because his eyes had failed, I read to him." Those times had been precious to Phaedra. Curled beside him in the oversized bed at Cherry Hill as they spoke of battles and bloodshed. "My father said I would have been a much better duke than my brother."

A bark of laughter came from Morgan. "You would have made an excellent duke." That softness in his eyes shimmered, tugging at Phaedra's heart. "Women are far stronger than most men give them credit for. Gertrude Van Rhys, for instance, was made of granite. Unbendable under even the worst circumstances. Firm in her convictions."

"Gertrude Van Rhys?" She recalled the conversation she'd overheard at the Rutherfords' about the mysterious Gertrude. "I met a man last night at Leo's party. Mr. Martin..." Several puzzle pieces, the one's comprising Morgan's existence, snapped together. "He doesn't like you."

"I expect he doesn't. Martin is Gertie's youngest half-brother." He shot her a pointed look. "I was nearly fourteen when she found me." There was such awe when Morgan said her name. Reverence, almost.

I sound like that when I speak of my father. As if no one had ever loved me but him. But in Morgan's case, that's likely true.

He took a deep breath and looked into the trees. "Gertie

was brilliant at business. The best teacher anyone could have hoped for. She remained unwed by choice. Took lovers when it suited her. Managed her own affairs. Despite an over-bearing father and four half-brothers, of which Martin is the only one left. Cholera outbreak." There was a sardonic note to his words. "I didn't kill them off."

"I didn't think you had."

"Liar. Gertie's family, especially Martin, decried every-thing about her. Hated the charitable endeavors which led to Gertie raising up those less fortunate."

"Like you."

Morgan nodded. "Just like me. Her father often complained that Gertie was training us all like lapdogs."

"You weren't the only one she took in."

"No. Only the worst. I tried to rob Gertrude. Steal her reticule. That's how we met. She could have had me hung for the crime, but instead she brought me to live under her roof. Sent me to school, determined I should become a lawyer. I found my studies useful, particularly for learning how to circumvent the law, not necessarily to practice it. But the others she saved stayed at the home Gertie founded for orphans. And before you ask, I'm definitely a bastard. I've no idea who my parents were. Born in a brothel." The rasp of his words hardened. "My mother was likely a whore and my father one of the men who visited her." The pale eyes hard-ened to a deeper gray.

"Oh, dear. I don't believe there's an entry for that in *Debrett's Peerage*."

If Morgan was hoping for her disgust, he wouldn't find it. The circumstances of his birth were not his fault. "You forget, we Barringtons have our own bastard. London does not let any of us forget it. Of all the things I object to, your birth is the least of them. Your personality, for instance, borders on boorishness. You carry about piano wire, and yet

I've never seen you tune a piano. And I won't even mention the offensive wager you placed."

The flintiness in his eyes faded once more to that pearly mist. "*This*"—the deep rumble of his voice lowered, the hunger for her engraved on his rough features—"has nothing to do with page seventy-eight."

Phaedra thought back to the dream of her father, who had calmly told her much the same.

Yes, but he's dead. And dreams aren't real. Also, he wouldn't share the strawberries.

"Why did Gertie take you in and not one of the others?" Phaedra asked, seeing for the first time the deep, aching sadness hovering about Morgan. It mixed oddly with all that ruthless brutality.

"Gertie never told me. Now she's gone, and I'll never know." He shrugged and turned away, but not before Phaedra saw the grief etched on his features.

She wanted to press matters further and ask how Gertrude Van Rhys had died but thought better of it.

"Perhaps," Phaedra said as the light dappled through the trees. "She saw something in you no one else did." Hidden behind the chilly mask he liked to wear. Buried under layers of menace and piano wire and wrapped in brutal ambition, was the spark of something else. Phaedra could feel it rubbing against her skin, tugging at her. "It explains why Martin Van Rhys doesn't like you. He didn't approve of his sister taking you in."

"Among other things. I watched you hang from his arm." His voice grew rough. "I want you to stay away from him."

"You don't dictate to me, Mr. Stewart."

"Nevertheless." The pale eyes grew shuttered once more, unwilling to debate the point further with her. Nodding at the pistol in her hand, Morgan said, "Clean it. Just as I showed you."

She did, cleaning the weapon carefully. He'd insisted before she fire a shot that Phaedra understand how to properly maintain and load the weapon. Once he'd been satisfied she could do so, Morgan had finally opened the sack he'd brought from the gig, pulling out an assortment of empty glass bottles. Placing the bottles carefully at intervals on a half-rotted tree trunk, he'd instructed her to take aim and pull the trigger.

Phaedra had managed to shatter one of the bottles, but only because her shot had knocked it from the tree trunk. Morgan hadn't grumbled or decried her lack of aim; instead, he'd spent the better part of an hour gently adjusting her grip on the pistol, pausing only to line up more bottles. She was no expert, but Phaedra felt confident in handling such a weapon in the future.

"I'll assume you have a use for this land," she said. "Just as you did the property in England you purchased from Mr. Cooke."

"You remembered what I told you at Cherry Hill."

"I do. But you also said Cooke didn't know he was selling to you. Which means you must have used a third party to complete the deal. So he wouldn't know."

"Clever thing. If it matters, I paid more than a fair price for the land. I didn't cheat him."

"You said you had a partner." She rubbed an oiled cloth over the barrel of the pistol. "Have I met him?"

"I imagine you have." Morgan didn't elaborate or disclose his partner's name, which had Phaedra thinking back to the dozens of gentlemen at The Barrington last night. The entire party had been made of Americans, save Phaedra and her family. Except...

"Mr. Lewis Armwood," she looked over at him. "He is the brother of Mr. Thomlinson's new wife. And it was Thomlinson who suddenly expressed an interest in that mill. On your behalf."

"Brilliant, savage, creature," Morgan whispered.

The warmth from earlier encompassed her entire system. Papa had often praised her mind. Tony on occasion, though he didn't understand her thinking. Leo grudgingly. But most gentlemen of her acquaintance simply decided that Phaedra's intelligence was merely another sign of her eccentricity.

Morgan *embraced* it.

"Thank you for today." Phaedra placed the pistol back in the finely carved case he'd brought. "My father always promised to show me, but he—"

"Died."

Phaedra swallowed. "Yes, and since then, I've badgered nearly every single person I know for lessons. The grooms. Footmen. Tony's valet. Even Pith wouldn't indulge me, and he was in the army."

"Pith?"

"Our butler, in London. He's been forced to play nursemaid to me for years. I can't move a foot from the Averell mansion without Pith finding out." Phaedra pointed to her chest. "*The Disastrous Barrington* and all that." Papa would have been quite pleased with her skill today. He was likely the only one.

"Come here." Morgan sat down beneath a tree and spread his legs open. He patted the spot of grass between them.

"Highly improper," she sniffed.

"Given you are in the middle of a marsh, in a remote area, and without a chaperone, having just been taught to shoot a pistol by the reviled Morgan Stewart, I'm not sure things can become any more improper, Phaedra."

"*Lady* Phaedra. And I would have said feared, not reviled. Perhaps I'd refer to you as a scourge."

A deep, melodic rumble came from him. He patted the

spot in the grass again. "*Schatje*." The word came from him like an endearment, soft and inviting.

"What does that really mean?" Phaedra took a step in his direction. "You could be insulting me in a foreign tongue, and I'd have no idea." She cast him a put-upon look but still came forward to settle between his muscular thighs. Leaning back against his broad chest, her body moved slightly with every breath he took, the beating of his heart solid along her back. Contrary to his appearance, his manner, and his habit of carrying piano wire, gentleness and warmth exuded from him, wrapping around Phaedra in a comforting embrace.

"You are not"—Morgan pressed a soft kiss beneath her ear—"disastrous. It is merely a word others use because you refuse to conform to their ideals. You would have made a *spectacular* duke. A duchess is debatable."

She turned her neck just slightly to smile up at him. "At least no one contradicts a duchess *except* a duke. Unfortunately, all the dukes presented to me thus far have been quite ancient and vastly unappealing."

A possessive rumble came from him. The arm at her waist pulled her closer.

She didn't want to be angry with Morgan. Nor think of the wager—or his reasons for it. Not here, where the sunlight had streamed over the grass as he'd taught her to shoot without so much as a hint of judgement. Called her brilliant. Praised her skill at Elysium. Her heart told her today had nothing to do with that bloody wager.

A squirrel scurried along the branches of the tree, rattling the leaves above them while a bird burst into song. But Phaedra heard little of it, only the steady heartbeat at her back. The silence between them lengthened, both lost to their own thoughts. Comfortable and whole. As if they had been together for a very long time.

One big hand danced lightly up her body, finally coming

to rest along the curve of her neck. The blunt fingers wrapped lightly around her throat, thumb pressing gently into her beating pulse. Morgan's other hand cupped the softness of her breast, the warmth of his palm searing her through the thin layers of Tony's old shirt.

Phaedra inhaled, drawing in a deep breath at the sudden tightening of her nipples. But she did not pull away. Impossible with the low, insistent hum vibrating between her thighs, aching with urgency and the need to be touched.

She twisted, wanting more of him.

"Stay still." The fingers curled more firmly around her throat, and a trickle of fear touched her. "I would never hurt you," he said fiercely. "The entire world, Phaedra. But *never* you."

There was the weight of truth to his words.

That is exactly what he would say to get you to capitulate.

Phaedra pushed away the thought.

"Morgan," she breathed, his name forced from her lips as he pinched her nipple.

He rolled the small peak between his fingers, teasing the tip until once more pinching, this time harder. The sting, surprisingly pleasurable, traveled down to her sex, the throbbing between her thighs becoming much more insistent.

"I think..." The fingers pulled from her breast and trailed down the length of her thigh, gently nudging her legs wider. "With practice, your aim with the pistol will improve even more." The thick fingers stretched over her mound, stroking at the softness hidden beneath the trousers.

She sucked in a small swallow of air at the brush along the area, sensitive to the light touch.

"Are you in the mood to learn something else today?" he whispered into her hair. "Negotiation tactics, perhaps?"

"I'm already brilliant." Her breath hitched at the press of his fingers and hand rotating between her thighs. "At negotiation. The wine merchant was surprised. As was the butcher. Elysium's chef was most pleased."

"Yes, but you've never had to bargain with me. I'll stop whenever you wish, *schatje*. You have only to say it."

Sensation rippled and flowed over her skin from the light teasing of his hand over the fabric of the trousers. Phaedra wanted to know where this tantalizing stroke of his fingers would lead her. Down a path of wickedness, she suspected.

I will embrace it.

"I've time for one other lesson today."

A deep sigh left him. "I love the way you smell, Phaedra." His lips trailed along her temple, nuzzled into her hair as his fingers plucked at the buttons on the trousers. "Your scent nearly blots out the odor of those trousers."

Phaedra's giggle came to an abrupt halt as his fingers tugged firmly at the fabric at her waist.

"We are at the bargaining table, Phaedra." The buttons opened, and the trousers parted, the air cool against her bare skin.

"And what is it you are challenging me for?" The words trembled out of her even as her hips lifted to his questing fingers.

"Your climax and ultimately your surrender. I want both."

"Oh." Phaedra sucked in a breath as the fingers found their way inside the trousers, tugging gently at the soft hair atop her mound. A slide of moisture between her thighs followed. "Your intentions are not honorable."

A wicked chuckle had her back bumping along his chest. "They never have been. I'm not that sort of man. I feel certain that if I were, you wouldn't find me half as appealing."

"I'm not sure I find you appealing now." Phaedra bit her lip to stop from whimpering. The sensations coursing over her body were that fierce.

"Liar."

Fingers stroked gently along the edges of her slit, exploring the outline of her sex. Every gentle touch increased the heavy, urgent sensation blooming inside her.

"No one has ever touched you here. Stroked this small bud." The very tip of his finger lingered over the most swollen part of her flesh before retreating.

"No," she stammered.

"That is exactly the right answer." Morgan pressed a kiss to her cheek.

Tilting her hips, Phaedra tried to shift so his hand would move back to that small bud hidden in her folds, but he resisted her efforts. A frustrated hiss came from her lips when Morgan deliberately continued his slow exploration, avoiding the spot entirely.

"We'll get to that, Phaedra. I promise."

"You are horribly controlling. It is yet another aspect of your personality," she panted, "which I do not care for."

"Agreed." Another soft kiss was pressed to her temple. His fingers moved lower, scratching his nails along the tender skin of her thighs. "Does that mean I should stop?"

"No," she choked out. "I do not yet concede."

"You will never concede. Nor do I ever want you to." Morgan's hips pushed up, enough so Phaedra could feel the thickness of him pressing into her bottom. "Well, perhaps in some things."

She gasped as a large finger sank inside her, unprepared as she was for the sensation of fullness. The first thing that came to mind while she lay sprawled here in the grass with Morgan's fingers teasing at her center was that bloody piece of ivory. The one she'd discovered at Elysium during her visit with Olivia so long ago, finally understanding the purpose.

The ivory was meant to be a substitute for a man's...cock.

Warmth teased at her cheeks, which, given the situation, should have happened some time ago. Morgan had his fingers

—and yet she was going to blush over the word *cock*. Good lord, she'd heard Leo utter that word numerous times. Possibly more. And Tony. Her brothers weren't cautious in tossing about vulgarities.

Morgan drew his finger over a spot inside her, causing a tingling, aching sensation, one that had her hips jerking. "There is also this to contend with." The finger rotated over the spot inside her.

"The piece of ivory," she stammered, her eyes rolling shut. "At Elysium. When I took Olivia—"

"You took Miss Nelson?" His lips brushed gently along her cheek, stirring the fine hairs along her ear. "And found an ivory cock? Shocking." But Morgan didn't sound the least shocked.

A low whine came from her as another finger joined the first, slowly moving back and forth. Her gaze flicked down, unsurprised that he'd managed to wedge his entire hand into the trousers, the fabric undulating as his fingers moved inside her. An unbearably erotic sight.

Pleasure coiled tight between her thighs, threatening to whip out along her body.

"I suspect that is how she met Mr. Cooke." Her breath hitched. "Ben. At Elysium."

The fingers rotated, stroking softly at that spot inside her, drawing each wave of sensation out until Phaedra's thoughts grew incoherent. She tilted her head back, as much as his hand on her throat would allow. The threat of impending pleasure pulsed along her skin.

"Interesting, my savage little creature." His voice roughened. "You can tell me more later, but at present, I feel our focus should be on the task at hand. All good negotiations should include disclosure of what each party brings to the table." His teeth nipped at her ear.

Phaedra moaned. Loudly. The birds above them scattered

at the sound. "I need—"

"Yes, I know." A soft hum came from Morgan. "Right here." His thumb moved along through her softness, finally stroking and teasing at the engorged bud. "So curious, that something so tiny creates such pleasure." Pressing down slightly, his thumb moved in a circular motion before retreating once more.

Phaedra was so very close to something. Bliss, held just out of reach. The ripples of it teased at her senses, making her feel as if she would erupt. Explode. She'd paid enough attention to her mother's pointed discussions on finding pleasure in the marital bed to know that this explosion of pleasure was the end game of physical relations. How appropriately that it be titled a climax.

Another tortured stroke across the poor aching bud.

This was why young ladies risked ruination. Not for kisses or hand holding. But this breathtaking, magnificent, mysterious feeling, which, up until now, Phaedra had thought exaggerated. She had never conceived of such intimacy before, thinking only of how awkward it would be—but not with Morgan.

Oh, Phaedra. The disappointed sound of Pith filled her head. *This will end badly.*

Another sound came from her. "Is this your offer, Morgan?" she gasped. "I must say, it's decent. Worthy of consideration. Little negotiation is required."

His thumb moved back and forth, putting pressure on the small nub that hummed and ached until Phaedra thought she might shatter. "My methods might be considered somewhat ruthless, but I am determined to gain the advantage." A shallow bite sank into her skin, right where Phaedra's neck and shoulder met. The fingers circling her neck tightened ever so slightly as his thumb pressed down, the digits still lodged inside her, curling at the same time.

Phaedra's body jerked. Bent. Arched and came off the ground. A thousand stars burst before her, or perhaps it was she who burst into bits of sparkling light. Her heart, which had been thumping in such an unsteady rhythm, halted in her chest, the air in her lungs unable to move.

"Morgan," she pleaded.

Hips thrusting upward, Phaedra's heels dug into the grass. She wrapped her fingers around his wrist, choking out his name, over and over. Blind was how she felt, to everything but the sharp waves of pleasure cresting over her skin. Morgan held her, whispering the most vulgar, glorious words in her ear, conjuring filthy, carnal images of the two of them together.

When at last Phaedra relaxed against his chest, body still pulsing softly, Morgan's hands left her throat, his fingers pulling carefully from her.

She could become a slave to this feeling. It was that magnificent. The sheer intensity of all one's senses halting at once so nothing could be felt but pleasure.

No wonder Romy had let Granby ruin her during a ball. *Good grief.*

When the last tremor finally abated, leaving her spent, sated, and now comfortably in Morgan's lap, the fingers at her neck traced the outline of her pulse. The hard length of him —*good lord, Phaedra. Just say cock*—pressed into her backside. What would that be like? To have him inside her? Morgan, naked and beautiful, like a large viper twisted around her.

She wanted that. *Him.* Her murderous suitor.

A shiver ran through her, though the day was warm.

"You make a strong argument, Mr. Stewart," Phaedra finally said, wishing she could stay here with him, beneath this tree, forever. For perhaps the first time in her life, there had been little consideration over her being a duke's daughter —or *The Disastrous Barrington.* Her feelings for Morgan, complicated since that first day at Hagerty's, were now doubly so. The entire situation was fraught with peril. The wager still sat, like a swirling, treacherous river, separating them from each other. Today had not erased it. Nor given a reason for it.

Morgan turned her mouth to his, lips brushing against hers. "Where does everyone suppose you are today?"

"In bed. With a female complaint," she said without thinking. "That's rather—"

"A good ruse." Morgan lifted her up before him, pausing only to tuck a stray strand of hair behind her ear.

Far too gentle for such a savage man.

Phaedra fussed with the shirt, making sure everything was tucked back in, feeling more self-conscious than she ever had in her life. "I suppose I've made things easy for you."

Lifting her chin with one finger, he allowed her to see, in the fraction of an instant, the depth of his longing for her. It was far more than ten thousand pounds would merit.

"Easy is not a word I would ever use for you, Phaedra Barrington. And you know that this"— he pressed his forehead ever so slightly to hers—"has nothing to do with page seventy-eight. Would that it did. Things would be far less complicated. Now, I want to hear all about your evening of debauchery and wickedness at Elysium. Tell me what you found in those second-floor rooms besides that piece of ivory." The heat in his eyes flared sharply.

Phaedra touched Morgan's hand, her fingers sliding over his. Feeling the solid warmth of him beside her.

"Drive slowly, Mr. Stewart," she said in a cheeky manner. "There is quite a bit of wickedness to discuss."

11

P haedra's singular thought, as Martin Van Rhys handed her into the carriage to sit next to her mother, was that she couldn't recall having agreed to this outing, though she must have during Leo's grand opening because it was the only other time she'd been in the company of Van Rhys.

Two long days had drifted by with no sign of her murderous suitor.

Fine. Perhaps merely *threatening*.

After driving back into the city after shooting pistols, Morgan had steered the gig once more into the alley behind The Barrington, dropped the reins, and then kissed Phaedra so savagely, she'd thought the gig might combust. Such intensity. So—*blistering* in nature. When at last Morgan had pulled away from her, Phaedra had found her fingers twisted around the lapel of his coat, panic filling her at the idea of leaving him.

"Is something wrong, dear? You look a bit flushed?" Mama sat beside her in Van Rhys's carriage.

"Only a little warm."

139

Try to behave. Or not, Morgan had whispered along her neck, reluctantly plucking her fingers from him. *Stay away from Van Rhys. I insist, schatje.*

Phaedra surveyed the elegant gentleman across the carriage. Van Rhys had dressed impeccably for their outing, his dark hair brushed back from his forehead showing just a hint of gray at the temples. The smile fixed on his lips absurdly polite. He'd charmed Phaedra at Leo's grand opening.

But now she knew why Morgan and Van Rhys didn't care for each other.

And possibly she would have refused today, if only Morgan hadn't used that *particular* word.

Insist.

Lady Dalton had *insisted* Phaedra temper her opinions so as not to infect those of her daughter. Phaedra's opinion, as it happened, was that Lady Dalton's daughter was a nitwit.

Mr. Riddle, the wine merchant, had *insisted* he would get better terms if only he could speak to the Duke of Averell directly. Phaedra had proved him incorrect, on more than one occasion, and found another merchant more agreeable.

Torrington had *insisted* she not enter Hagerty's unescorted.

Very well, that could have gone horribly awry. But only in that one instance.

Mama had *insisted* Phaedra learn the violin, though she'd had not an ounce of interest or talent. Instead, she had been forced to accompany Olivia's flute playing while everyone, including Pith, stuffed cotton in their ears to mute the sound.

The list was rather endless. Phaedra was exhausted by the *insistence* of others. Now Morgan was insisting, and her immediate inclination was to defy him. Though in this instance, Phaedra should have heeded his request.

It was a bloody command.

Van Rhys clearly hadn't agreed with his sister Gertrude's adoption of Morgan and bringing him into her home. He struck her as a gentleman for whom appearances mattered greatly. Having a pickpocket living under his sister's roof had likely been humiliating for Van Rhys.

I should have begged off.

Van Rhys leaned back and said something to the driver, who slowed the carriage as they made their way down Broadway. He smiled to a pair of gentlemen, leaning nonchalantly out the side of the carriage to greet them.

Both dipped their hats in his direction as the carriage passed, eyes gazing in curiosity at Phaedra and her mother.

Van Rhys beamed, sitting back on the leather seats like some emperor as he showed off his conquests, a dowager duchess and a duke's daughter.

"Friends of yours, Mr. Van Rhys?" Phaedra ventured, knowing he was waiting for her to comment.

He gave a careless wave. "Business acquaintances. Both are clients of New York Loss & Life, my insurance company."

"Insurance?" Mama said. "A venture with ups and downs, I'm told."

"Challenging, Your Grace. New York has been visited by a series of events which affected us all. Fire. Financial collapse." His brows drew together. "Not to mention cholera. But enough talk of disaster. The day is fine, and a visit to The Battery is in order, just as I promised."

"The Battery?" Van Rhys had mentioned the place to her previously, the night of the grand opening, but she'd been too intent on Morgan to pay him much attention. That must have been when she had agreed to this outing, or at the very least, hadn't objected.

"The Dutch—my ancestors," Van Rhys stated in a lofty tone, "first occupied the area, and according to historical record, it was there that they purchased Manhattan from the

Lenape tribe, though I'm not sure the Lenape knew they were selling anything, let alone this." Van Rhys gestured to the city around them. "A fort once stood at The Battery, housing George Washington and the Continental army. Years later, while you were attempting to invade us," he said, giving them a wry smile, "five additional forts were built at the site to guard New York. We didn't want you sailing up the Hudson, you see. Now, The Battery is a park, with an amphitheater and The Castle, where a vast assortment of entertainments take place. Circus performances. Hot air balloons. The Marquis de Lafayette visited once. Quite an honor for the city."

"I'm sure we'll find it delightful, Mr. Van Rhys," Mama said. "Even if we English were on the losing side in that particular matter. Don't you think so, dear?" She smiled at Phaedra.

"Sounds lovely." Phaedra turned to admire the passing scenery, the sprawl of the city, which was so different from London. Her mind went to Gertrude Van Rhys, Martin's sister, who had been brave enough to take a man like Morgan Stewart under her wing. What had happened to her?

If there was an opportunity to ask Van Rhys in a discreet manner today, Phaedra meant to find out. Morgan hadn't shared the information.

Once they arrived at Battery Park, the afternoon passed in a pleasant fashion. The Castle was indeed splendid, though there were no entertainments planned for today, which was rather disappointing. But Van Rhys proved to once more be a charming companion. He entertained Phaedra and her mother with amusing tales of a childhood spent with older brothers who were always in trouble. He spoke fondly of his parents, mentioning that his entire family had perished during the cholera epidemic, including the young lady to whom he'd been betrothed.

"My goodness, Mr. Van Rhys. You have had your share of tragedy." Mama touched his arm.

"Indeed, I have, Your Grace."

"Didn't you have a sister, Mr. Van Rhys?" Phaedra said as they paused on a bluff overlooking the river.

Van Rhys stiffened beside her.

"My apologies," Phaedra quickly added. "It is only that I heard Gertrude Van Rhys mentioned at a dinner I attended. I assumed—well, the cholera."

"My sister and I had a rather complicated relationship," he said, looking out across the water. "She was older and the product of my father's first marriage. Gertrude died much later under"—he cleared his throat—"other circumstances." The charming, polite tone went cold.

Mama wisely changed the subject by pointing to a building in the distance. "And what is that, Mr. Van Rhys?" She took his arm and led him away from where Phaedra stood.

The sun glistened along the surface of the Hudson as she contemplated Morgan, Van Rhys, and Gertrude. An image of Morgan's savagely cut features, the pain in his eyes so clear to her at the mention of his adopted mother flashed before Phaedra.

I should have declined today.

A tiny ruffle of unease passed through her. The nature of her relationship with Morgan had undergone a shift two days ago. Not only because of the physical intimacy taking place between them, but—there was an absolute *rightness* to being with Morgan.

"Phaedra," her mother waved. "Hurry along."

When at last the carriage started back towards The Barrington, Van Rhys was busy telling yet another amusing tale concerning a visit to the circus. Phaedra would even dare to say she was enjoying herself, which did nothing but make her feel disloyal.

He made a bloody wager on me. One that could bankrupt my brother.

Morgan didn't own her person. Nor did he dictate her time.

The constant back and forth, the argument Phaedra was having with herself, consumed her so much, she hadn't even realized the carriage was approaching a park.

"I thought we'd take a different route back to The Barrington." Van Rhys smiled at her. "Through The Row," he said with a wink. "And Washington Park."

"Goodness, Mr. Van Rhys," her mother said. "Is this akin to Rotten Row in Hyde Park, where everyone rides about to be seen?"

Phaedra hid her smile. Mama had certainly figured out Van Rhys, who had strutted about introducing them to nearly everyone they came upon today, which was no small number.

"No, Your Grace. Not at all. Over the course of the afternoon, you mentioned your affinity for architecture as well as history. The Row and Washington Park have a bit of both. The area was once a cemetery. German in origin, I believe. Then the area was used for executions." He gestured to the lovely park towards which the carriage rolled. "But it is the homes along Washington Square that should interest you, Your Grace."

"Her Grace does enjoy a good Grecian column," Phaedra interjected.

"Doric, dearest," Mama corrected.

Phaedra rolled her eyes. Honestly, the only other person who'd ever cared about such things had been Papa. And Phaedra thought he'd done so merely to humor her mother. No one gave a fig about window shapes, the pitch of a roof, or what sort of column you stuck outside your house.

"The wealthy have built a row of homes along the North side, which we in Manhattan refer to as The Row." A soft chuckle. "I confess, my home is one of them."

Of course, it is. Braggart.

Van Rhys would expire on the spot if he saw Cherry Hill. Or the Averell mansion in London.

"How extraordinary." Mama surveyed the residences as the carriage passed by. "I've always admired the Greeks and their contributions to design."

"There is a distinct Grecian style, don't you agree?"

Mama narrowed her eyes, taking in every house as they passed, nodding slowly as she admired all that brick and stone.

Phaedra stifled a yawn.

Van Rhys pointed out his own home, a red brick building with towering columns in the front. Flowers bloomed from pots lined up along the steps. "Would you care to stop?"

"We are expected back at The Barrington, Mr. Van Rhys, though your home is certainly beautiful." Her mother surveyed the residence before them. "Another time, perhaps? When I can truly admire the artistry." Mama softened the blow.

"I look forward to it," Van Rhys replied smoothly. "And what are your thoughts, Lady Phaedra?"

"Your home is quite lovely, Mr. Van Rhys, though I confess I don't share my mother's understanding of architecture." Honestly, Phaedra thought all the homes resembled each other, built side by side, much like many of the residences in London.

The carriage slowed at each of the houses while Van Rhys pointed out small but significant architectural details to her mother. At least Phaedra imagined them important, by the questions Mama asked. Van Rhys mentioned the owners of each residence and their importance in relation to his own.

So tedious.

As they approached the end of the street, the carriage slowed to barely a crawl, nearly halting at the final house, undistinguished in comparison to the others and lacking the flourishes decorating some of the previous homes.

"That one is rather plain." Mama leaned forward. "Older than the others, I would guess. The brick isn't the same."

"You would be correct, Your Grace. One of the first homes built and much less modern. Ruins the look of The Row, in my opinion. But the house has some sentimental value, I suppose."

Phaedra watched with dawning horror as a gentleman exited the front door of the house, walking stick in one hand. Broad shoulders stretched the fabric of his coat, threatening to burst the seams, though surely it had been made for him. The sun caught at the smoky topaz of his hair, glinting along the line of his jaw. Even from this distance, Phaedra could make out the scar on his chin.

Morgan looked up, his eyes lighting on the carriage as it passed at a snail's pace. There was no sign of recognition or anger in the pale gaze. Only a chilling cold, so blinding Phaedra shuddered as it fell on her.

Oh, dear.

"You asked about my sister, Gertrude." Van Rhys shook his head sadly. "That house was once hers. My entire family lived there at one time before we moved to a larger home. Gertrude was a kind, charitable woman. She started a home for orphans. Gave large sums of her fortune to good works with moderate success. Many of those she helped could not be saved. Her home is now inhabited by one such failure. Worse than all the rest."

Mama looked towards Morgan standing on the steps. "He is one of her foundlings?"

"Morgan Stewart was taken in by my sister. I believe she

gave him the name. If he had another name at one point, no one knows it. She left her entire fortune to him. Coerced, no doubt."

Phaedra composed her features into boredom, just as she'd been taught to do when faced with an unpleasant situation, and this certainly qualified. The envy leaking from Van Rhys, the utter loathing, was difficult to miss. More than having a mongrel at the Van Rhys dinner table, then.

Gertrude had chosen Morgan over her own brother.

"Stewart inherited Gertrude's home, which my father built, along with everything else. A terrible shame. He never even bothered to return those things which should have remained in the Van Rhys family. Heirlooms and such." A frustrated sound left him. "You can imagine my upset, as I am the sole remaining member. My sister wouldn't have wanted me to be treated so poorly."

But yet she'd left everything to Morgan. Not Van Rhys.

"And of course, there was gossip."

Phaedra's stomach lurched, knowing she was about to hear something incredibly unpleasant.

"Gossip?" Her mother gave him a sympathetic look.

Van Rhys looked down for a moment, allowing the silence to sink in.

"Stewart was not a child when Gertrude took him in." He slowly raised his chin. "She was unwed, you see. A spinster, but far from elderly. Stewart was...I believe fourteen, possibly older." He cleared his throat, letting the ugly insinuation to take root. "Forgive me for being indelicate. There are other accusations—far worse." He waved a hand as if distraught.

Phaedra was certain he was not. Van Rhys had planned the drive through Washington Square, and The Row. How he'd known Morgan would come out of his house at about this time was another matter.

"Mr. Van Rhys?" Mama leaned forward.

He shook his head. "I've said too much, Your Grace. Far more than I meant to. It is only that the very sight of him dredges up such unhappy memories. I should have known better than to take us down The Row, but I thought you'd enjoy seeing the houses. Please tell me I haven't ruined our afternoon."

"Of course not, Mr. Van Rhys."

"At any rate," Van Rhys said, composing himself, "Stewart is determined to infiltrate the ranks of polite society despite his notoriety. He is a man of means now, thanks to Gertrude. There is a rumor that he means to wed Iris Beekman, but I can't countenance her father approving the match. I doubt she'd survive living under the same roof as Stewart." Then quietly, under his breath, "My sister did not."

Mama studied Van Rhys for a moment but did not rise to the bait. The dowager duchess had dealt with her fair share of posturing wealthy gentlemen. She would return to The Barrington and seek out Georgina rather than ask Van Rhys anything more.

"Let us return to The Barrington and put this behind us," Van Rhys said cheerfully. "I'm sure you're ready to return, are you not, my lady?" He gave Phaedra an innocent look.

Van Rhys had *seen* Phaedra and Morgan together, whether at the grand opening or when Phaedra left the city in Morgan's gig. This was his way of letting her know he had. What he meant to do with the information was anyone's guess. But she thought it had much more to do with Morgan than her.

As for Morgan, he hadn't shown a flicker of recognition at seeing Phaedra in Van Rhys's carriage. Nor given any outward indication he was bothered by it. But she had noticed the blunt fingers twitching in agitation against one muscular thigh. Morgan's tell.

Phaedra turned back to Van Rhys with a bland look. "I am. It is nearly time for tea, and I'm famished."

Never show distress or they will eat you alive.

Papa had often equated society to a pack of wolves intent upon tearing you apart, as if it were their sole duty. She'd learned from a young age that being a Barrington, particularly *The Disastrous Barrington*, meant you could never bend. Never care what others said. If she had been a weak girl, Phaedra would have collapsed into a fit of tears at the wagers in the Red Book.

Van Rhys didn't take his eyes from her. "Of course." With a flick of one wrist, he instructed his driver to return to The Barrington, waiting for any sign the arrow he'd launched at Phaedra would find its mark.

Van Rhys would get nothing from her.

Phaedra already knew Morgan had an innate brutality. A violent side to his nature. That was no surprise. She was only partially joking when she referred to him as her murderous suitor. But those savage features had been filled with love when Morgan had spoken of Gertrude, the sort a son has for his mother. Phaedra might not be certain of many things at the moment, but she was *positive* Morgan and Gertrude had never been lovers.

She looked out at the passing street, trying to collect her thoughts while her mother and Van Rhys conversed on the grand opening of The Barrington and those who had been in attendance.

Nothing more was said about Morgan Stewart. Thankfully.

"What a glorious day," she said to Van Rhys as they arrived at the hotel and he helped her out of the carriage. "Thank you so much for taking us to The Battery, Mr. Van Rhys. I enjoyed seeing it very much."

"I hope our little detour appealed to you, my lady." His

eyes caught hers with nothing but polite inquiry, though Phaedra saw the glint of malice he couldn't hide. "I was certain you'd find the drive through the park to be of interest."

"I confess, Mr. Van Rhys, that I don't care for architecture nearly as much as my mother." She lowered her voice so that only he could hear. "Or you, for that matter." A brilliant smile was bestowed on him.

Van Rhys inclined his head, lips curling just slightly at her words.

Phaedra didn't care.

"Thank you again. Good day, Mr. Van Rhys."

Phaedra observed the residence before her, taking a deep breath to help bolster her resolve. Three stories of cold, gray stone, a shade darker than Morgan's eyes. Devoid of ornamentation. Door knocker not even in the shape of a wolf or a lion, which would have been appropriate. Even the shrubbery looked menacing. It was no surprise to Phaedra that Morgan hadn't sold Gertrude's former residence and perhaps opted to move somewhere else after her death. Whatever this house might mean to Van Rhys, *this* was Morgan's *home*, something he'd never had until Gertrude. It would be akin to Phaedra selling Cherry Hill, for instance.

Morgan wasn't about to leave this house, not even with Martin Van Rhys living at the other end of the street.

In the week that had passed since the trip to The Battery, Phaedra had debated long and hard about the outing with Van Rhys. If Morgan was angry, it was his own fault. He didn't have the right to dictate to her, even if she didn't particularly care for Van Rhys or his mysteriously dropped hints concerning the relationship between Morgan and Gertrude. *Her* relationship with Morgan was vague at best. He wasn't courting her, at least not in a respectable manner. There was no understanding between them. Only a wager.

When he appeared, she meant to tell him so. In the meantime, Phaedra would keep occupied. She had busied herself by insisting Rosalind show her how to make a lemon tart. The results were mixed at best. She'd also attended two teas on behalf of Mrs. Rutherford.

Van Rhys had lingered about, dining with Leo at least twice.

Phaedra had avoided him.

She drummed her fingers along one thigh, eyes never leaving the gray stone before her, and took a halting breath.

Morgan, as it turned out, had not laid siege to The Barrington. Nor had he appeared outside in the gardens where he'd lurked during Olivia's wedding. He wasn't the sort to send flowers or sweets, but Phaedra had thought at least he might send another knife. Perhaps a pistol. Or a deadly hatpin.

Absolutely *nothing* had happened.

His silence spoke volumes.

Phaedra had been prepared for coldly biting anger. A bit of menace, perhaps. Morgan might have displayed possessive behavior, which she would have combatted with her carefully prepared speech.

But not this terrible, unexpected silence which tore at her heart.

Arrogant, slightly murderous Morgan was one thing.

Wounded Morgan was quite another.

"Don't be a coward, Phaedra," she whispered under her breath, staring at all that gray brick. "Even the lion tamer must enter the beast's cage now and again, risking dismemberment."

Placing a hand on the hack's door, she took a deep breath, holding it to the count of ten before expelling. It did nothing to calm her. Yesterday, Phaedra had swallowed her stubbornness and sent Morgan a note.

There had been no reply.

This was *not* about page seventy-eight in the Red Book. Teaching her to shoot a pistol had not been about the bloody wager. Morgan taking intimacies—well, if that was about the wager, he could have just ruined her beneath the tree. Instead, he'd bared part of his soul to her.

And she'd gone to The Battery with Van Rhys.

Which was why Phaedra was here, an unwed young lady from a good family, visiting a gentleman's home at night without escort. The hack driver didn't count. Reckless, to be sure, but Phaedra reasoned she wasn't well known in New York, at least not by sight. The fact that Van Rhys lived six houses down was problematic, but she'd waited until complete darkness before venturing out, with the hood of her cloak pulled tightly around her features. Phaedra's rooms at The Barrington were opposite the quarters of the rest of the family. She'd retired early. No one would miss her.

Return to the safety of The Barrington this instant. Consider your reputation.

"Why must the voice of reason sound like Pith?" she said under her breath. "It's rather annoying."

"Beg your pardon, miss?" The hack driver, an older man with tufts of white hair sticking out at odd angles from beneath his hat, gave her a look.

"I said, you don't have to wait." Hopping out of the hack, Phaedra pulled the hood of the cloak more securely around her face. The street was completely deserted. No one to bear witness to her irresponsible behavior. Each step had her reconsidering the current course of action but...

I hurt him. Unintentionally.

Phaedra, in all her obstinance had never once considered a man like Morgan Stewart, who could walk the streets of St. Giles or Five Points without fear, could be hurt. And by her.

Her palm pressed against her fiercely beating heart.

The hack pulled away, the sound rattling her nerves. Another deep breath which failed to do anything but make her lightheaded. She didn't move for a few minutes, just contemplated that this evening would likely end in her ruination.

Freely given.

Phaedra had only just raised her hand to the knocker, a plain thing made of brass, when the door flew open suddenly.

A small, wiry man, hair the color of gunmetal and dressed in a plum-colored coat, eyed her with suspicion. He took a step forward, carefully peeking behind her to study the street. There was a pistol stuck into his waistband.

Lovely.

"Can I help you, miss?" He didn't seem as if he actually wanted to assist Phaedra, given his distrustful glare. More that he was being forced to. This had to be Morgan's butler, but he wasn't dressed in any sort of uniform or even a decent coat. Plum did nothing for his complexion.

"Is Mr. Stewart at home?"

He raised a brow. "Who wants to know?" Sharp eyes lingered over her. "Let me see your face."

She peeled back the hood just a bit and dared to take a step inside with one foot so he couldn't close the door on her. "I've business with Mr. Stewart. He's expecting me."

A disgruntled sound came from him. "Didn't mention he'd be having a visitor tonight."

What a rude little man. Completely lacking in manners.

Phaedra shrugged, reasonably sure she could brazen this out. "I am Lady Phaedra."

A snort. "Sure, you are." He waved her forward. "I'm Dabble, Stewart's man. Don't need to explain yourself." He held up a hand. "Usually tells me if he's expecting your sort, that's all. Must have forgotten. You sound like a governess, not that I ever had one."

Your sort. Whatever did that mean?

"Stewart is in his study."

Phaedra's spine snapped straight, the realization dawning on her. *Your sort*. Mr. Dabble thought her to be a...*doxy*. One Morgan had *ordered*. Such as asking for your meat to be cooked rare. How utterly *unexpected* was the surge of rather virulent irritation pulsing beneath her skin at the thought that Morgan had invited or *ordered*—

"Something wrong with you?" Dabble stopped, itching his scalp. "You look funny."

Phaedra realized she'd come to a complete stop in the narrow hall, her fists clutched at her sides. She felt rather *savage*.

"Not in the least." Lifting her chin, she nodded for Mr. Dabble to continue through the labyrinth of a hall, admiring the fine furnishings and artwork scattered about. Understated. Nothing too lavish. She had a suspicion Morgan hadn't picked out any of it, but rather Gertrude Van Rhys had.

"I'll warn you." Dabble paused. "He ain't in the best mood. I'll wait in case you decide to leave. Wouldn't blame you if you did."

"I won't."

"As you wish, *my lady*." Dabble smirked a bit before knocking on the door.

An unwelcoming growl was the response. A bear whose hibernation had been interrupted. Rather terrifying.

"Told you. Lady Whatever." He snorted.

"Phaedra. Lady Phaedra."

"Fancy name for your ilk. You read that in a book or something?"

"I am *not* a courtesan," Phaedra snapped at him.

Dabble's brows drew together in confusion. "A quart of what?"

"Never mind." Phaedra forced her features into a look of cool disdain. An apology had been prepared for Morgan. A confession that she...had possibly behaved thoughtlessly in accompanying Van Rhys. That she hadn't meant to hurt him. Now she felt nothing but foolish. Perhaps Morgan had decided after their day of pistols and pleasure that Phaedra didn't suit him after all.

There could be droves of women filtering in and out of his house for the purposes of lewd acts. Scores of them fluttering about. All of them much more well-versed in physical relations than Phaedra. Well, what had she expected? Clearly—

"You're making that face again." Dabble's hand sat on the doorknob. "Do you need to...relieve yourself, afore you go in there?"

Dear God. She was going to stab Dabble. "Open the door."

Dabble coughed and swung the door wide.

Stewart sat behind a massive desk, coat discarded, the sleeves of his shirt rolled up to display muscled forearms with thick veins running beneath the skin. There was a dark spot just above one wrist. A mark of some sort.

A tattoo.

The space above Phaedra's heart fluttered about like a butterfly trapped beneath her skin. Intoxication, the sort only Morgan seemed to create, made her dizzy. Her eyes drifted to the tattoo once more, arousal flushing her skin. Peckham, Leo's floor manager at Elysium, sported a tattoo on his hand. She'd never been the least interested in it. Or Peckham. And of course, pirates had tattoos. Criminals. Dangerous men. Maybe even those from Five Points.

A bolt of warmth burst across her chest and spread down the length of her body.

Morgan's fingers, the very ones that had lavished so much attention on that spot now aching between her thighs, were curled around a glass of what looked like whiskey. There was no welcome in his rough features. He glared at her, eyes like shards of ice.

None of that stopped the swaying of her form in his direction. Shocking, that was the best way to describe how Morgan affected her. Her legs became quite unsteady.

Phaedra pressed the heels of her half-boots into the rug.

Not a lick of emotion showed on that harsh-cut mouth. His gaze flat, reflecting the light, like the surface of a frozen pond. But the entire study smelled like Morgan, the woodsy scent, the sweetness of apples filling her nostrils.

"Now is not a good time, Lady Phaedra. Dabble will escort you out."

He *never* addressed her as *Lady* Phaedra. That alone was confirmation that she had indeed wounded the large, dangerous, beast before her. Anger came off him in frosty waves, coating her face and hands.

"Expecting someone else?" she retorted, daring to match his chilly tone.

"No sense of self-preservation at all," he growled. "I'm busy."

"How unfortunate." She pulled off her gloves.

Morgan sat back in the chair. Tipping his glass, he swallowed the remainder, pale eyes not once leaving her. His shirt was unbuttoned at the top, revealing a tiny swath of dark gold hair. She followed the motions of his naked throat as he swallowed, fascinated by the movement.

"It would be better for both of us if you returned home, *my lady*. Given my mood." Each word was covered in frost. "Run along." He flicked the wrist bearing the mark.

"As it happens"—Phaedra stepped forward and flung off the cloak—"I'm in a somewhat murderous mood myself. I didn't encourage a carriage ride with Van Rhys. And I certainly didn't ask him to drive down The Row in order to torment you."

A low rumble came from Morgan.

Phaedra stood her ground.

"Van Rhys. Jesus." Dabble's eyes widened.

"I don't care." Morgan slammed the glass on the desk so hard, Phaedra thought it might shatter. "Please have the carriage brought around, Dabble. Lady Phaedra is departing,"

"Ignore that order, Mr. Dabble." Phaedra's tone was crisp.

"Just Dabble," he muttered, glancing between the two of them.

"I'm not leaving. Even if I must tolerate an *entire parade* of your female companions this evening." She had the presence of mind to stamp her half-boot into the carpet.

"Female companions? What are you...? What did you say to her?" He glared at Dabble.

Dabble wisely didn't reply, instead exiting immediately and shutting the door with a hurried click.

Phaedra went straight to the sideboard, poured something that looked like brandy, took a sip, and made a face.

"Bourbon whiskey." Morgan held out his glass. "As long as you are sampling my sideboard, spill some more of it in my glass. I'll have Dabble bring you some tea."

"I don't want your bloody tea." She poured more of the bourbon in her glass before setting the decanter on the corner of his desk.

"So bad at following directions."

"Only when they are rudely given." Taking another careful sip, she tried not to make a face. "I didn't know you had a tattoo." Phaedra nodded at his wrist.

"This is more a brand. Like one does with cattle or

sheep." He looked into the fire, shoulders tense, and Phaedra could almost *feel* how painful that tattoo was for him.

"I didn't mean—"

"You can ask me later." Morgan turned back to her. "I might even tell you."

"Van Rhys requested a carriage ride the night of the grand opening. I wasn't paying him the least attention. I've no idea if I agreed. But my mother took it upon herself to accept the invitation when he sent a note. On my behalf. It isn't as if I encouraged him." She took another swallow, kept from coughing, and allowed the warmth to spread along her limbs.

"You should have declined."

At least he was speaking to her and not threatening to have her thrown out. "Probably."

"And you didn't refuse *because* I asked you to stay away from him." His eyes narrowed.

"No," she lifted her chin. "You didn't ask. You *insisted*. Demanded I obey without giving me the courtesy of a good reason to do so. I am not unintelligent, Morgan. I will not be dictated to."

"Christ, you'll never obey me, will you?"

"It is highly unlikely," she answered.

"I want you anyway," he snarled, stroking the glass of bourbon with one blunt finger, eyes darkening to that odd blue-gray. "As maddening as you are. As horrible as I am."

"You are quite horrible," she agreed. He wasn't. Not entirely.

"You've no idea. Nor do I wish you to." Morgan's voice caught, the deep roar lowering to a mere whisper.

"Morgan," she said softly.

"If I had an ounce of decency, I would never see you again."

"You aren't at all decent, either." Phaedra wanted so badly to touch him. Kiss the scar on his chin. Sink her fingers into the muted gold of his hair. The pull in his direction could no longer be ignored.

"There are no other women. No Miss Beekman. No mistresses. No doxies." The rough features softened on her. "No others since Hagerty's. My affections are decided." He raised his glass and drained it. "Lucky you."

Affection was such a tame word for what had bloomed between her and Morgan. Fixed from that first meeting at Hagerty's. Phaedra was exhausted with trying to pretend it didn't exist. "As are mine," she finally said, meaning every word.

"This is not about page seventy-eight. Nor..." He paused as if considering what more he might say. "...Anything else." His voice thickened to a rasp.

"I know it isn't." She took another cautious step forward.

"You are worth far more to me than ten thousand pounds." The misty gaze flicked over her. "Your value is incalculable." Morgan pressed a palm over his chest as his voice grew tortured. "A great treasure. Come here my ferocious creature."

Phaedra moved towards the desk, body and heart both aching. Weighted with everything she felt for Morgan, which was bloody substantial. The air filled with the inescapable force of their connection to each other.

"*Schatje*," he whispered.

"I still don't know what that word really means. It could be anything. What you would name your favorite horse, for instance."

A bark of laughter came from him. "I've only ever used that word with you." He held out his hand, begging her fingers to wrap around his own. "And you are my favorite everything."

Another burst of warmth stretched out across her limbs,

heating the blood beneath her skin. "Are you still put out with me?"

"Entirely. But it will fade."

A tear threatened to fall, but she blinked it away. Phaedra laced her fingers with his, ready to fall into the abyss, as long as it was with him.

13

Beautiful, brave girl.

There were grown men who, upon hearing of Morgan's displeasure, had pissed themselves, afraid for their lives. One snarl from him, and they would fall away and scatter, like a flock of crows. He was the thing that lived in the dark, roaming Five Points for amusement and then returning to eviscerate someone unlucky enough to cross him in business.

Oh, but not Phaedra.

Steel. Fire. Brilliance. All wrapped in silk and smelling of wild roses.

There wasn't anything Morgan wouldn't do for her.

Dread, so thick and overgrown he could barely breathe, took hold of him. The same terror that had taken root the moment he'd seen her with Van Rhys, who had grinned at Morgan like some demented clown.

Van Rhys had found Morgan's weakness.

I'm going to have to kill him.

"I'm not the least troublesome," Phaedra murmured, her slender fingers tightening on his.

The statement was such a bold lie, Morgan laughed again. "I don't mind a bit of trouble, as it happens. I'm not afraid of you, Phaedra Barrington."

"Perhaps you should be." She sighed into him, pressing a palm to his cheek.

When Morgan had been that poor, starved boy, more wraith than child, he had never imagined one day sitting in a fine house, drinking bourbon, with his heart's desire before him. The other half of his blackened, ruined soul. He had cared for so little before meeting Gertie, only how best to survive with the least pain. Since her death, Morgan had cared even less. Ambition drove him. Petty revenge amused him. If someone stood in his way, he removed them.

But now Morgan had something to protect. Someone who belonged to him, though Phaedra was unlikely to ever admit it. He would never let her go. Not after tonight.

Morgan had enemies. More than a few. He and Benjamin Cooke, for instance, had been at each other's throats since finding that fucking coat years ago when they were children.

But Van Rhys was different.

He didn't want a coat, but a railroad. The controlling shares of Mohawk & Hudson, to be specific. Shares Van Rhys had sold to Gertrude years ago but, since her death, had decided he should have back. Morgan's study was littered with letters demanding the return of those shares. He could have papered the wall with them, but if Van Rhys had any legal power at all to take them, he already would have.

"Morgan," Phaedra breathed. "I feel as if I don't have your complete attention."

He roughly pulled her into his lap, situating her limbs so she straddled him, her skirts rucked up, exposing her legs. "You have *all* my attention." When Morgan looked at Phaedra, all the chaos and bitter rage inside him, forged over years, became muted. Silent. Quieted to barely a whisper.

Phaedra had all of Morgan. He would do anything to keep her.

Cupping her face, he stared into those magnificent eyes, with their distinct ring of indigo, seeing her intelligence, her desire. The beat of his heart picked up at the knowledge that this glorious creature wanted him. Morgan Stewart.

Greedily, he pulled her mouth to his, enjoying the gentle sway of her body. "Mine," he whispered against her lips, feeling the truth of it in his heart. "Admit to it."

"I belong to myself," she replied tartly. "But I *will* grant you liberties with my person." Phaedra pressed a careful kiss to the hollow of his throat. "You need only to ask."

His hands slid down Phaedra's curves, beneath her hips, to cup the plump cheeks of her bottom. Such a delicious bottom. He meant to sink his teeth into every inch of it. "Mine."

She made a breathless sound and wiggled about his lap in response.

Morgan's cock hardened to marble, thick and pulsing with desire. He tamped down the need to claim her as savagely as possible, terrified he might hurt her.

Not Phaedra. Never her.

Contrary to what most of Manhattan thought of him, Morgan was not a brute with women. He was careful with them. Conscious always of his bigger size. His strength. His need for control. Morgan had disposed of dozens of men, in bloody, brutal ways, but he'd never once harmed any female.

Not even Sister Bridget.

An oily, unwelcome sensation curled in his stomach, as if he were a young lad once more. His failure to be able to face that particular nightmare was one he'd buried deep inside, covered with a thick layer of ice, and tried to ignore.

"*Do* you wish to take liberties with me?" Phaedra's thumb

stroked the scar on his chin, dispensing all thoughts of the past. "You don't seem at all inclined to do so."

Morgan pressed her more fully into his lap so she could feel the throbbing of his cock. "I thought you were more observant than that."

Phaedra rotated her hips, watching him with a great deal of concentration. She was bold and reckless, his *schatje*, but in this, she was innocent. "I will," she said, her voice trembling just slightly, "grant you permission for all. Liberties." Small white teeth nipped at the skin of his neck.

Morgan wanted *those* marks on his flesh, all made with Phaedra's delicate white teeth. She could cover his body with them. Cover the scars already imbedded there. A groan left him as she nibbled on the lobe of his ear.

"You won't leave here with your virtue intact," he said solemnly.

"It would be rather disappointing if I did." Another soft kiss was pressed to the scar on his chin.

"I don't want to hurt you." She was so small and delicate in his arms, though she had a ferocious heart.

She bit him again, this time just below his ear, and whispered, "Do your worst."

14

Phaedra's mother would be mortified.

Years of careful explanation. Books. Drawings, even, for goodness's sake. There was no telling what Pith would think of Mama's efforts if he were to find those diagrams.

All because the dowager duchess had *despaired* that her youngest daughter would go *uninformed* to a future husband. To be fair, Mama had Phaedra's best interests at heart. Tales abounded in society of virgins fainting and weeping on their wedding nights because they hadn't known what a man's anatomy looked like. Mama believed, strongly, that physical relations were meant to be appealing. Enjoyable. But her mother's rather detailed explanations had always seemed so awkward to Phaedra. Where should one place their hands, for instance? What about noses? Feet? Then she was to wait for proper instruction from her husband.

She wasn't good at taking instruction under the best circumstances.

Phaedra had always assumed the loss of her maidenhead would be performed in a polite, mildly satisfying manner on her wedding night. A trifle boring, but with practice, she'd learn to enjoy the attentions of her husband.

Mama had planned and instructed Phaedra for a titled gentleman.

Not Morgan.

Phaedra had not anticipated the violent need to fuse herself to him. To bite Morgan, scratch at him, sink her teeth into every inch until they were firmly fixed together. She wanted those big, blunt fingers on her skin. The cruel mouth trailing over her body.

Surprisingly, the voice of reason, usually full of caution and sounding like Pith, had gone silent. Not a whisper of protest, though it was a terribly scandalous thing to be ruined.

As a Barrington though, ruination was almost an expectation. But this was not London. She wasn't at some ball or fête in a darkened alcove. Phaedra was not *The Disastrous Barrington* in New York. The loss of her virtue would be done far more quietly.

Her brows drew together.

There was the matter of the wager.

Morgan would have her surrender, and good lord, Phaedra wanted that as well. But she wasn't going to run off with him, as the wager dictated. The lines in the Red Book said nothing about her losing her virtue or taking a lover.

Or...*wedding* him.

Morgan pulled her up, holding Phaedra before reaching behind her to the desk. One sweep of his hand and papers spilled. Ledgers. And unsurprisingly, two tiny spools of piano wire.

He licked at her bottom lip, teasing Phaedra until her mouth parted beneath his, claiming the soft whimper she made. Such hunger lingered in that kiss, the sort that would never be satisfied. Another sound came from her as Phaedra rubbed herself sinuously against him, trying unsuccessfully to stanch the ache between her thighs.

Fingers made their way beneath her skirts, skimming over her legs, finally stopping to grab hold of her hip once more. Jerking her forward, Morgan's other hand spilled across her spine, undoing the buttons that started at the base of her neck.

"Only one hand," she moved closer as the buttons popped. "Impressive."

"I have some experience."

Phaedra's dress parted, dipping over her shoulders, trapping her hands at her sides.

"I can't move my arms."

"Rather my point."

"Morgan—"

"No sign of a corset. Can't say I'm shocked." His mouth nibbled along the side of her neck while one hand toyed with her breast beneath the thin fabric of her chemise. "I applaud your thinking, Phaedra." His thumb teased at her nipple. "Though I had looked forward to cutting you out of your corset."

Sensation bled from the small peak, sending jolts of pleasure down the front of her body at his words. The thought of the cool blade barely touching her skin as he cut away her corset conjured up an incredibly erotic image, along with a spill of wetness between her thighs.

Morgan's mouth closed over the taut peak of her nipple, sucking and licking through the nearly transparent fabric of her chemise. The heat of his mouth had her twisting about in his lap, frustrated she couldn't touch him with her arms trapped at her sides. The length of him was...well, it was pulsing beneath her bottom and quite thick...heavy. Morgan was a big, broad man. It would stand to reason that his—

A whimper left her at the graze of his teeth across her breast.

"What if I had tossed you out?" he murmured.

"I would not have permitted it." Phaedra's breath hitched at the motion of his mouth, suckling her through the chemise. The hand beneath her skirts moved between her thighs, searching through her underthings until one blunt finger touched her mound. Gently he stroked along her sex as his mouth found hers once more.

"So easily aroused. So responsive to me." The words pressed along the seam of her lips as his fingers moved, slowly sinking two digits inside her. An almost unbearable stretch that pulled at her muscles. His thumb flicked gently over the tiny swollen nub while the fingers thrust, opening her slowly, until Phaedra moaned.

"Much like playing the violin," she said in a low voice. "One must learn the correct placement for one's fingers."

"You did absorb something in your lessons. And you told me you had no musical talent." Morgan added a third finger, making her thrash about. The insistent ache spilling over her mid-section screamed for the same completion she'd experienced before.

"I want—" The press of his mouth silenced her.

His thumb moved more purposefully, teasing and stroking while Phaedra continued to struggle on his lap, her breasts skimming the heat of his chest but unable to get too close. Lips falling to his neck, Phaedra nipped at the smoke of his skin, smelling bourbon and restrained violence.

"Stay away from Martin Van Rhys," Morgan whispered as his thumb circled the small nub hidden in her folds. The first tremors of her impending climax jerked at her limbs. "Don't use him to rebel or piss me off, Phaedra." He ran his teeth over her bottom lip. "Promise me."

She let out a soft moan. "I was making a point."

"Defiant to the end. Your point has been made. Don't do it again."

Phaedra buried her face in Morgan's neck, choking out his name as she found her release, writhing and shaking in his lap. His hand continued to tease at her until the last wave of bliss subsided, finally drawing away as she sat, sated, in his lap.

The buttons at her spine were tugged at once more, loosening the remainder of her dress. Morgan removed every stitch of her clothing, moving her about like a doll until Phaedra was left only in her stockings. She stayed seated in his lap throughout her entire disrobing, her assistance brushed away by his big hands. His hold on her only loosened once, to remove her half-boots, which he unceremoniously tossed over one big shoulder.

Naked and exposed, Phaedra's first inclination was to cover herself, but at the slightest attempt to do so, Morgan stopped her.

"No." Taking her hands, he pressed a kiss to the pulse beating in each of her wrists before releasing her.

"Take down your hair." His eyes were that strange hue once more, misty slate.

Phaedra's fingers pulled at the pins holding the simple chignon twisted at the base of her neck. The heavy mass of hair spilled over her shoulders.

"Like worn leather." His hand fell through the strands. "With bits of copper strewn throughout. Or a sunset over the East River. The day growing dark but streaks of red still hovering over the water." His nose fell into the thick waves, inhaling her with a deep sigh.

"It was once nearly the same hue as my mother's. But when I got older, it darkened. I always wished it had not."

Morgan picked her up and set her bare bottom on top of his desk. "I happen to adore the color of your hair as it is. I want it wrapped around me when I'm buried inside you."

Oh. Her nipples tightened painfully.

"Don't spill the bourbon, *schatje.*" He inclined his head towards the decanter at the far corner. "No matter what happens."

Phaedra looked at the decanter. The ceiling. The window at Morgan's back. Anywhere but at her own nakedness and the still clothed man before her.

"Phaedra," he purred, gaze full of hunger. "You are beautiful."

"I'm the least attractive Barrington." The words came flying from her. "In looks and deeds."

"Not in my eyes. I'll take you as you are." Pushing her legs apart with his palms, thumbs pressing into her flesh, Morgan stared down at her before nuzzling the hair atop her mound with his nose. "You smell delicious."

A quiver ran through her. "What do you intend to do?" His nose and mouth were very close to...*everything.*

The fingers of his hand tangled in the soft hair, tugging lightly until Phaedra whimpered at the tiny sting. "You're mine," he rasped. "*Say it.*"

Phaedra stubbornly shook her head even as the brush of his lips sent a bolt of desire pinging through her body. "I'm not a thing to be owned."

A grunt followed her response as his fingers toyed once more along her flesh. "We'll see."

Morgan pushed her thighs up until she was rather horribly exposed. Moving in one swift motion, he bent, dragging his tongue along the length of her slit. One big hand cupped her bottom, squeezing the flesh, pulling her more firmly against his mouth.

"Bollocks." The word came out in a low moan.

Morgan's amusement at her curse caused a vibration along

her exposed flesh, the flat of his tongue doing the most interesting things...the sudden tightening in her mid-section, the sense of her pleasure coiling into a knot only he could—

"Bollocks." Phaedra shouted as her entire body arched upward from the desk, nearly knocking over the bourbon decanter. She clawed at his shoulders, managing to grab the collar of his shirt. Writhing like a wild thing beneath his ministrations. Her impending pleasure had formed into a sharp, vicious point.

Morgan paused, stopping her release before it could break free, one hand pinching the nipple of one breast. "Say it."

The sting sent another wave of pleasure down her body. "I'm yours," she panted as the ripples pulled at her limbs. She thrust her hips forward, begging for his mouth once more. "I am. You know it." Phaedra thumped a fist on his shoulder.

"Ferocious creature. Finally, you admit it." The tip of his tongue barely touched the tiny, swollen bud before Phaedra broke apart. Her fingers threaded through his hair, holding him shamefully as pleasure drove every other thought from her mind.

When at last she opened her eyes, enough to see that there was a small crack in the ceiling above her as she lay sprawled across Morgan's desk, she sighed at the feel of his mouth trailing along her naked skin.

"Is that—normal?" The pleasure ebbing from her skin was almost painful. Already she longed to call it back.

"To find your release more than once? Not for every woman. Or every time she's bedded. But you and I..." He cupped her cheek.

"Are a good match," she said.

"Because you're mine and you finally admitted to it. Don't you feel better now?" He winked at her.

"So bloody arrogant." She lifted her chin stubbornly but didn't bother to deny his claim.

"I'm yours as well," he murmured. "I've no shame in admitting it, Phaedra." Morgan lifted her from the desk, holding her naked body against his entirely clothed one, and pressed a kiss on her temple. Concern wrinkled his brow, along with hesitation. "I've done what I could to prepare you." Fear glinted in his eyes over hurting her. "But I don't—"

She cut off his words with a small kiss. "You won't hurt me." Her heart ached for this brutal menace holding her so gently. "You won't." Phaedra pulled away from him and lowered herself to the rug before the fire, entirely naked save for her hair and stockings.

"You're so sure?" A shadow crossed the silver of his eyes.

"Positive. I've ridden astride nearly my entire life. I'm told that prepares a young lady."

And even when Phaedra did feel it—because she would, given the enormous bulge in Morgan's trousers that might well break her in half—she would never tell him.

"Now who is being arrogant?" He leaned against the wall, bracing himself in order to pull off his boots, which he threw across the room. Morgan took a halting breath and stared at her for some moments before pulling his shirt out of the waist of his trousers. He hesitated again, as if considering something, but finally tore the garment off, tossing it to the floor.

Oh, but he was magnificent.

All broad shoulders and chest, built as if he'd spent a lifetime hauling stones from a quarry with thick, heavy arms. Carved hollows of hard muscle crossed his torso, the dusting of hair trailing over his stomach only marred by scars. Slices across his ribs and chest, as if someone had repeatedly cut him with a knife. There were dozens of them.

Phaedra stared at the pattern of stark white lines. Each one had been meant to cause pain and make him bleed but not kill him.

He regarded her with hooded eyes, waiting for her to comment.

She gave him a steady look.

Hooking his thumbs into his trousers, Morgan halted once more. There was a defensive cast to his features before he stepped out, exposing thighs heavy with muscle and more scars.

Oh.

She could not have looked away had her hair been on fire. But not because of the scars.

Good Lord.

Mama, in her desire to be completely forthcoming, had drawn the male anatomy, several versions of it, for Phaedra. The piece of ivory at Elysium she'd discovered with Olivia was meant to mimic a man's...*phallus*.

But Morgan's *cock* didn't resemble—it was much larger, for one thing and—

Morgan abruptly turned, giving her his back. Taking a deep breath, as if resigned, he otherwise stayed silent, pressing his forehead against the wall. And waited.

Phaedra covered her mouth before any sound at the horror before her could escape.

"If you decide..." The words were painfully quiet and tentative. So unlike Morgan. "...That it is too repulsive—that I am too repulsive—I'll understand. I won't be angry. I promise, *schatje*."

Phaedra had expected scars, such as the ones she'd seen on his chest. Considering the life she suspected Morgan had led prior to being rescued by Gertrude Van Rhys, she was frankly surprised he had all his limbs. But *this*—this was mutilation. Phaedra hadn't considered until now how full the world was of cruelty. Or how much of it Morgan had experienced.

"Not a pretty sight, is it?" he said over his shoulder. "You wouldn't be the first to scream."

"No." Phaedra kept her voice steady. "But it is a map of your survival, Morgan."

Streaks of ropey white scars decorated his back and buttocks, extending down his thighs to his calves. Pitted. Like the ruts in a country road.

So many.

He'd been caned. Repeatedly. Or whipped. Difficult to tell. Small round marks sat puckered between those longer, ancient wounds. The exact size of the end of a cheroot. Or a fireplace poker.

Damaged, indeed. Far more than Phaedra could have possibly imagined.

The faded look of those scars, the way they stretched across the muscles of his back, told her Morgan had been a child when this violence had been inflicted on him. Completely at the mercy of someone else. Unable to fight his way out. No wonder his need to control everything around him. Or why he'd wrapped himself in ice. A shield, against this brutality.

Oh, Morgan.

"Don't feel sorry for me. I don't want your pity," he advised her in a chilly tone.

"Good. Because you don't have it," she snapped back. Empathy was another matter. "You survived."

This was what Morgan kept hidden from the entire world. The child who had not been able to defend himself, one who had been weak. Whoever had done this had likely also given him the mark he bore on his wrist. What had he called it? A brand.

No one will hurt him again, her heart whispered. *I won't allow it.*

Phaedra shot him an annoyed look. The best way to deal

175

with this situation and stop the tears she longed to weep for him. He might tell her one day, but not tonight.

"Am I staying a virgin, Morgan?"

"No." The flat, nasal quality of his voice was clipped and cold "You are not."

15

"I've always thought," Phaedra whispered as he dropped to his knees before her, "that physical relations would be a bit awkward." She tried to ignore the length of him bobbing in her direction. The task before her seemed impossible, considering his size and hers. "There are so many body parts that must be put in their proper places."

"I'm aware, Phaedra." Morgan was smiling at her. "You tend to babble when you are nervous."

"I do not. It is only that when observing the size of—"

The brush of his mouth stopped her from speaking further. The big, brutish body laid hers down carefully on the rug before the fire, bathing her in his warmth. Morgan's lips trailed down her neck, worshipping the rise of her breasts with his tongue, adoring every inch of her with such care, Phaedra sighed into him, her heart swelling, wanting to find his and hold it.

"I surrender," she gasped as his mouth sucked on one taut nipple before circling the peak with his teeth. The sting sent a jolt between Phaedra's legs, the ache once more returning.

He did it again, until she moaned softly and clutched at his hair. "But only to you."

"Fair enough."

Fingers pressed at the space between her thighs once more, urging her to open.

She cautiously traced the scars along his back with her fingers, feeling the ragged tissue. She bit his bottom lip when his mouth met hers once more. "Are you going to ravish me? Or merely talk about it? I confess—"

Morgan wrapped the length of her hair around his wrist, tugging at the ends and pulling her mouth back to his. "Why can't I do both?" he murmured, placing himself at the entrance of her body.

Phaedra widened her legs farther. "My murderous suitor. Get on with it, then."

A smile flitted at his lips. A flicker of worry in the pale mist of his eyes. Then, one thrust, the force of which pushed Phaedra halfway across the rug.

The air left her lungs at the sudden intrusion. A mewling sound came from her, though she tried to stop it. Prey trapped under the paw of a wolf, perhaps. That's how she thought of herself. "Well, that settles it," she choked out. "Riding does not make it hurt less."

"I'm sorry," he whispered brokenly into her hair. "I'm sorry, *schatje*."

The sensation of fullness, the stretching and pulling, that was the worst of it. Her muscles fluttered about, struggling to make sense of the invasion. She tried to focus on the pleasant scratchiness of his chest hair along her breasts. The strange, musky taste on his lips, which could only be *her*. The comfort derived from his solid weight atop her.

Morgan stayed still, cock pulsing, lips moving across her collarbone, whispering to her as the pain slowly receded.

Attempting to soothe her. But the feeling of being *impaled* did not abate.

"Awkward. Just as I expected," she finally said. Much less pleasurable than his mouth or fingers. But—tolerable.

"I promise it will get better." He caught her mouth. "But maybe not this time."

Phaedra sighed as he withdrew, instinctively lifting her hips as he thrust once more, this time sinking deeper. The shock lessened to a dull ache, the stretching sensation subsiding in small increments as her body adjusted. But that tenuous, persistent ache between her thighs, the stirring of her own pleasure, had gone dormant.

Well, that's rather disappointing.

"Better?"

Her nod was the only incentive he needed to start again, teaching Phaedra how to match his movements, which became increasingly rougher.

She did not object.

Forcing her legs up he hooked one over his shoulder, nearly bending her in half. Each thrust hit that spot inside Phaedra, teasing at pleasure. Nearly in reach.

He clasped her tighter, his movements becoming jagged before he buried his face in her neck. Groaning her name, he stiffened and withdrew as warm stickiness covered her stomach and thighs.

Phaedra closed her eyes as he collapsed alongside her, all muscle and heavy bone, curling protectively around her smaller form. He hadn't spent inside her, which, considering Phaedra still didn't know what the future held, was for the best. Mama had also covered such measures in her lectures.

Morgan rolled to the side and grabbed his discarded shirt, wiping carefully between her thighs to clean her. Dabbing at the small bit of blood.

"You didn't—spill inside me." A consideration few gentlemen might give.

"No, and I won't. I grew up in a brothel, remember? I saw women who...didn't want the child they carried. A great many of them. One of the many disadvantages of being a whore, among others. There are ways to rid yourself of a child you don't want. None are pleasant. I would not foist such a burden on you."

Phaedra wrapped her fingers around the brand on his wrist, watching as he pressed a kiss to her hip. Morgan Stewart would never allow a child of his to be discarded as he had been, she knew that with certainty. Nor would he force an unwanted child on Phaedra.

Unprincipled, brutal men don't give a fig about such things. They ravish curious virgins without a care to their well-being. Spend inside them unworried about the consequences. Discard their bastard children.

How wrong everyone was about Morgan.

"You made a strong case this evening, Mr. Stewart, for my affection." Phaedra snuggled against him. He was solid and warm, a protective barrier guarding her from the world.

"I should let you go back to London and wed some titled twit. An earl or something. Wear frilly gowns and dance at balls. I'm not good."

All of that sounded quite terrible to Phaedra. Besides, given Morgan's possessive nature, she couldn't fathom him waving her goodbye as she made her way back to England. "You are quite terrible. I think we've already agreed, I'm not sure why you keep belaboring the point. Little decency. Threatening manner." Phaedra crawled atop him, pressing a kiss to his cheek, knowing that her heart belonged to Morgan. Wager or not. No matter what the future held.

"Mine," he said against her temple.

"Yes," she agreed. "Brute."

PHAEDRA GRINNED AT HIM, NAKED AND SPLENDID, bourbon colored hair spilling over her shoulders in glorious disarray. A dream, or a wish, appearing to Morgan in human form. The ache for her, the certainty that he might not survive if she were gone from his life, pressed against his chest. The need to keep her beside him, protect her, was far worse now. He would be hard-pressed to even send her back to The Barrington.

"A terrible man," he agreed.

"But not for me." Her eyes on him were serious as she cupped his cheek.

"Never for you." Phaedra anchored Morgan in much the same way Gertie had, though his feelings for the woman lying atop him were vastly different. He had been a good son to his adopted mother, encouraged by her affection, but he'd never left behind his true nature.

He would make an effort to do so for Phaedra.

There was no washing away the stains of Canal Street or Sister Bridget. Nor any of the terrible things he'd done, of which there were many. He still had no reservations about removing those who might get in his way, whether with money or some other method. Nor would he tolerate any threat to Phaedra. Those would be dealt with in his usual fashion.

But for this one girl who made his heart beat harder inside the cage of his chest, Morgan would *try* to be better. Or at least keep his more questionable traits well hidden.

Phaedra jokingly referred to him as her murderous suitor. She'd no idea. Not really.

She'll think I'm a monster.

"I do not regret the loss of my virtue." A soft kiss to his lips. "If you feel the least guilt."

"None, *schatje*."

A wrinkle formed between her dark brows. "You once said the word means troublesome, which makes me seem a pest or an enraged infant. Can't you find something else to call me? Sweetheart, perhaps? Darling, even. Honestly, I don't mind ferocious creature."

Of course she didn't. Phaedra *was* ferocious. She liked that Morgan saw it. Admired her for it. "I like *schatje*."

My treasure.

That was the literal meaning in Dutch, but it was used interchangeably as an endearment between lovers or parents to a child. Seemed fitting to use it for Phaedra. She was *his* treasure. Stalwart. Loyal. Fierce when required. Intelligent and quick witted. Far wiser than her age would dictate. She hadn't even made a sound upon seeing Morgan's back. Even his previous mistress had been hesitant to touch that horror.

"Hmm. We may need to renegotiate that point." Her nose pressed into his shoulder, cuddling to him like some small cat, unmindful of the larger animal she teased.

Tonight had put a definitive end to his plan of using Phaedra to get at Murphy and thus Rutherford. Besides, he'd found another way. One not half as threatening, but it was the only option open to him at present that didn't involve Phaedra directly.

Investment in Murphy's future enterprises. As a partner. Along with taking control of some of The Barrington's more important suppliers. Lew was already making arrangements. He would have Phaedra *and* make Rutherford answer for Gertie.

Morgan stood and helped Phaedra back into her dress, pressing his lips along her skin as he buttoned her up. She smelled of him and her. What they'd done together. He firmly wrapped the cloak around her, batting away her small hands.

"I can take a hack," she insisted.

"You will not." He kissed her before she could argue, already missing her and resisting the urge to just keep her here. But Morgan couldn't claim her, not yet. Murphy was extremely interested in the proposal Lew had made, but no papers had yet been signed. He needed another week, possibly, at most to push the deal through. Then Murphy and Averell would officially be Morgan's partners, whether they liked it or not. It wasn't nearly as perfect as bankrupting Elysium and threatening to destroy Murphy to get what he wanted, but it would have to do.

"I'll see you back to The Barrington."

Phaedra threw a panicked glance at the clock sitting on his desk. "Bollocks."

"Are you uttering a curse or demanding their attention?" Morgan pulled her into the circle of his arms. "You need only ask."

She giggled. A most beautiful sound. One Morgan wanted to hear for the rest of his life.

He drove her back to The Barrington in the same gig he'd used the other day for pistols as she curled against him, yawning sleepily into the night. Leaving the gig some distance away, he walked her down the alley to the servants' entrance at the hotel, snarling at some footpad who'd been stupid enough to approach them.

"Light the lamp in your room and place it by the window so I know you made it safely inside." Morgan kissed her hard, pushing her against the wall, part of him fearful he'd never see her again.

Phaedra rubbed herself against him. "Stop ordering me about."

"Please." He kissed her gently this time, cupping her cheek. "Go inside."

She lingered at the door as he walked towards the gig—he

could feel her eyes on him. Finally, Morgan turned to Phaedra, motioning for her to go in. "Go inside."

"I love you." The words echoed along the stone of the alley. "I love you, Morgan." Then she went through the door before he could respond, closing it behind her.

Once the door shut, Morgan returned to the gig, his pulse unsteady. He took the long way home, past the front of The Barrington, where he waited, a palm over his heart, counting the seconds until light filtered through the window he knew belonged to Phaedra.

"Goodnight, *schatje*."

16

"**V**an Rhys is in trouble," Lew said as he stepped into Morgan's office. "New York Loss & Life is facing another storm of creditors."

"No great secret." The city had faced a collapse of financial institutions some years ago, along with several well-known insurance companies. Martin Van Rhys was still afloat, barely surviving on his family name and connections. It would have been an easy thing to purchase most of New York Loss & Life without Van Rhys knowing, but it was far more amusing to watch Gertie's brother circle the hole of oblivion. "If this keeps up, he'll have to sell his fancy house on The Row."

Lew pushed a packet across the desk in Morgan's direction. "This was waiting for you out front. I paid the messenger."

"He's becoming more desperate," Morgan said, taking the packet. "This is the third time in a month he's made his demands known." Opening the envelope, he pulled out correspondence from yet another lawyer stipulating the immediate return of all the shares of Mohawk & Hudson to Martin Van

Rhys. The shares, declared the letter, had been gifted to Gertrude Van Rhys and upon her death were to be returned to her *rightful* heir.

"That's a nice touch. *Rightful* heir." Lew was reading the document from the other side of the desk.

"Gifted. Martin sold those shares to her at an inflated price when he decided to build that pretentious mansion he inhabits. At the time, the bargain was in his favor. She paid twice what the shares were worth."

"His interest in Mohawk & Hudson didn't start until the railroad suddenly became worth a king's ransom." Lew moved away from the desk, no longer interested in Martin's demands. "An impressive feat, considering the opposition you faced in building the track along the canal. So many others tried and failed."

"Shrewd negotiating." Consisting of threats. Intimidation. Piano wire and a bit of blood. Morgan regretted none of it.

"I'm not sure why he continues to waste his rapidly dwindling fortune on the multitude of lawyers he's hired," Lew said. "It's obvious he doesn't have a copy of his grandmother's will stipulating the shares were to stay in the family, or he would have produced it by now."

"Because it doesn't exist. Gertie would have told me. I suppose he hopes eventually a judge will listen to him. Or I might give in."

"Out of the kindness of your heart? Doubtful. On another note," Lew said, "Murphy and Averell are still reviewing the proposal I've made, though both expressed how pleased and generous the offer is. I can't fathom they won't sign it. You won't have a controlling share, but enough so that you can make things difficult."

"And the importers? The main spirit supplier for The Barrington?"

"Yours. Along with his closest competitor. I'm working on the others."

Morgan wouldn't control The Barrington, but his shares, combined with owning the supply lines leading to the hotel, would be enough to cause problems. He could hold The Barrington hostage, if need be, until Rutherford faced Morgan.

"I'll take him the papers today," Lew assured him, strolling to the sideboard. "A celebratory drink?" He stopped and moved around the bottles before him and made a disgruntled sound. "Why isn't there any brandy? Or scotch. Maybe a nice cognac?"

"Learn to like bourbon," Morgan answered.

"I'm trying, but I find it a slow process. By the way, will you be offering for Lady Phaedra? Or do you have something else planned?"

God. Damn. It.

"Naughty of her, visiting you late at night. Alone. I'll assume you made her acquaintance at The Barrington grand opening. Or was it London? Does she have a role in your scheme?"

A word with Dabble was required. "She isn't part of this."

"You could hold her reputation up as a threat. That could be useful."

"Best to have those papers signed as soon as possible," Morgan grunted in response, refusing to give Lew any information about his relationship with Phaedra. The fewer people who knew, the better.

"So she has no idea what you're up to." Lew swilled the bourbon around in his glass, putting off that first sip as long as possible. "Or that you're attempting to become partners with her brother."

Morgan didn't answer at first, too busy thinking of the way Phaedra had looked with her skirts rucked up around her waist yesterday when he'd caught her throwing knives in Murphy's English garden. She'd been shredding some poor tree to bits. At the sight of him, Phaedra had broken into a run and thrown herself at Morgan, wrapping her arms around his neck.

"Murderous suitor," she'd said, kissing him. "I did wonder when you would appear."

"Ferocious creature," he'd answered. "Damaging Miss Nelson's hard work."

All his hard edges, the jagged raw bits of him, quieted once more at her touch. A risk, to seek her out at The Barrington, especially when he had to wait out the deal with Murphy. Make sure the papers were signed so he'd have some leverage. Force Rutherford's hand. Then Morgan meant to offer for Phaedra. Properly. As she deserved.

But he'd missed her. Terribly.

"Pull up your skirts," he'd growled, pushing her against another tree with a much stouter trunk.

Phaedra had done so immediately, kissing Morgan as if they'd been apart months instead of merely a few days. It was always like that between them. The almost violent need to touch and meld into each other.

She had already been wet when he'd thrust inside her. Warm. Morgan had buried himself in Phaedra, making sure that this time, they'd find their pleasure together. He'd stroked her, just above the place they were joined, watching as her eyes widened in surprise at climaxing while he pounded into her. She screamed her pleasure into the folds of his coat.

Madness. Anyone could have seen them, and Morgan hadn't cared.

Once more he'd withdrawn, careful not to mar her skirts.

Lew set the glass of bourbon down with a sound of disgust. He opened the cabinet door and riffled through whatever spirits were contained inside. Triumphantly, he pulled out a bottle of brandy, covered with a thin layer of dust. "Thank God."

Morgan had stood next to that tree after adjusting their clothing, worried he'd hurt her by being so rough, but Phaedra had glowed. "I enjoyed that very much," she'd said, tugging at his coat.

"You worry that you'll hurt me, Morgan," she'd murmured. "But you wouldn't." Then she'd very boldly placed her slender hand on his still throbbing cock.

Phaedra Barrington was a naughty thing. And his.

Morgan shifted in his seat.

Lew took a sip of the brandy. "This isn't bad. You didn't answer the question. About your intentions towards Lady Phaedra."

"None of your affair." He picked up the letter from Martin Van Rhys and tossed it in the fire, watching the paper crinkle and burn. "Just get the papers signed."

17

"Get on your knees. On the bed."

Phaedra gave him a saucy look, completely naked save for her stockings, guessing correctly that he enjoyed the view. She pranced about his bedroom, bourbon-colored hair glinting with copper as it flew about her hips and breasts.

She had a surprising lack of inhibition for a woman who had been a virgin barely two weeks ago.

"So grouchy." She spun about once more.

Desire for her struck him so fiercely, Morgan had to put a palm on the wall of his bedroom to steady himself. His cock might burst free at any moment.

"You interrupted an important business dinner." He tried to sound coldly disapproving, but in truth, Morgan had been rather delighted by her unexpected appearance. Phaedra occupied every thought he had, even blotting out his plans for Rutherford. She made him soft in ways Morgan hadn't expected, which was unsettling, to say the least.

Last night, a thief had slashed at his coat near the ferry,

meaning to take his purse. Morgan had only broken the man's wrists instead of snapping his neck.

"It was only Mr. Armwood." Phaedra shrugged, lifting the rapier he'd bought her. "Your dinner guest."

He'd presented the weapon to her while they lay together in his bed, limbs entwined, hearts beating as one. Pressing his cheek to her chest, Morgan had listened to the steady rhythm of her breath, soothed by the scent of her—wild roses and defiance. After he'd given her the rapier, she had turned and pushed Morgan to his stomach so she could gently trace every horrible scar decorating his skin with her mouth and lips, holding him all the while in her embrace. Whispering to Morgan that no one would ever hurt him again.

Morgan's heart squeezed tight, thinking of how she'd surprised him right after breakfast that day, making the air halt in his lungs at the sight of her. Sometimes he had difficulty breathing around Phaedra.

"And no," she said smartly. "I haven't told a soul you and Armwood are partners. That would lead to an entire host of questions I don't want to answer."

Well, that was certainly true.

The papers had not been signed. Lew had called on Murphy earlier to find out if there was a problem but had been told Murphy and Averell were both out. Lew had come to relay the news and stayed to dine.

"Armwood is still important. You shocked poor Dabble by popping out of my bedroom, and he grew up in the Bowery."

Phaedra flashed the rapier back and forth, spinning about with her curtain of hair.

Morgan's cock twitched at the gentle bounce of her breasts. Once this business with Murphy was finished, once he'd had the chance to confront Rutherford, Morgan meant to take her away. Somewhere remote. Where she could wear as little clothing as possible, with no Dabble wandering about.

Dabble, slightly red-faced, had informed Morgan, just as he and Lew had tucked into the roasted chicken, that there was a visitor waiting for him upstairs.

Lew had arched one brow, not the least surprised. "Just elope with her. Now. Before Murphy or anyone else can stop you."

He couldn't. Or rather, he wouldn't. Elopement, according to the wager, would constitute 'running away with an American.' He'd win. Bankrupt Elysium.

And Morgan no longer wanted to.

"You can see yourself out, Lew." He left the dining room, trying to keep from taking the stairs two at a time, knowing Phaedra was in his bedroom.

She'd already been naked except for her stockings, parrying with her rapier when he entered, threatening to slice off his cravat before the thin blade dipped to the buttons on his trousers.

"Get on the bed, Phaedra. Now."

Phaedra winked at him and set down the rapier, obediently going to the bed, though she took her time. Crawling atop the coverlet, she lowered her head, the mass of dark hair spilling across the pillows. "You see, I *can* be obedient, Morgan."

Christ.

Her delicious bottom wiggled at him, pushing aside thoughts of anything but her.

"You shouldn't be here." He shrugged out of his coat before grabbing at the silk of his cravat.

Tomorrow, Lew would return to The Barrington. The papers *would* be signed if he had to bribe Murphy or hold a gun to his overprivileged head. He'd have his leverage, hopefully.

But most importantly, he wouldn't lose Phaedra.

Morgan brushed his lips over the back of her neck, trailing his fingers over one plump buttock. "I adore you," he whispered reverently. In truth, Morgan knew it was far more than adoration. But he couldn't describe the emotion adequately. Love was an abstract concept to him. Any sort of affection, really. He'd felt a deep connection to Gertie but not a romantic one. This was far different. An intense combination of possessiveness and the need to keep Phaedra close.

She made a delicious sound and arched her back. "I know."

"Do you trust me?"

"Yes." She didn't even hesitate.

Morgan pulled off the cravat, trailing the silk along her skin. He leaned forward. "You can't go about interrupting my business dinners." Taking her wrists, he pulled them behind her, tying her hands loosely with the cravat. Not tight. Phaedra could get away if she wanted to. But his *schatje* had a spark of darkness inside her. His nature aroused her. He'd found out the day he'd taken her pistol shooting.

"I protest." A sound came from her. "I think I'm more important than a roasted chicken."

"You are more important than anything." The weight of those words slammed into him. The truth of it. This beautiful girl who should run from Morgan instead of dancing about him naked, letting him tie her up with his cravat. Phaedra deserved to know everything. About Gertie. Rutherford. Why he'd sought her out. Sister Bridget. How he and Benjamin Cooke knew each other, though surely she'd guessed by now.

Morgan placed a pillow beneath her hips.

She turned her head to the side and pressed a kiss to the mark on his wrist. Sister Bridget's brand. Her lips took away the sting.

He swatted one plump cheek with his palm.

Phaedra made a soft moan as his fingers ran down her slit.

Morgan flung away his trousers and pulled her gently to the edge of the bed. He played with her, running his fingers along her wetness until she begged for relief. When her body grew taut, he stopped, pressing a line of kisses down the length of her spine.

"Do you know what it did to me, knowing you were up here while Lew and I were down there with a roasted chicken?" He touched her again, feeling the wetness slide over his fingers.

"I thought you would need dessert," she gasped at the pinch of his fingers. "Phaedra a la rapier. Not something just any gentleman gets to have."

"No other man. Ever. As a matter of fact."

You should just take her. Tonight. Find a minister.

Morgan laid his cheek at the base of her spine, fingers moving over her. "I will never stray from you, Phaedra. You need never have that worry." He wasn't sure why he said so, though it was the truth. The idea of bedding another woman repulsed him.

A soft whimper followed as his head lowered and breathed in the scent of her sex mixed with wild roses, letting all those thorny vines sink into his skin. His tongue flicked out. God, she was delicious. Every inch of her.

"Do you want me to fuck you, Phaedra?" he said crudely. "Put my cock inside you?"

"Please."

That one word nearly undid him. "Next time you'll take me in your mouth."

Phaedra squeezed her thighs together, pushing herself into the mattress. "Yes. And in return, I promise to disrupt all your future business dinners and meetings."

"There's my girl. Ever defiant."

He placed his hand on the back of her neck, pressing another kiss into her hair. "I desire you beyond anything else." Morgan buried himself inside her with a groan, holding her tightly before rocking his hips into her.

Taking her slowly, he listened for every breath she made, absorbing each sound, inhaling the scent of wild roses coming from her skin. Stroking the tiny bud between her thighs, he waited for her limbs to tremble, her body tighten, before he would stop.

"You are being," she panted, "vastly unfair."

"A bit of punishment would do you good, Phaedra. You've been indulged your entire life."

He teased her for an eternity, nuzzling into her hair, stroking her breasts until she pressed her mouth into the bed, panting out her release.

As much as he knew *how* to love, Morgan loved Phaedra.

His own release struck him, blinding him with singular intensity, and Morgan attempted to withdraw, spend himself in the sheets.

She grabbed at his hip, keeping him in place. "Don't leave me."

A growl came from him as he spilled inside her. She'd chosen this. *Him*. Possibly a child. Hope, always so elusive and foreign, spread across his chest. There was happiness here, with Phaedra.

Morgan nuzzled the side of her neck, waiting for his breathing to return to normal, feeling the grip of her muscles along his cock. He pulled away, pausing only to remove the silk of his cravat from around her wrists. Pressing a kiss to each palm, he discarded the remainder of his clothing and flopped beside her on the bed, pulling her close.

"That was rather marvelous. Well worth whatever punishment you inflict on poor Dabble for having allowed me into your bedroom." Phaedra placed the flat of her hand against his cheek, stroking the hair along his jaw. Such love for him shone in those magnificent eyes. More than he would ever deserve. He vowed to never allow anything terrible to touch her.

Morgan would consider later that he, who resolutely controlled every outcome and made allowances for every possibility, had failed to anticipate that his happiness, so long in coming, would also be short lived.

His sins would refuse to stay buried.

Morgan pulled a sheet across his hips as Phaedra walked over to grab at her things.

"I suppose I must get dressed and return to The Barrington." A smile teased at her lips.

"You do, else there will be an uproar that you're missing. Come, *schatje*. I'll do up your buttons. Where did you tell your family the rapier came from?"

"I didn't." She walked to the bed and presented him with her back. "No one has asked. Tony is too busy making preparations for the return to London to wonder what I may be up to." Her eyes met his. "Do you have anything to say about that? My return to London?"

"Only that it is unlikely you'll be going." At least not without him. "I—"

A loud noise coming from downstairs stopped the speech Morgan had been about to make. He'd meant to tell her some of the truth. Ask her to marry him, to stay in New York.

Another bang sounded, as if the front door was being torn from its hinges.

Dabble's raised voice made its way up the stairs, threatening whoever had invaded Morgan's home.

"Morgan?" Phaedra turned, worry etched on her features.

He immediately rolled over and grabbed a pistol out of the side table, then reached behind the headboard for the knife strapped to the bed frame. Morgan lived in the darkness. He had enemies. Dabble was armed, as were most of Morgan's staff. But Phaedra could not be put at risk.

"Put on your boots. Hurry. I don't know who it is, but you don't need to worry, *schatje*. Behind the armoire is a door that—"

"Where is she?" The furious voice thundered up the stairs. "My sister. Where is she?"

Phaedra went white, dropping the half-boot in her hand. "It's Leo."

Heavy steps echoed on the stairs, marching with purpose towards the bedroom.

"What happened to your boundaries, Stewart?" Cooke's voice came from the other side of the door. He was probably covered in knives.

"Ben and Olivia shouldn't be back yet," Phaedra whispered. "Not until late tomorrow. Why is he here?"

Morgan had an inkling. Dread bloomed inside him.

"It will be all right, Phaedra," he assured her, though he knew it wouldn't be. Murphy hadn't signed the papers. Cooke had returned to Manhattan early and was now in Morgan's house.

"Put on your boots. Look presentable." Morgan reached for his trousers. "Maybe this is for the best."

She was ruined. There was a slim chance Murphy would ask him to be honorable.

"Nothing about this is for the best," she choked, staring warily at the door.

The heavy wood flew open, banging against the wall and sprinkling the rug with plaster.

Cooke stood there, his eyes as cold and dead as Morgan had ever seen them. This was just like the damned coat. Except it was Phaedra they were going to fight over this time.

"Don't you know how to knock?" Morgan's fingers tightened on the knife.

"You miserable prick," Cooke stated. "I told you to stay away from her. Warned you in London." He launched himself at Morgan, hitting him squarely in the jaw. "I suppose you think you've won your wager."

Morgan snarled, holding up his own knife, the blood from his split lip dripping down his chin. "You get one for free, *Twist*."

"Stop, this instant." Phaedra stepped between them, her hands out.

Murphy appeared at the door, brandishing a pistol, looking more like the thug Morgan thought he really was beneath all that aristocratic veneer. He took in Phaedra's dishevelment and leveled the gun at Morgan. "If I shoot him," he said to Cooke, "can you get rid of the body?"

"Yes," Cooke snapped.

"Are you mad? There will be no shooting. Of anyone." Phaedra stepped towards her brother, not the least cowed. "You are not going to hurt Morgan." She clutched the place over her heart. "I *love* him, Leo. I am here of my own free will. He is *my* choice."

Murphy blinked. "Christ, you don't mean that."

"I do."

"He's using you, Phaedra," Cooke said blandly. "I'm surprised you haven't yet realized it. You're leverage for some scheme he has planned. I've told Leo about the wager." He jerked his chin towards Murphy. "The one meant to bankrupt Elysium. Page seventy-eight."

"You should have told me well before this," Murphy snapped. "I would have kept her in London."

"Pay attention to your own books, Leo," Cooke replied without looking away from Phaedra.

"This isn't about the wager." Phaedra looked at Morgan, her lovely features panicked. "Tell them. It isn't."

"You knew?" Leo thundered. "That this mongrel made a wager, one that could destroy Elysium and yet you're still—"

"This isn't about the wager," Morgan stated, eyes never leaving Phaedra. "It hasn't been for a very long time."

"It doesn't matter," Leo roared. "You were going to take Phaedra. Elysium. The Barrington." He shook his head. "Oh, yes, I found out about what you and Lewis Armwood had planned. Most of my enemies come at me directly, not by seducing my sister."

"This has nothing to do with you, Murphy." Morgan glanced at Cooke. He *had* to know. Rutherford wouldn't have kept the secret of Gertie from his precious nephew.

"Really? Because if Martin Van Rhys hadn't come for dinner this evening, I would never have guessed that you purchased two of the largest importers of wine and spirits in New York. Along with more than a handful of businesses that supply The Barrington. Meaning you can choke the life right out of my hotel if you choose. I knew Armwood's proposal reeked of suspicion."

Martin. Of course it had been Martin.

"I find it strange Van Rhys is keeping tabs on your sister," Morgan drawled. "Oh, but wait. Let me guess." He could hear the blood thundering in his ears. "He also is interested in investing in The Barrington."

Leo's face reddened.

Phaedra lifted her chin, studying Morgan, a slight quaver in her voice. "Is it true, Morgan? About the importers? And Armwood?" She bit her lip. "You said you wouldn't hurt—"

"I didn't take Elysium," he snapped, ignoring the disappointment in her eyes. "Or bankrupt him."

A small cry was her response.

"Why don't you explain, *Nubbs*, what this is really about." Cooke leaned against the wall, the hilt of his blades flashing.

"I confess I'm curious. The only thing I'm sure of is that it has nothing to do with either Leo or Phaedra."

Morgan froze at the sound of that name, the one he'd used before Gertie had made him into Morgan Stewart. The last person to call him Nubbs had been Sister Bridget.

His stomach clenched.

"Don't call me that, *Twist*. Phaedra isn't a coat you've found on Canal Street. One you steal from your best friend, leaving him nothing but this." Morgan trailed his finger over the scar on his chin.

Phaedra and Murphy looked between them, she with rapidly dawning realization and Murphy with confusion.

"Did you tell her about Gertrude Van Rhys?" Cooke said conversationally. "How you murdered the woman who took you in so you could inherit a fortune? Never tried or convicted, though. You went free. There's the mystery."

A pained gasp came from Phaedra as she backed away from the bed. "No. He wouldn't have."

"Not just an inheritance, but all those shares in Mohawk & Hudson," Cooke continued. "Shares that were supposed to stay in the Van Rhys family. But you made sure Gertrude gave them to you. I suspect she was going to return them to her brother, and you made sure she did not."

"That isn't true." Morgan glared at him. "None of it."

"Her murder was declared an accident, I suppose through bribery or threats. The only witness besides yourself was Gertrude's maid. Conveniently, she went missing."

"You *know* I didn't kill Gertie." Cooke's attitude, more than anything else, confirmed that Rutherford was guilty and Cooke was protecting his uncle.

Cooke shrugged. "Do I? There were signs a man had been in her bed. A lover's quarrel, perhaps. You lost control. A rarity, I agree."

Phaedra shut her eyes, as if she could no longer bear to look at him. "It can't be true."

"She was my *mother*," Morgan bit out. An image of Gertie, lying dead on the floor, flashed before him. How he'd kneeled at her side and begged her not to be dead. Rutherford had been there. He— "My God," he said in surprise as the truth hit him. "You *don't* know, do you?"

Cooke narrowed his eyes. "I know enough."

"Rutherford and Gertie were lovers. *He* was in her bed that night."

"You're lying," Cooke said quietly, but he shifted against the wall. "Jacob would have told me."

A bitter laugh erupted from Morgan's lips. "Jacob Rutherford? Doubtful. You're merely his errand boy."

"It doesn't change the facts."

"The facts? There are no facts except those spouted by Martin Van Rhys, who resented everything his sister did for me. I was more surprised than anyone that Gertie left everything to me. Of course I was in the house that night. I lived here. I had just finished my last term at law school." Morgan leaned back against the headboard. "How easy it is for you to think the worst of me. I couldn't possibly have been worth saving, not like *you*, Benjamin Cooke."

The old bitterness roiled inside Morgan, returning with a vengeance. Even Phaedra could no longer soothe it. Or stop the coldness inching over his skin. She was slipping through his fingers, fading into mist as he watched.

So much for love.

"You should know I stopped by Hagerty's before I left London." Cooke's lip curled as he turned to Phaedra. "Hagerty was puzzled over the bodies of two of his regulars. Found them garroted in an alley. Probably with piano wire, unless I'm mistaken. The same two who'd boasted they were going to speak to the lady who came to watch the fights."

Phaedra shook her head. "No." She looked at him, color draining from her features. Pressing a palm to her stomach, she begged him to deny the accusation.

"That's who he is, Phaedra." Cooke pierced him with a look. "You should know that."

"Jesus, Phaedra," Leo uttered. "You went to Hagerty's? Alone?"

"I won't apologize." Morgan snarled like some wounded animal. "They were going to hurt you. Would have come at you again. I made sure they did not. Nor anyone else."

Phaedra inhaled, horror clouding her face. "I never asked you to do something so terrible." The light in her eyes that had glowed only for him, faded. "Have there been others?" Her fists curled. "Answer me, Morgan."

"Morgan Stewart is a brilliant man of business." Cooke lifted his chin. "The string of bodies behind every deal he makes is proof of that."

Shrugging, as if it were of no import, he didn't try to defend himself. Phaedra's mind was made up, at any rate. Morgan didn't bother to protest that he would change. Not be so inclined to solve challenges in unpleasant ways. And he would not apologize for relieving the world of anyone who would harm her.

"You called me your murderous suitor. What exactly did you think that entailed? Or do you not know the definition of the word?" he hurled at her.

A tear ran down her cheek. "I never really thought—"

"Yes, you did." He cut her off. "You knew what I was."

Phaedra covered the sob erupting from her mouth and backed further away.

Honestly, Morgan wished Cooke would just slice him to ribbons. Let him bleed to death on the fine rug covering the bedroom floor. The pain of losing Phaedra, of having her despise him, was akin to having someone hack off one of his limbs. He'd rather endure another beating from Sister Bridget than this.

"And don't pretend you're any better," he finally said, looking up at his former friend. "You aren't. Does your little doe know the things you've done, Benjamin Cooke?" He looked at Leo. "Does he? I recall the riverboat gambler who toyed with Georgina years ago. Not to mention the others. Tell me, did Mr. Clarkson, that lascivious gentleman who had the audacity to take liberties with sweet Cousin Lilian, really go visit relatives in Ohio? I'm told he never arrived."

Cooke's lips tightened. "That has nothing to do with this."

Phaedra averted her eyes. She thought Morgan a monster, just as he'd always feared. A horrible, callous thing, unworthy of her or—

"*Schatje.*" He reached for her one last time. "I didn't hurt Gertie. If nothing else, believe that."

"Don't," she whispered painfully, as if he'd broken her heart. "I'm not sure I can trust anything you say. You promised me."

Morgan's lungs wouldn't work. Every breath caused a great deal of pain. This was far worse than finding Gertie. He should have kept Phaedra at arm's length. Never gone to Cherry Hill and realized what she was to him.

His fingers twitched in her direction, even as he struggled to hide the anguish of losing the only thing that had made him human. He should have told her everything. Never even attempted the business deal with Murphy. Forced Peckham to rescind that damned wager at gunpoint. The coldness sank into his bones. It might never leave.

Leo took Phaedra's arm and led her to the door. "You won't be winning your damned wager. Nor Elysium. The Barrington. None of it."

Morgan wanted to laugh. He'd never really wanted any of

those things. Only Phaedra. "It isn't about you, Murphy. That's the only truthful thing my dear friend Twist said."

"Tell Armwood to stay out of The Barrington or I'll have him shot."

Unlikely, since Chipplewit and several other members of The Barrington's staff were actually in Morgan's employ, but he doubted it would matter.

The sound of their footsteps echoed on the stairs as Murphy took Phaedra away, her chin lowered, unwilling to look at him. Morgan stared at the empty space where she'd stood before taking all the color of his world with her, only jerking his gaze away when the sound of the front door slamming echoed up the stairs.

Cooke didn't follow, only regarded Morgan curiously with those murky eyes of his.

"Staying to pick over the bones? Well." He looked up. "Let me know when you're finished gloating. I've got an appointment with a bottle of bourbon. A rather important one." Morgan came to his feet, uncaring that he was naked.

"This is about Jacob Rutherford."

"So fucking astute, aren't you? It's *always* been about Rutherford. He knows what happened to Gertie. I suspect he killed her. And I want his confession. They were lovers for years, *Twist*. She wanted him to leave Cordelia. But don't take my word for it. Ask your prick of an uncle." He gave a bitter laugh. "That's right, he isn't really your uncle. Your keeper, perhaps." He turned around and grabbed at his trousers.

Cooke made a sound.

Morgan looked over his shoulder. "Pretty as a picture, isn't it? My back. The day I returned to Sister Bridget after losing you to a coat and the promise of a hot meal, she beat me so hard with a cane, I fell to the floor and broke my nose. Fireplace poker came next." Morgan made a hiss. "I couldn't walk for weeks. While I was lying on my stomach, trying not to scream from the pain, she lined up the regulars and had them take turns using me to put out cigars. I entertained them for hours."

Cooke took a step back, his features like stone.

"I had to bring in twice as much, after, to make up for you. Suffered ten times more. That's why I've hated you for the coat. If Gertie hadn't found me, I'd be dead. Ask me again, Twist. Would I really have harmed the person who saved me from that? Rutherford knows what happened to her. He killed her—or maybe he had someone do his dirty work. But either way, I need to know. And I ran out of ways to force him to speak to me." Morgan pulled on his trousers. "I am tired of having everyone in New York think I murdered Gertie for a fucking railroad." He was yelling at Cooke and didn't care if the entire house heard him.

"Now, if you don't mind, get out of my house before I garrote you."

18

Phaedra sat in the carriage waiting for Ben, ignoring Leo as he frowned at her from across the carriage. Finally, she said, "Go on, Leo. Berate me."

"What were you thinking, Phaedra?" Leo drummed his fingers along the leather seat. "Morgan Stewart. It's as if you deliberately picked the worst sort of individual possible. How could you not have heard the gossip about the murder of Gertrude Van Rhys? It is all anyone ever speaks of."

"I don't listen to gossip." Would it have made a difference, given the pull in Morgan's direction?

"Had I seen the Red Book before leaving for New York, I would never have allowed you to come with us. Ten thousand pounds." He ran a hand through his hair. "It would have ruined me."

"You're being dramatic." He wasn't. Phaedra had done the books for Elysium, after all. The gambling hell wouldn't have been completely bankrupted, but very close. Enough so Leo wouldn't have been able to continue to operate so lavishly. The majority of his funds were tied up in The Barrington.

"I'm thrilled you can be so calm about this." Leo slammed

206

his hand against the seats. "Not to mention, he's ruined you, Phaedra. Don't bother to deny it."

"I won't." There wasn't any point. "Do you want me to collapse into a heap on the carriage floor, weeping, because I've taken a lover?" The air in Morgan's bedroom, the scent of him on her skin, had been proof enough. She was mortified. Ashamed. She'd been taken in by him.

Not true. Pith's voice once more.

"So glib. Tony should have wed you to Emberly and been done with it."

"Emberly wouldn't survive a marriage to me. I can punch better than he, for one thing."

Leo shot her an exasperated look. "Stewart is *dangerous*. He could have hurt you. And now you're..."

"Soiled, I believe, is the word you're looking for." She thought of the way Morgan had looked at her, as if she were the only thing he could see. The only thing that mattered.

His nostrils flared. "I warned Tony something like this would happen. You're far too headstrong. Marcus let you run wild at Cherry Hill. Then Tony. You were exposed to all sorts of things at Elysium. I'm not sure what I can tell Amanda. That you fancy yourself in love with a monster."

No. Her heart screamed. Loudly. "He isn't a monster."

Ferocious creature. I adore you.

Morgan was quite a lot of things. Damaged, most assuredly, but not, she thought, beyond repair. Given to brutality. More murderous than she'd previously considered. But also loving. Gentle. He *listened* to her. Respected her. And there was reverence when Morgan spoke of Gertrude Van Rhys. He'd *loved* her. Her death must have destroyed him. Now that the initial shock had abated, Phaedra knew Morgan could never have hurt Gertrude.

And she'd waltzed out of his life without allowing him to explain.

She put her hand on the carriage door, and Leo grabbed it. "Don't you dare think of going back to him."

Ben arrived just as Phaedra pulled her hand away, climbing into the carriage and folding his lean body next to Leo's. The anger and violence that had been in evidence earlier was now gone, muted and once more hidden behind the blandly pleasant look on his features. But Phaedra could still see it, hovering in the murkiness of his hazel eyes.

Ben and Morgan were much the same. Olivia had certainly guessed what lay beneath her new husband's skin, coiled up and only waiting for an opportunity to strike. But Ben had been gifted a family. Georgina and Lilian were more sisters to him than anything else, though Phaedra could guess what it had been like to be raised by Jacob Rutherford. Ben's mask of civility was much better than Morgan's, perfected after trailing behind Georgina in society while pretending to be a flirtatious rogue.

Morgan's nature was more clearly stamped on his features, and he made little attempt to hide it.

"How have you known Morgan since childhood if you are Jacob Rutherford's nephew?" she asked bluntly, already suspecting the truth. It was the only thing that made sense. Benjamin Cooke *wasn't* Benjamin Cooke. He'd been born Twist.

Ben regarded her coldly. "I don't believe its relevant at the moment, Phaedra."

Like Morgan, Ben rarely used her title. Almost as if he were spitting on his betters. "Five Points," she murmured.

"Specifically, near Canal Street." He jerked in her direction, eyes flinty.

"Who cares?" Leo interjected. "You've been ruined, Phaedra. God knows how many times."

"A handful. But all with the same man. That should put you at ease," she retorted. "No need to continuously remind me of my soiled state, Leo. I'm well aware of what has occurred."

"You've always been reckless." His nostrils flared.

"I take after my brothers."

Leo's nostrils flared wider this time, lips taut with anger. When had he become so staid? He was the bastard. He'd been involved with Georgina well before she was widowed. They'd had a child out of wedlock, though a great deal of money had fixed that little problem. Not to mention Leo owned Elysium, a notorious gambling hell, and had allowed wagers on his *infant sister*. Phaedra was sure there was more, but that was quite enough.

"You'll have to wed." Leo was drumming his fingers once more. "There isn't any way around it. Either here or in London. You could be with child. Emberly would take you, I suppose. Or Van Rhys."

"Van Rhys." The cause of this entire mess.

"He's in the market for a wife. You like New York. I could keep an eye on you."

Ben stayed silent, muddy eyes glinting with a bit of gold as he watched her.

"No to marriage." Phaedra turned to the view outside the carriage. "Neither you nor Tony can force me, even if I become as round as a melon. Papa left strict instructions I was to have the ability to choose my own husband. I cannot be forced to wed."

"I don't think Marcus planned for this particular circumstance," Leo thundered, the vein in his forehead protruding in that alarming manner.

"You're insane, Leo," Ben said quietly, "if you think Stewart would let his child be raised by some titled twit in London. She'd be a widow in a trice. I'm not even sure he'll let her leave New York."

Leo shook his head. Good grief, he really was terribly distressed.

"Calm down. If you collapse in the carriage, Georgina will never forgive me," Ben said, looking at Phaedra. "No one knows about..." He waved a hand in her direction. "Except for you and me, Leo. My suggestion is we keep it that way. Don't go running to Tony or Amanda with this. At least not at present."

"Van Rhys knows she's been ruined," Leo shot off. "He's the one who told me what my *infant sister* was up to."

"Highly convenient." Ben glanced at Phaedra. "He comes to dine, drops the information Armwood is Stewart's partner, makes you a proposal of his own, then tells you, regretfully I'm sure, that Phaedra is at Stewart's home."

Listening to Ben lay things out so plainly, Phaedra's own suspicions were aroused. The timing *was* incredibly convenient.

"Van Rhys is connected. Wealthy. I'd be fortunate to have him as a partner in future endeavors," her brother insisted.

"Only one of those things is true, Leo. His business has been failing for years. Connections are all he has. He doesn't have the funds to invest with you, but perhaps he thinks you'd waive the stake if he were to wed your sister. He hasn't survived this long by not being ruthless, though he is much more polite about it than most. He's used his influence to put off those to whom he owes money and put aside claims the insured have made. Tell me, has he even paid the fee for the private club at The Barrington?"

Leo fell back against the seat, deflated. "No. But Van Rhys behaves as if he's about to come into a great deal of money. He wants to expand his business interests in London, which is how Phaedra came up in the conversation."

"You are usually much more perceptive than this, Leo."

Ben looked out the window with a frown. "Van Rhys has charmed you."

"But not me," Phaedra said. "And you aren't giving me to him. I'm not a piece of spoiled fruit to be tossed from the bowl."

Leo's mouth hardened into a grim line.

"If you tried to give Phaedra to Van Rhys," Ben murmured, "he wouldn't live to see Christmas. All things considered, he still might not."

🦋 19 🦋

"**I** suppose you deserve to know, Phaedra. So here I am."

Phaedra looked up from the book in her lap to see Ben standing in the doorway of the small parlor she had once shared with Olivia.

Surprised at his unexpected appearance, she shut the book and put it aside. She'd reread the same paragraph at least six times this morning and was happy to have an interruption. Her concentration on anything other than Morgan seemed impossible. Phaedra had felt pummeled after Leo's arrival and Ben's accusations the other night. Unsure how to proceed at loving a man who might have betrayed her and was far more murderous than she'd suspected.

Piano wire, Phaedra. A tool for garroting others.

The voice of reason, always belonging to Pith, derided her.

Upon waking after that terrible night, with her heart still broken, Phaedra's first thought had been Morgan. She had to see him. But The Barrington was the most luxurious sort of prison. Her every move was watched. A lumpy, rough man in a coat that barely fit him followed Phaedra as she moved about the hotel, dogging her steps when she walked in the garden. Far worse than having Pith constantly sniffing about.

Leo had not told Tony about Phaedra and Morgan, nor Mama. Not yet. But it was only a matter of time.

"This is rather unexpected, Ben. What is it I should know?"

Phaedra, though happy to have an interruption to her swirling thoughts, wasn't pleased the intrusion was Ben. Not after he'd stormed into Morgan's home with knives gleaming from his hands, prepared to skewer her lover. He had taken great pleasure in detailing Morgan's sins, not all of it for Phaedra's benefit. Ben had wanted to hurt Morgan. The hostility between them had nearly shimmered in the air, so thick it could be cut with one of Ben's knives.

"Not exactly welcoming, are you?" Ben took a seat across from her, long legs crossed, the glimmer of a knife shining from one coat pocket as he settled.

"Not at all," Phaedra agreed.

"I've done quite a bit of thinking as of late." Ben took a deep breath. "I want to tell you about the coat." His eyes were that strange combination of green and brown, shining with flecks of gold. The arresting color added to Ben's attractive mask, one that hid his nature so well.

"The coat?"

"I thought he might have told you, but he hasn't. So I will. I doubt a recitation of the past will deter your affections for Stewart. Knowing he's garroted two men hasn't. No telling what else he's done for you."

"I'm sure you've matched him in brutality at times, *Twist*."

That flintiness crept into Ben's eyes. "I don't care for piano wire. I prefer knives. I'm going to tell you about two orphaned boys and a coat. Pay attention."

Phaedra clasped her hands together. "Raised in a brothel."

Ben's eyes narrowed. "So, he did tell you some of it. We

were best friends. Brothers. Clinging to each other because there was no one else. Sister Bridget owned the brothel where we were born. In addition to her whores, she kept a collection of children to pick pockets. We were expected to work for her if we wanted to eat. Once the girls were old enough, they took clients upstairs. We lads..." He spread his arms. "We were taught a different set of skills from the beginning."

Cruel, brutal skills. Phaedra thought of the scars decorating Morgan's back and chest. The mark on his wrist. The suffering he'd endured now had a name, a source—Sister Bridget. And he'd grown up beside Ben, who had once been Twist. Both abandoned to the care of a brothel owner.

"You still haven't told me how you came to be Benjamin Cooke. Or about the coat."

"I'm getting to that." He shook his head. "Your lack of patience must drive Stewart half-mad. He's spent a lifetime scheming, patiently spinning webs to trap the unsuspecting in highly complicated ways. It's one of the reasons he's been so successful in business. Stewart is always two steps ahead of everyone else. Like a giant spider in an expensive coat."

"I think him more as a murderous wolf. Or a large cat. Not an arachnid."

"Believe it or not, Stewart was smaller than me when we were children. Sickly, much of the time. Always hungry. Weak. I often thought I would wake one day, and he'd be..." Ben's words tapered off, his fingers curling and uncurling against his thighs. "Not sure how he ended up so big. I—took to protecting him as best I could. I had a knife and knew how to use it. The bigger lads let us be. We were inseparable. Shared everything. Slept beneath the same blanket in the same spot before the fire, when Sister Bridget allowed it. I..." His voice grew choked and thick. His hands curled into fists. "I didn't understand, Phaedra. I didn't realize how Nubbs—

Stewart"—he corrected himself—"depended on me. I didn't know."

Until he'd seen the result of his abandonment. Morgan's poor ruined back.

"I would like to think that had I known, I wouldn't have left him in that alley off Canal, but the truth is..." Ben's gaze grew misty, looking at something in the past only he could see, desolation pulling at his handsome features. "I don't think I'd have chosen differently."

Phaedra knew, beyond a doubt, that were she to relieve Ben of his coat and shirt, his own skin would tell a story similar to Morgan's. Not quite as bad, possibly, but the scars would still be there.

"We thought she was dead." His voice grew distant. "The woman in the alley. She was raving. Sick. Dying and covered in sores. The smell was horrific, most of it from the body beside her. No more than a bag of bones the rats were chewing on. She kept speaking to that rotting corpse. It was her son." Cooke stopped again and cleared his throat. "We were going to take her boots. Sell them for something to eat." A mournful sound left him. "We were so hungry."

Phaedra tried to picture the scene in her mind. Two ragged children who didn't flinch from a rotting corpse and an obviously mad woman. Starving and cold. Desperate.

"Jacob Rutherford had a sister who ran away with a sea captain. Alice. That was who we found in that alley. Alice Rutherford, though I didn't know it at the time." He turned back to Phaedra. "In her madness, she mistook me for her dead child."

"Benjamin Cooke." Phaedra wanted to take the hand trembling along Ben's thigh, but she didn't dare.

He nodded. "She put the coat on me while Nubbs was picking through the trash and keeping watch. She called me Benjamin Cooke and begged me to find my uncle, Jacob

Rutherford, on Lafayette Square. A note had been pinned to the inside of the coat. One she'd written for her brother. I couldn't read. Had no idea what it said. Nubbs and I fought for that coat. I gave him the scar on his chin." He looked away. "And I ran. All the way to Lafayette Square. The servants tried to shoo me away, but Georgina came to the door. I gave her the note, which said I was her cousin, Benjamin Cooke. No one had seen Jacob's sister in years. And they'd never met her son."

Phaedra regarded him for a few moments. She'd known or at least suspected Ben and Morgan had come from the same place. "Have you told Olivia?"

Ben nodded. "Georgina knows too. And of course, Jacob. I understand Stewart's bitterness now, his hatred for me, after seeing—what Sister Bridget did to him."

"You left him." Phaedra tried to keep the anger out of her voice and failed. Gertrude had not been the first person Morgan had ever loved. Ben had been. And the betrayal of that trust had lasted half their lives.

And now I've deserted him as well.

Phaedra's chest constricted.

"He would have done the same." Ben savagely turned on her. "Can you imagine what it is like to fight over the bones of a chicken? Hoping for a bit of meat? Always cold. Your stomach constantly aching because it has been days since you've eaten." He looked down at his hands. "In the alley that day, I thought *only* of a hot meal and a warm place to lay my head. Not my best friend."

What had Phaedra been doing as a child? Terrorizing her nanny. Demanding Papa buy her a horse. Pretending to wage a war with her dolls. Not picking through trash looking for food. She had no right to judge Ben for his choices.

"How old were you?"

"Ten. I think? Sister Bridget wasn't one to celebrate a

birthday." He ran a hand through the russet of his hair. "I should have considered what she would do to him for losing me. I was her best pickpocket."

"Sister Bridget sounds lovely," she finally said.

"Not anymore, she isn't. Lovely." Something ugly flashed across Ben's face, giving him a feral look. "Nor was she happy to see *me*."

He'd gone to that woman and done—*something*. For Morgan.

Phaedra's breath hitched, and she rubbed at the spot above her heart. Because Ben hadn't protected Morgan then, but he could now. And somehow Ben knew his former friend couldn't do it himself.

"The next time I saw Stewart, I barely recognized him as Nubbs. Not because Gertrude Van Rhys had taken a slug of lead and shined it to silver, but physically, he looked nothing like the boy I'd once known. Only the eyes were the same. Amazing what regular meals will do for a person, isn't it? This was some years after I'd gone to Rutherford."

"Morgan didn't kill Gertrude," Phaedra insisted.

Ben continued as if she hadn't spoken, as if he stopped talking, he wouldn't be able to start again. "Jacob wasn't sure. But he bribed the police commissioner to release Stewart all the same. Had it all wiped under the rug."

"He's why Morgan didn't hang." She sat back in surprise.

"Oh," Ben assured her, "he didn't do it for Stewart's sake, but Gertrude's. And before you ask, Jacob didn't kill her, and I believe him. But Stewart—Jacob speculates that maybe he and Gertrude had a disagreement and he hurt her accidentally."

Phaedra shook her head. "Impossible."

Ben stood and smoothed down his coat. "As to why he won't speak to Morgan, I think he can't. He went white at the mention of Gertrude's name. He confirmed they had been lovers. No one knew. He was afraid the gossip of their affair might impact his business and cause trouble with Cordelia. Even so, Jacob *loved* Gertrude Van Rhys. The look on his face when he spoke of her...I think her death—I don't think he ever recovered from it, Phaedra. Stewart reminds him too much of that time. Of her. What Jacob gave up in the pursuit of power and wealth. Gertrude used to call Jacob *schatje.*"

Phaedra's chin jerked up.

"Such an odd thing for him to admit to. The word is Dutch. Gertrude still spoke the language. It's an endearment. It means *little treasure.* Can you imagine anyone thinking Jacob Rutherford a treasure?"

"No," she whispered. "He told me it meant troublesome. Morgan." Definitely not the words of a man using her for his own ends, but Phaedra had already stopped believing that. "It was never about Elysium. Or Leo."

"Spider web." Ben wiggled his fingers. "He's been trying to flush out Rutherford for years. Tormenting me. Ruining business deals. Stewart even appeared at my uncle's office, demanding a meeting. I suppose threatening his son-in-law seemed a viable option to force my uncle to speak to him."

"Leo thinks he's a monster." Phaedra looked up at Ben.

"Even monsters can love." Ben rolled his shoulders. "I would know." Something menacing shifted in his hazel eyes before it once more disappeared. "Stewart *will* come for you. He isn't about to let you go back to England."

"Why are you telling me this Ben? Guilt?"

His chin hardened. "When he does, I have no plans to stop him. I'll try to keep Leo out of it. And Averell if it comes to that."

Phaedra stayed still for a moment, letting Ben's words sink in.

Did she want Morgan to come for her?

A pair of maids chattered just outside the partially open

door. The two would knock at any moment to enter and clean Phaedra's rooms.

Ben's demeanor changed in an instant, once more becoming Georgina's flirtatious, wicked cousin, shrugging off Twist as if he never existed. But Phaedra had seen who Ben had once been, who he still was, despite loving Olivia.

"Your mask is so much better than his," she said.

"Isn't it?" Ben winked at her before stepping out the door, greeting both maids effusively while they giggled at his attention. He directed them down the corridor in the other direction, stating that his sister-in-law had asked not to be disturbed.

Phaedra stood and moved to a chair closer to the window, directly beneath a patch of sunlight. Ben's recitation of the shared past had brought with it a great deal of darkness, a glimpse at a world far different from the one in which Phaedra had always existed. But once the conversation settled, she doubted it would change anything.

Morgan *did* love her, though his love didn't take the shape of the romantic platitudes Phaedra had been taught to expect. His version was more menacing, possessive, and horribly overprotective.

But it was still love.

"Most women concern themselves that their husband might take a mistress. I will worry that mine would garrote any gentleman who touches me."

A great deal of guilt filled her over those two men at Hagerty's. Had she only listened to Torrington and not visited the boxing establishment, she wouldn't have caught their attention, and she felt indirectly responsible for their deaths. But Morgan was right. Ratty Coat wanted to hurt her. He would have sought her out once more if Morgan hadn't taken care of the situation.

In Morgan's world, the one in which he still had one foot

firmly fixed, a response to such a challenge was expected. She understood it. Now that the shock had worn off, his actions left her feeling protected. Safe. Not horrified.

I should probably be horrified.

Phaedra plucked at the pillow beside her, tugging at a few stray threads. Love meant accepting all of Morgan's sharp edges.

She only wished there weren't so many of them.

❧ 20 ❧

An hour or so after Ben's visit, Lilian, Georgina's sister, arrived with Olivia in tow. Olivia had sent word earlier about a visit to a confectioner's shop that was all the rage and suggested taking their nephews, Freddie and Daniel, to enjoy the experience. Phaedra had agreed and took on the task of inviting the two boys.

Freddie, Tony's son, ever serious and cognizant of being a future duke, nodded solemnly at the invitation. Daniel, Leo's boy, more exuberant than his cousin, jumped up and down in excitement.

After instructing Freddie's nanny to make both boys ready, Phaedra returned to her rooms to change. Nothing would be served by sitting by herself all afternoon dwelling on Ben's visit. Or worrying over the decision Phaedra knew she must make.

"Let us collect our escorts," Olivia said as Phaedra entered the lobby. "And make our way to the carriage. It isn't far."

"Mr. Chipplewit!" Lilian waved at Leo's manager. "Shall I bring you back a bag of lemon drops?"

221

"If you are going to Amberson's Confections." Chipplewit bowed. "Most assuredly, thank you, Mrs. Harrison." He took in Phaedra and Olivia. "Lady Phaedra. Mrs. Cooke."

"Come along." Georgina's sister was especially lovely today, all blonde wispiness and tragic melancholy. Irresistible to any male. At Leo's grand opening, Phaedra had watched as one young man, struck dumb by the sight of Lilian, had walked into a servant carrying champagne, knocking the entire tray to the floor.

Lilian had only danced once that night. With Mr. Armwood.

Speculation for another day. Phaedra had quite enough to occupy her at the moment.

"I think we should take the longest way about to the candy shop, don't you, Olivia?" Lilian said loudly as they approached Freddie and Daniel, hovered over by their nanny. "Our nephews will want to see the houses and fine people walking about. No one wants to look at sweets."

"Indeed," Phaedra exclaimed, pretending not to see Freddie and Daniel waiting impatiently with the nanny, Mrs. Phipps. "I can't imagine anything worse than an entire shop dedicated solely to sweets. Perhaps our time would be better spent on something else." She tapped a finger against her lips. "Hats. Can we shop for hats instead?"

"Hmmm. Gloves, possibly." Olivia pretended to consider Phaedra's suggestion.

"No. We must see the sweets, Aunt Ollie." Freddie inclined his head, looking very much like Tony. "I don't care overmuch for gloves."

"Auntie Lil." Daniel grabbed at Lilian's skirts, nudging aside Freddie. "Your bonnet is very becoming; you don't require a new one. You all look quite fetching."

Lilian rolled her eyes. "Good lord, he'll be as bad as Leo one day. Paying all the ladies compliments." She turned to

Freddie. "I suppose I must give in to your demands and direct us to Amberson's. Are you ready for our adventure, Lord Welles?"

"Yes, Auntie Lil," Freddie answered, with a small blush. "Mama says I may call you Auntie Lil as Daniel does because we are all one family."

"We most certainly are," Lilian agreed. "I would be delighted to have you address me as Auntie Lil."

Freddie smiled up at her. "And you must call me Freddie."

"Come, my loves." Olivia took Freddie's hand. "There are sweets to be tasted."

Lilian took Daniel, glancing wistfully at both boys, her desire for a child of her own clearly stamped across her lovely face. When Leo and Georgina had been apart, it had been Lilian who'd cared for Daniel. She was good with both boys, chatting away about dirt and bugs, describing the sweets at Amberson's.

If anyone deserved another chance at happiness, to be a mother, it was Lilian.

The sweet shop, as it turned out, was only a short ride from The Barrington. Lilian listened with rapt attention as Daniel pointed out what he called "interesting sights" to Freddie, who exclaimed over nearly everything to please his cousin.

When they exited the carriage, Phaedra stared up at the large sign above the door, declaring the shop, in bright red letters, to be 'Amberson's Confections.' The scent of sugar reached her nose, though they hadn't yet walked inside. The windows alone were enough to tempt a saint. Rows of delicate cakes, all with marzipan flowers, were displayed to any passerby. Tall jars, filled with lemon drops, peppermint sticks, violet drops and rose drops, were surrounded by bags of sugared almonds.

Daniel started jumping up and down in his excitement. Freddie joined in as Lilian led them into the chaos inside.

Chocolate hit her nostrils as Phaedra dodged two children who were running from their mother. Amberson's was much more crowded than she'd anticipated. Olivia and Lilian held Daniel between them while Phaedra, holding tight to Freddie, was led over by her nephew to an enormous jar of cinnamon sticks.

"Marvelous," Phaedra breathed, taking in the jar which had to be at least as tall as Freddie.

"Auntie Phae." Freddie looked up at her, about to burst he was so excited. "Might I have a small bag of those?" He pointed to a jar of candy drops in every color of the rainbow.

"What shall we try first?" Lilian mused, coming up behind them, her hand curled around the top of Daniel's coat to keep him from running off. "How about one of those tiny flowers?" She pointed to a row of confections shaped to look like roses behind the glass case. "Or those. They look like tiny seashells."

They all made their way to the counter, both boys pressing their faces to the glass to catch a better glimpse of what the cases contained. Phaedra leaned over to view the candy drops and an entire case of taffy.

"Licorice, too," Freddie said, looking like a miniature of Tony. Even his hair had the same windblown appearance as his father's. "You promised. Some of those." He pointed to the glass jar.

"Yes, of course." Phaedra straightened. "Stay right here beside me while I place our order." She released his hand. Goodness, there was so much to choose from. "I think those might be cherry, Freddie. You adore cherries." When Freddie didn't answer, Phaedra looked down, the spot beside her empty.

"Freddie?" She scanned the area around her, catching sight

of Lilian, Olivia, and Daniel near a barrel full of Turkish Delight on the other side of the shop, but not Freddie. Phaedra had only looked away for a moment. Trying to tamp down her rising panic, she wound her way through another row of barrels and cases, searching for her nephew. He wouldn't go outside without her, would he?

She hurried towards the door, searching the area just outside. There were dozens of people milling about, but no Freddie. "Freddie," she called. "This isn't amusing."

Fingers wrapped lightly around her upper arm as a voice murmured next to her ear, "Lady Phaedra, what a pleasant surprise."

Her first inclination was to shake him free as one might a rodent caught in her skirts. She hadn't seen him, thankfully, since their outing to The Battery, though he'd continued to visit The Barrington.

"Mr. Van Rhys." She wanted to grind her heel into his toe, a reward for informing Leo of her relationship with Morgan.

"You don't look pleased to see me." He made a tsking sound. "Now what could I have done to offend you?" His minty breath fanned her cheek. "I can't imagine."

She might punch him simply for being smug and pompous.

Attempting to wrench her arm discreetly and unsuccessfully from his grasp, Phaedra looked around her in desperation, hoping to see Lilian or Olivia. She didn't care for Van Rhys, especially after his little stunt the day of their visit to The Battery and had avoided him ever since. Now that she knew more about Morgan's past and his relationship with Gertrude, Phaedra liked him a great deal less. Morgan's admonition to stay away of Van Rhys was one she meant to obey.

"Excuse me, Mr. Van Rhys." Phaedra tried to move away but he held her tight.

"Are you looking for little Lord Welles, by any chance?" He shot her a look of concern. "He's wearing a coat of green. Carrying a string of licorice."

"Where is he?" She turned, considering whether anyone would see her kick Van Rhys.

"I saw him right over there." He made a vague gesture with one gloved hand. "Don't be distressed. I'm sure he's fine. Come, I'll show you."

Phaedra looked helplessly towards their carriage, some distance down the street her worry over Freddie overcoming her common sense. The crowd was so large that Leo's driver couldn't stay in front of Amberson's. Nor could he see Van Rhys escorting her away.

"I must say, Lady Phaedra, I think you've been avoiding me." Van Rhys steered her in the opposite direction, away from the waiting carriage and the confectioner's shop.

"He would not have gone this far." She halted, digging in her heels.

"I offered him licorice so we could play a game. Hide from his aunt," Van Rhys said smoothly. "Deceitful, but I wished to speak to you, Lady Phaedra. I thought we'd established quite a rapport earlier, so much so I've made my interest in you known to Mr. Murphy."

"Where is Freddie?" Phaedra demanded as a sickening dread filled her. "His father is the Duke of Averell. When I inform my brother—"

Van Rhys rolled his eyes and made a dismissive motion with his hand, still dragging her along. "Yes, yes. I'm supposed to be completely overwhelmed that your brother is a duke." A piffing sound came from him. "Impressed by his arrogance and wealth." Van Rhys snapped his fingers. "Just as I should pretend not to notice Murphy was born on the wrong side of the blanket." He gave her a bemused look.

"Frankly, I'm far more important on this side of the Atlantic than you are."

Turning a corner, he dragged her down a slim alley where a carriage sat.

Phaedra twisted about, struggling to get free. She didn't know what Van Rhys wanted her for, but whatever it was, it couldn't be good. "Let go of me this instant." Her free hand slid down her dress before remembering she hadn't brought her knife. Because this bloody dress didn't have pockets. And she'd only been going to Amberson's.

"You are quite a challenge, my lady. I'm abducting you," Van Rhys said in a mild tone. "Don't worry about little Lord Welles. I told him to take his licorice and show it to Mrs. Harrison. Awfully trusting. I've only met his little lordship once, but he remembers me. While you've been rolling about with that overgrown street urchin my sister took in, I've made great strides in my relationship with Mr. Murphy."

She kicked out at him as they drew closer to the carriage. "Is that why you saw fit to inform him of my whereabouts the other evening?"

"I saw it as my duty. You should be more careful going about unescorted, Lady Phaedra. I think you wanted me to catch you." He pulled her forward. "Have I ever shown you the handkerchief my late betrothed embroidered for me? It's a keepsake."

A handkerchief was thrust before her eyes, then against her nostrils.

"Doesn't it smell sweet?"

"My brother—" She tried to push the handkerchief away from her nose and mouth.

"Yes, yes. Duke of Averell. You're Lady Phaedra. I don't care. You are a means to an end. I've waited quite a long time to find Stewart's weakness. Now I have. Here, take another whiff."

The handkerchief was pressed harder into her nostrils.

"I'll be honest with you, my lady. You should have been more enthusiastic about a match between us. The end result, I fear, would still be the same, but less unpleasant. At any rate, I'm not certain you'll survive long enough to complain." The handkerchief was shoved in her face once more, and Phaedra became dizzy. "A pity."

"What?" She stumbled at the sweet odor invading her nostrils. She tried to push his hand away but her movements had become slow.

"Oh, dear, my lady. You're stumbling. Allow me to help you inside."

Phaedra's limbs felt heavy. Languid. The corners of her vision had black edges. She struggled to keep her eyes open.

Van Rhys shoved her unceremoniously into the carriage. Once he settled beside her, he held the handkerchief to her nose again while Phaedra gave a futile slap. Her hands wouldn't work properly. And her fingertips felt numb.

Van Rhys is not a gentleman, Pith's voice confirmed, which was entirely unhelpful.

"There we go," he said as her head rolled against the leather seat. "I don't want to give you too much. I have a physician friend who has cautioned me against doing so, and I need you alive for this next part. I am truly sorry about your disappearance, my lady. It will appear that Stewart abducted you. Surely, he'll hang for murder this time. I'll be grief-stricken for you, of course. But there isn't any other way, I don't think."

"Where are you taking me...?" She could barely form the words.

"Now, your role is that of a wiggling worm on a hook, my lady. Bait, to catch a much larger fish."

Van Rhys's handsome features blurred again. She was so incredibly tired. Her eyelids grew heavy, as if weighted down.

"I want you to understand—this is purely a business matter. Not at all personal. Stewart has something of mine he refuses to return. I've tried everything. But I think now he'll understand the seriousness of my request."

Phaedra's eyes finally slammed shut, her mind going blank as darkness overtook her.

21

Morgan reclined in the chair behind his desk, idly sipping on a glass of bourbon, thoughts more on Phaedra than the contracts he was supposed to be working on. He liked contracts. Everything laid out in black and white, with few gray areas. There were always loopholes, of course, but Morgan had grown masterful at spotting them. Gertie had been right to have him study law, though he would never practice it.

Still, a useful skill to have. Law.

Morgan took in the contract before him, along with the letter, from one of the city's most prominent lawyers. Another demand for the return of the Mohawk & Hudson shares stating that Gertie had been pressured to give them to Morgan. The shares were never to have left the Van Rhys family. A rule stipulated by their grandmother, who had been the original owner of the shares. Identical to the letter he'd received a few weeks ago at his office.

Morgan had to give Martin credit for being tenacious. He supposed Gertie's brother had no other choice when his accusations of murder had fallen flat, after making Morgan a pariah—*fine, I was already a pariah*—hadn't produced the desired results. Martin had resorted to other means. He'd employed nearly every lawyer in New York since then, none of whom had been able to refute Gertrude's ironclad will. His failure to provide proof that his grandmother had decreed the shares to stay in the Van Rhys family was ridiculous. Martin's father had sold his own shares to Beekman.

He snorted. Martin didn't have the funds to pursue this further.

If Murphy would just put aside his outrage over having found Phaedra in Morgan's bed, he'd see that the offer Lew had made to be part of The Barrington was a good one. Solid. Yes, Morgan had made it to get close to Rutherford, but that didn't take away from the fact that the proposal was generous.

He shut his eyes for a moment, pressing a palm to his chest. Willing his heart to cease this endless ache for Phaedra. She'd be his soon enough. He meant to retrieve her whether she hated him or not.

I can't bear for her to hate me.

So, Morgan waited, willing her anger towards him to abate before he approached her once more. Chipplewit kept track of Phaedra for Morgan. So did one of the upstairs maids. And a groom. She hadn't left The Barrington, not even to practice with her knife.

After that night, when his heart had been ripped from his chest, Morgan had ingested an entire bottle of bourbon, glaring at Dabble, who'd dared to interrupt. He'd sat in this same chair, allowing every bit of chaos and bitterness to erupt out of his body. Plans had been made to dispatch a business rival in Philadelphia. He'd scratched out a scheme to take over a list of businesses he didn't even want. Sent Armwood to Boston to assess a piece of property he would use for his own hotel.

None of it had made him the least happy.

The ugly edges of his life were sharp, piercing his own skin now that Phaedra was no longer here to soothe them away. It was daunting, knowing that no matter how hard he'd tried, even after Sister Bridget and vowing he would never be at anyone's mercy again, that one reckless girl, ferocious to her core, held Morgan in the palm of her hand.

So much so that Morgan feared how terrible he might become without her.

One more day.

And he would simply take her. A minister would wed them before he spirited her away. If she wasn't already with child, she would be. He didn't care about the wager, Murphy, or fucking Elysium.

The Duke of Averell would kick up a fuss. So would Murphy. Cooke might come at Morgan with his blades. So be it. He might never find out what happened to Gertie, and he was sorry for it. Maybe, at some point, he would just hold a knife to Rutherford's throat and get his answers that way. The only reason he hadn't resorted to violence was that Gertie wouldn't have approved. She'd loved Rutherford, though he wouldn't leave Cordelia.

There would be no more complicated schemes. No more webs to weave. Because none of it gave him pleasure any longer. Yes, he'd still be ruthless, but he'd temper his more savage instincts. Him being wed to a duke's daughter wouldn't stop Manhattan from sticking their noses in the air when they saw him, but what did it matter?

He only cared that Phaedra would come back to him.

A pair of knuckles rapped on the door a moment before Dabble's head appeared, a large envelope clutched in his hand. "This is for you, Stewart." He gave a twitch, holding out the packet.

"What is it?" Dabble looked unsettled, never a good sign. His mood was a barometer of sorts, like the way the birds flew before a storm.

Dabble's lips twisted. "Messenger brought this to the front door. Didn't bother to wait for a response. Seems odd, is all."

Morgan took the packet.

"Something ain't right, Stewart."

Dabble had lived his entire life on the streets until coming into Morgan's employ. You didn't survive that long without trusting your instincts. Or knowing how to use a weapon. Morgan's unease increased tenfold. "Send one of the boys after the messenger. Let's see who sent him."

The older man nodded and rushed out.

Opening the packet, he pulled out a stack of documents, nearly identical to those already scattered across his desk, except for the absence of a demand letter. Just a legally binding contract, transferring all of Morgan's shares in the Mohawk & Hudson to Martin Van Rhys.

Morgan tossed back the remainder of the bourbon and placed the papers on his desk.

A note fell out, stuck between the pages. There was no greeting or signature. Not that one was required.

You've repeatedly ignored my demands to return what rightfully belongs to me. So now, we will strike a bargain. I have Lady Phaedra Barrington. Sign the papers and bring them to me at that lovely spot where you do your pistol shooting.

A punch to his gut left Morgan breathless.

He read the note again, trying to discern a hidden meaning or if there was something he'd misread.

Martin hadn't just admitted to abducting Phaedra, had he?

Over a stack of shares in Mohawk & Hudson? Had he lost his mind?

Unfortunately, Gertie's brother wasn't mad. Not even close. He wasn't suffering a fit and in need of a good dose of laudanum. Nor was he stupid. He was only very, *very* determined. A dog with a bone, one he was not releasing for any reason.

And he had Phaedra.

"Stewart?" Dabble had returned. "We lost the messenger. He must have had someone waiting for him, knowing you'd follow." There was a grim set to Dabble's craggy features. "What do you need me to do?"

Morgan took out a piece of paper, pen hesitating for a moment. But he had no other choice. Lew was in Boston. He hoped his writing was legible. It often wasn't. Scrawling a name across the front, he handed it to Dabble. "Deliver this to him yourself. Pearl Street."

"Should I summon Mr. Armwood from Boston?"

"Only if I don't return, in which case Lew will know what to do." Morgan had laid plans years ago for his eventual demise, just as he did everything else. But the idea it may come at the hands of Martin Van Rhys was irritating. "Have my horse brought around. There is a matter that requires my urgent attention."

Martin was smart. Gertie had often said he approached each challenge with a singular focus. He would have already put things in motion so Morgan would eventually be blamed for Phaedra's disappearance. Or worse. Had the situation been reversed, that's what Morgan would have done.

A weakness was a terrible thing.

He marched out of his home, the only one he'd ever had, wondering if he'd see this house again, and decided it didn't matter. Martin couldn't return Phaedra to The Barrington without implicating himself, which meant he had no intention of allowing her to live. The thought of a world without her in it, her light being extinguished, had his steps falter.

He inhaled, letting the ice flow back into his veins.

Morgan meant to offer much more than Mohawk & Hudson to induce Martin to release her.

He had just the thing.

22

Phaedra rolled her neck around, wincing at the stiffness. Opening her eyes, she took in her surroundings, blinking away the fuzziness clouding her mind. Definitely not The Barrington. She was in a cottage of some sort, one in a state of complete disrepair. Or a shack. The smell of rotted vegetation with a hint of brine reached her nostrils, tugging at a memory. Where had she caught that scent before?

Morgan.

Harsh features softening as he took her hand, leading Phaedra down a trail buffeted on either side by trees and marsh. Warning her not to wander off as they passed by a dilapidated building. A shanty of some sort.

There was a window facing her, across the crumbling floorboards. Filthy. Cracked at the edges. Scores of thick trees sat outside, with only a small bit of light making it through the canopy.

This was Morgan's property. The place he'd taken her to shoot pistols. Which meant Phaedra was well out of the city and far from The Barrington.

A bubble of fear threatened to pop inside her.

You are a daughter of the Duke of Averell. Afraid of nothing.

Phaedra allowed her father's words to soothe her. She tilted her chin up, determined to face her circumstances with as much bravery as she could muster. If nothing else, her captor would not see her panic.

"Finally awake, I see." Van Rhys stepped into view, a tiny glass of what looked like brandy clasped in one elegant hand.

I really dislike him. I can't believe Leo thought he'd make me a good husband.

He lifted the glass, peering at her through the amber liquid before chuckling softly. "Just celebrating my impending success. I finally managed to outsmart him. And I have you to thank. I'd ask if you'd like a glass, but"—he gave her a helpless look—"I'm afraid I can't risk you running off. You might grab a stick and stab me. Stewart has rubbed off on you."

"This is his property." Her voice sounded scratchy.

"Rather a perfect spot, don't you think? For practicing pistols." He gave her a smart look. "Among other things."

Nausea roiled inside her, spoiling the memory of that day. "You followed us."

Van Rhys gave her a look of disbelief. "I wouldn't waste my time doing so. Hurtz took care of that for me. He described your outing to me in great detail."

"Hurtz?" The sting of a rope burnt into her wrists when she tried to move. Phaedra couldn't feel her fingers. "Have you lost your bloody mind?" she said, wiggling against the ropes. "Release me this instant. You can't kidnap the sister of a duke."

"Seems I can. And an insane man wouldn't have been able to trap that mongrel so neatly. It has taken me years to force Stewart into this position. A decades-long game of chess. Unfortunately, in order to win this match, the queen will need to be sacrificed."

Phaedra sucked in a breath. "You can't be serious."

Van Rhys ignored her. "Ah, there's Hurtz now."

A thin man with hair so sparse Phaedra could see his scalp stepped inside the shanty. He leered at Phaedra, his tongue running along his lower lip.

"Hurtz, may I introduce you to Lady Phaedra? Officially, at least. I believe you are already acquainted with her and her pistol skills."

The slow smile Hurtz gave Phaedra informed her that not only had he seen her practice shooting, but he'd witnessed what came after. A slow roll of heat swept up her cheeks, though she tried to stop it.

"A bit late to be embarrassed, isn't it Lady Phaedra?" Van Rhys gave her a disappointed look. "You've been a scandal for quite some time. Mrs. Pitchwick and her daughter visited London just last year. When I mentioned my friendship with Mr. Murphy, she was only too pleased to relate the gossip surrounding *The Disastrous Barrington*. An entire family mired in scandal and eccentricity, and you are the *worst*. At least your eldest sister had the sense to be ruined by a duke and not the son of a whore."

Phaedra took a painful breath but refused to let Van Rhys see her fear.

"Stewart's coming," Hurtz stated in a flat tone. "I waited at the end of the trail, as you said. Saw him on his horse. He's alone."

"Good. I was afraid he'd bring that tiny rat who runs his household."

Dabble. He means Dabble.

"I'm glad Gertrude managed to instill some decency in Stewart. At least he has a shred of honor, though he needed a push in the right direction. A part of me worried he'd abandon you to your fate. In any case, I'll finally have back what is rightfully mine. Mohawk & Hudson. Maybe I'll even wed Iris Beekman, now that I'm assured Stewart hasn't defiled her. Can't say the same for you, Lady Phaedra."

"The railroad." She wet her lips. Her mouth was dry, as if she'd had a wad of muslin shoved inside.

"*My* railroad, which he inherited illegally from my sister. Gertie should have left those shares to me, along with everything else. I am the last Van Rhys. The house is mine. The paintings gracing the walls are mine. And Mohawk & Hudson most assuredly is *mine*."

"Then why weren't you Gertrude's heir instead of Morgan?"

His face reddened. "You should mind your tongue, Lady Phaedra. Regarding things about which you know nothing."

Hurtz watched them, his gaze focused on Phaedra's bosom. He licked his lips once more.

Well, this trip to New York had certainly exceeded her expectations. Murderous suitors. Clandestine physical relations. Now to be used by one of Manhattan's most respected gentlemen to realize his revenge-fueled ambitions.

Altogether, it made Phaedra miss London.

"Why go to the trouble of informing my brother about my relationship with Stewart if you meant to kidnap me all along? You told Leo you wanted to wed me. I suppose your pride was wounded that I preferred Morgan. I'm sure I'm not the only one."

Van Rhys laughed. "Nicely done, my lady. Marvelous set-down. If you must know, it was far easier to get you alone once Stewart was busy nursing his broken heart and not lurking about. I don't have a death wish. Marriage to you would have been easier, I confess. But in either case, your fate was assured."

Phaedra looked away.

"This way is better, I think. There is the future gratitude of the Duke of Averell and Murphy once this is done. You see, I tried to save you, Lady Phaedra. A young lady I once hoped might be my wife. Yet another tragedy I've had to withstand." He gave her a mournful look. "But I was too late. I'll grieve you—and what might have been—with your entire family. Maybe I'll offer comfort to the dowager duchess. She's still a lovely woman."

Phaedra bit into her lip so hard, she tasted blood.

Van Rhys had no intention of allowing her to survive. He couldn't afford to. The authorities might not believe Morgan, but they would believe Lady Phaedra if she claimed Van Rhys had kidnapped her.

"Stewart will be found next to your body. Unconscious or dead. We'll see how things go. Either way, the authorities will be summoned by Hurtz." He nodded to his henchman. "They'll find me here, gun pointed at Stewart, weeping over you, of course."

"Of course." Leo would believe him. So would Tony.

But Ben wouldn't.

Phaedra held on to that thought. It was the only thing that kept her from becoming hysterical.

I am a daughter of the Duke of Averell.

She repeated the words over and over, taking what little comfort they offered.

"I'm considering running for office. Senator Van Rhys has a lovely ring to it, doesn't it? But I need a war chest, of sorts. Allies, like Mr. Murphy and a duke. Who will be only too grateful to support my endeavors after I tried to save you."

"What a well thought out plan, Mr. Van Rhys." Phaedra returned her gaze to his. It *was* rather perfect. No one would suspect him of any misdeeds. Had he not kidnapped her, she would never have assumed Van Rhys had the stomach for such things.

Hurtz suddenly moved to the side of the door, raised a pistol, and cocked it. "He's here."

The door opened slowly. Morgan stepped inside, blatantly ignoring Hurtz and the pistol as if they were of no import. His eyes fixed on Van Rhys.

A tiny sound came from Phaedra. Relief mixed with the utter hopelessness of the situation. Still, she had to warn him. "Morgan, he's going to—"

Morgan's pale gaze turned to her, shaking his head just slightly, a command for Phaedra to stay silent. There was an iciness to him, one she hadn't seen or felt for some time.

"I'm here, Martin." He walked towards Van Rhys. "Just as you asked."

Hurtz cocked the pistol. "That's far enough."

"Did you bring the contracts?" Van Rhys held out one gloved hand. "Signed, I hope."

"Not yet. I'm not a fool, Martin."

A snarl left Van Rhys. "Sign the contracts now, or Hurtz will shoot her."

Phaedra shut her eyes, thinking of all the things she hadn't gotten to say to Morgan. Her family. Poor Pith. He'd be so distressed at her death. But Lord Richards stood to win a large sum. He'd placed the wager in the Red Book that she'd be kidnapped and held for ransom. Congratulations were in order.

I am a daughter of the Duke of Averell.

"Calm down, Martin. I didn't say I wouldn't sign them, only that I hadn't yet. Not until you listen to my own proposal for how this will work. One I think you'll like better. A bargain, of sorts."

Van Rhys walked over and grabbed the pistol from Hurtz, pressing it against Phaedra's temple. "I'm listening. But speak fast. My patience is thin."

She winced at the sudden press of the gun barrel against her temple.

"I think we can both agree," Morgan said smoothly. "I didn't kill Gertrude."

Van Rhys's lips thinned. "You are to blame for her death, all the same. Gertrude knew full well that the shares of Mohawk & Hudson were meant to stay in the family. But she gave them to you, along with everything else. Can't you see how wrong that was? *I* am the last Van Rhys. I should have been her heir. Not you. Not one of her projects, fished from Five Points. I asked her one last time to give those shares back to me—" Van Rhys clamped his lips shut, eyes blazing with loathing at Morgan.

"What did you do?" Morgan said quietly.

"You should be more concerned with what I *plan* to do." He nudged the pistol once at Phaedra. "What is your proposal?"

"I just need to know, Martin. Before we conclude our business. What happened to Gertie? It won't matter if you tell me now, will it?"

The pressure of the pistol against her temple eased.

"I suppose not. It was an unfortunate accident, Stewart. I didn't mean...Gertrude was so stubborn. I only went to her that night to plead my case. Give me back the shares. New York Life & Loss had recently paid out several large claims. I needed—it was what our grandmother and father would have wanted. But Gertrude was far too upset when I arrived. The sheets of her bed were rumpled as her lover"—he glared at Morgan—"had only recently left. My sister was with child. *Your* child."

Morgan's broad frame fell back a pace. "Gertie was—she never told me. And I was never her lover."

"Liar."

"No. She was a mother to me, nothing more. It was Jacob Rutherford." Sadness etched Morgan's words. "They were lovers for nearly two years before she died."

Van Rhys's hand holding the pistol trembled just slightly against her temple.

"Jacob Rutherford. I should have guessed. Gertrude always had terrible taste in men." He cast a dubious look at Morgan before composing himself. "Well, it wouldn't have changed anything, my knowing it was Rutherford and not you. She wouldn't sign the shares to me, and the thought of an heir—well, I never considered *you* were already her heir. We argued. She fell and hit her head." A small measure of regret edged his words. "I didn't mean for her to die. But I stayed with her until she passed."

A sound came from Morgan, though his lips remained tight, with only the hint of a half-smile on his lips. "Good of you."

"I told her I was sorry, but dying was better than bearing a bastard and shaming our family. I gave her some laudanum for the pain. Held her hand. I wasn't about to let her die alone."

"How noble," Phaedra hissed. Poor Gertrude. Killed by the greed of her own brother. At least Morgan knew the truth now. Finally.

"Thank you," Morgan said, without any hint of anger, though his eyes on Van Rhys were cool, like tiny chips of ice. "I appreciate you telling me."

"Now, about your counterproposal."

Morgan nodded slowly. "First, shooting Lady Phaedra will not benefit you in the long run. I assume you intend to blame me for her disappearance and murder?"

"I do. The rabid dog from Canal Street. Not one person will defend your character."

"True, true," Morgan agreed. "But there is a problem, Martin. Benjamin Cooke. When you sent Leo Murphy to my home to retrieve her, he brought Cooke. Who will eventually figure things out, if he hasn't already, and come looking for *you*. He's married to Lady Phaedra's sister. You know how protective he is about family."

Fear shadowed Van Rhys's features. The pistol wavered just a bit. He had forgotten about Ben in all his perfect planning.

"But I have a better idea. One that gives you *everything* you want. And more importantly, Cooke won't slice you to bits after."

"Always willing to make a deal, aren't you? I've long admired your business acumen, Stewart. It's unfortunate I object to everything else. I'll assume this plan leaves Lady Phaedra alive?"

Morgan kept his gaze averted from hers, not even acknowledging Phaedra was in the room.

"I will sign over my *entire* fortune. Everything amassed since Gertie's death. *Including* all the shares of Mohawk & Hudson. Along with the house facing Washington Park and everything in it."

Van Rhys's brows drew up into his hairline. "Everything?"

"I will also sign a confession, one you can dictate if you like, admitting to the murder of Gertrude Van Rhys."

Van Rhys drew in a breath. The greed shining from his eyes. "A confession?"

"Think of it. You'll be a wealthy man. Vindicated in your assertion that I killed your sister. In return, Phaedra goes free and returns to The Barrington without a mark on her. Alive and well. But until I know she's safe, I won't sign your papers. Hurtz"—he jerked his chin—"stays where I can see him when she leaves, as do you. We'll have a drink or two. When an hour has passed, I'll sign everything over."

"Or I could shoot you both. Now. Forge your signature."

An ugly laugh came from Morgan. "You've often mocked me for my handwriting, Martin, but it's nearly impossible to duplicate my signature. Armwood and my lawyer would know if you forged my name. You *need* me to sign."

Van Rhys narrowed his eyes. "What's to keep you from rescinding your agreement, once I let her go? Or stabbing me on my way home? You can easily overpower me and Hurtz once I lower this pistol."

Morgan kept his features averted from her. "Because I'll be dead."

Phaedra swayed in the chair she was bound to. "No."

"That's the best part of my proposal. Once Lady Phaedra is safe," Morgan continued, "you can march me half a mile to the marshes and shoot me. There won't be a body. I'll wash out to sea. You'll have everything you want, even a confession, and I'll be dead. Once she's gone, Hurtz can take my weapons and bind my wrists. As part of our deal, I won't fight you."

"No," Phaedra said louder. "You can't possibly be serious about letting this fop shoot you."

"Shut up, Phaedra." Morgan finally looked at her, giving away nothing. As if he wanted Van Rhys to drag him out to the bloody swamp and shoot him.

"Yes, shut up, Phaedra. And I'm not a fop." Van Rhys nudged her in the temple with the pistol again. "Honestly, Stewart. How do you tolerate her insolence?"

"Do we have a deal, Van Rhys?" Morgan leaned forward. "My life and everything I have, including Mohawk & Hudson, in return for Lady Phaedra leaving unharmed."

No. No. No.

Phaedra felt the punch of his words. "You can't mean to do this, Morgan." She strained to catch his eye, but once more he refused to look at her. "Please."

Van Rhys let out a laugh. "I must say, that is quite an offer." His eyes gleamed with avarice. "As much as I hate to admit it, your signature does present a problem. Far too distinctive, or else I would have forged it years ago. My sister paid for tutors and a fine education, neither of which did anything to remedy your poor penmanship. So, I agree to your proposal." Van Rhys lowered the pistol, nodding at Hurtz. "I'd be a fool not to."

"Follow the trail, and you'll see my horse," Morgan said, finally looking in her direction. "Once you find the road, go left and ride until you see the Collect Pond. Then take Broadway to The Barrington. Don't look back." Morgan turned once more to Van Rhys. "Hurtz stays where I can see him, or I won't sign a thing."

"Don't make me regret letting you go, Lady Phaedra," Van Rhys drawled. "Remember, I'm good friends with your nephew Freddie. I've gotten to know Daniel as well."

"Don't you dare threaten—"

"Phaedra," Morgan said in a soothing tone, stopping her next words. "Averell and his family are returning to London, Martin. At the end of the week. She won't be in New York much longer. And I doubt she'll return. Nor will she say anything about what has happened today."

"Morgan," she pleaded. "Don't."

Van Rhys nodded. "Very well. Cut her bonds, Hurtz."

Hurtz took his time, his hand lingering over her calves and arms as he sliced through the ropes. When she was free, Phaedra came unsteadily to her feet.

"Do as I ask, Phaedra. Just this once. Pretend some semblance of obedience," Morgan said in a low tone. The pearly mist of his eyes had gone a deep slate. "Everything will be fine. Now, make a vow to Martin that you won't breathe a word of what happened today."

Morgan had to have a plan. A scheme. Something he'd concocted to trick Van Rhys. But Phaedra couldn't see it. "I agree." She nodded and whispered to him, "*Schatje.*"

He jerked, fingers twitching against his thigh. He'd heard her.

"Get on your knees, Stewart. I've been waiting a long time, and I want to enjoy this." Van Rhys pulled up a chair and sat down. "I plan on making your confession quite splendid."

"I haven't any doubt." Morgan went to his knees, eyes pleading with her now. "Run, Phaedra." He hesitated. "Behave, or not."

Phaedra blinked back tears and stumbled out the door, wondering if she could somehow double back, because under no circumstances was she going to allow that arrogant Dutch dandy to hurt Morgan. She tripped over her feet, eyes shifting along the trees, looking for a rock. Or a large stick. Maybe she could disarm Hurtz.

A blade suddenly whizzed past her ear, lifting the strands of her hair. A thud followed behind her. Turning, she caught sight of Hurtz falling to the ground. Blood spewed across his shirt from the knife protruding from his neck.

❧ 23 ❧

Martin. What a pompous, self-important idiot. Petty to the core.

At least if Morgan was dead, which seemed more the case than his original plan, he wouldn't have to tolerate Gertie's brother any longer. That would be a relief.

Phaedra would be safe. All that mattered. If Morgan was gone, she'd end up married to some titled prick who would make her dance at balls and insist she ride sidesaddle. Probably discourage her weaponry skills. But she would be alive.

Schatje.

Morgan had never told her what the word meant, but someone had. The memory of her, using that endearment for him, was one that would comfort Morgan if he did end up being marched out of this shack at the end of Martin's pistol. Phaedra loved him. He'd seen it clearly in her stricken features as Hurtz led her to the door.

The beat of his heart intensified.

And now he knew what had become of Gertie. Rutherford had been there that night and left after they'd argued. Had she told him about the child? How foolish Morgan had been to discount Martin. He never would have thought him capable of murdering his own sister. Gertie's life, a worthy one, cut short so her brother could puff his chest out as majority owner of Mohawk & Hudson. No one would ever suspect him of having killed Gertie. Her lady's maid was probably the only one to have seen Martin in the house that night, and he'd probably paid her to leave New York. Or tossed her in the East River.

Martin had counted on Morgan being hung for her murder. How disappointed he must have been when things hadn't worked out.

Over-privileged twit.

If Morgan didn't return home, if the hurried plan he'd concocted and his request for assistance went unheeded, Martin's triumph at Morgan's death would be short-lived. Within the week, his carriage would end up on a deserted street near the Bowery where the beasts that lived nearby would tear him limb from limb. Dabble would see to it.

Morgan had only promised to sign over Mohawk & Hudson, not allow Martin to keep it.

"Drink?" Martin asked. "It's the least I can do."

"Yes, thank you." He needed to drag this out as long as possible. He didn't entirely trust that Hurtz wouldn't go running after Phaedra or that Martin wouldn't shoot her purely out of spite. He seemed to think himself untouchable, forgetting that Morgan would have made his own arrangements.

Hurtz pushed Phaedra out the door.

Morgan tensed, waiting for Hurtz to reappear.

"It was always going to come to this, Stewart." Martin pointed the pistol. "Take out every weapon on you, including that tiny spool in your side pocket. Place it all on the floor where I can see. You hesitate or make a move in my direction, and I'll have Hurtz hunt her down like a wild animal."

He did as Martin instructed.

"Good." A kick of his foot and the knives along with the spool of wire flew across the shanty, well out of reach. "Place your hands flat on the floor. When Hurtz returns, we'll begin."

Hurtz was a few feet outside the door, turned in the direction Phaedra would have run. It seemed that for once in her life, she had listened and not decided to do something stupid. Like attempt to save him.

My brave, ferocious creature.

The road wasn't far. His horse was in plain sight, and Phaedra was an excellent rider. Which was good, because as the minutes ticked by, Morgan became less sure that—

Hurtz jerked suddenly. He twirled around as if dancing, then fell to the ground, feet kicking as he grabbed at the knife sticking out of his throat.

Relief flooded Morgan. His hands tensed as Martin whirled about, his face a mask of fury.

"I should never have trusted—" He raised the pistol.

Another blade gleamed as it flew through the air of the shanty, pinning Martin's wrist to the wall.

He howled in pain and anger, trying unsuccessfully to wrench his wrist free, grabbing at the pistol to keep the weapon aimed at Morgan. Blood splattered across the wall as he struggled.

Morgan dipped to the floor and rolled to the side, reaching for his knife.

Another blade of silver flew through the air, lodging itself in Martin's shoulder. He shrieked, dropping the pistol.

"You're late." Morgan came to his feet. "Though I didn't think you'd come at all."

Cooke stepped over Hurtz's body, pausing only to retrieve the knife embedded in his neck. He wiped it on the dead man's coat before walking towards Martin, who struggled like a bug stuck on a pin.

"I'm right on time." Cooke cocked his head at Martin. "And you should be more grateful. She's safe, at any rate. I told her to wait down the trail a bit. I doubt she'll listen."

"Probably not." Morgan looked at the man who he had been at odds with for most of his life—and didn't want to be any longer. When he'd sent Dabble with a note for Cooke, Morgan had trusted his former friend to come for Phaedra, if nothing else. "Thank you."

"I owed you for the coat," Cooke stated blandly.

One day, he and Cooke would open a bottle of bourbon and discuss the past. Rutherford. Gertrude. Maybe Morgan would even ask about Sister Bridget, who had been found, bled to death from dozens of small cuts. Impaled to the headboard of her bed. According to Dabble.

"You don't," Morgan replied.

Cooke shrugged. "I'll see Phaedra home, unless you need my assistance." He motioned with his knife in Martin's direction. "With this."

"I'll handle things myself, but I appreciate the offer."

"You're both dead men," Martin snapped, kicking at the wall, trying to free himself. "I'll make sure neither of you can ever show your face in Manhattan again. I am Martin Van Rhys. I am important. If I go missing, there will be questions."

"I won't be bothering Rutherford any longer," Morgan said, ignoring him. "I have my answers. Martin killed Gertie."

"For the railroad." Cooke's brows raised before turning to Martin once more, his features hard. "Jacob Rutherford owns the police. And the mayor. I can assure you that once he finds out you murdered Gertrude, no one on earth will be looking for you. Besides, you fled to Canada due to the bankruptcy of

New York Loss & Life. I'm afraid your reputation is about to be muddied with accusations of embezzlement."

Martin let out a wail.

Morgan raised a brow. "Clever."

Cooke inclined his head. "You'll have to see to some details when you are...finished."

A frustrated sob came from the wall. "I am Martin Van Rhys."

"So what?" Cooke jerked his chin towards the door with a resigned sigh. "Stop lurking about, Phaedra. Mind the dead body. Don't get blood on yourself. It will ruin the story we'll have to tell your family."

Phaedra stood, fingers only trembling slightly as she stepped over Hurtz. But she didn't flinch, only lifted her skirts away from the blood.

"You can't be a party to this," Martin roared. "You're a duke's daughter."

Her brows drew together as she focused her gaze on Morgan. "Not an hour ago you had a pistol pointed at my temple. So forgive me if I am not invested in your future, Mr. Van Rhys." Her fingers reached out to Morgan before she jerked them back.

"You wandered away from Amberson's because you got it in your head to visit Stewart," Cooke stated. "Leo won't question you defying him. Stewart wasn't at home. Thankfully, Olivia summoned me immediately. I found you and brought you back to The Barrington. That's what we're going to tell everyone. I'm sure Leo has already told Tony about you and Stewart."

"Go back with Cooke," Morgan said, not daring to touch her. She was in a state of shock, far too calm given the circumstances. As much as Phaedra loved him, and Morgan was certain she did, this might be too much for her. *He* might be too much. And his nature was unlikely to change completely.

Could he keep her, knowing Phaedra might be terrified of him?

"There are enough rocks scattered outside to weight his pockets," Cooke said helpfully. "And his." He nodded to Hurtz. "The water is deep and washes out to sea. There might even be some quicksand."

"You won't get away with this. You won't." Martin gave a futile tug at the knives pinning him.

"I'm fairly certain I will," Morgan returned. He took a deep breath and looked at Phaedra. "*Schatje*." His voice was gentle. "Go with Cooke. It's all right if...if you go back to England. Marry some aristocratic nitwit. I won't be angry."

A sob left Phaedra. "You—"

"I'll understand. And I don't want you to see this—*or* me," he snarled at her. "Go."

"I already see you," she choked. "And if you think I'm going to wed some—"

The rest of her words were cut off as Cooke dragged Phaedra outside.

Morgan counted to twenty, listening to Martin hurl his useless threats before his words devolved into shaking sobs as he pleaded for his life. None of it moved Morgan to spare him. He picked up the spool of piano wire from the floor, taking great care to unwind it slowly while Van Rhys let out a scream.

"This is for Gertie."

24

A few days after her unexpected abduction, Phaedra wandered into Leo's English garden, needing a bit of air after recent events. She was unsurprised to find Olivia in a worn pair of trousers, digging around the base of a flowering shrub. The entire area, including her sister, smelled of manure. Clumps of it were heaped everywhere.

"You aren't going to roll around in that, are you?" Phaedra kicked a clod in Olivia's direction.

"I'm not sure what it is you have against good fertilizer, Phaedra. It's necessary for happy plants. Just look at the garden. It's flourishing. Thriving. I thought you'd be packing."

Phaedra frowned at her. "That's what I've come to discuss."

The departure to London was set for the end of the week, just as Morgan had informed Van Rhys. So she couldn't blame her murderous suitor's absence—*so murderous*—on the fact that he was not informed of her plans. If anyone had asked prior to her being abducted by Van Rhys if Phaedra was returning to England, she would have laughed. Morgan would never allow it.

But now?

It's all right if you go back to England.

That entire speech from Morgan had sounded more like a goodbye than anything else. He'd expected her to shun him now, and frankly, there must be something wrong with her that she still ...*loved* him, even knowing the alternative uses for piano wire.

"Terrible about Martin Van Rhys, isn't it?" Olivia interrupted her thoughts. She didn't look up, just continued to efficiently tuck manure around the base of some flowering shrub. "Who would have thought he'd do such a thing? Defrauding some of the most important members of Manhattan society."

The disappearance of Martin Van Rhys had been the headline in yesterday's newspaper. New York Loss & Life, his insurance company, was completely bankrupt. Martin had fled to Canada to escape his creditors and the authorities. There were vague whispers of searching for him, but that was all they were. Whispers.

"Terrible," Phaedra agreed. She'd heard Van Rhys screaming as Ben had led her towards the road. She'd tried to feel badly about his death, if not the method of his demise, but couldn't. He *had* been meaning to kill her, all so he could have a bloody railway. Still, Phaedra kept trying to force out some emotion, just as she had about the men who'd threatened her at Hagerty's.

Phaedra pressed a palm to her mid-section, demanding her stomach settle.

She had said not a word when Ben had returned her to The Barrington, her mind on the violence she'd seen in both he and Morgan. Knowing it was there, beneath the surface, was one thing. *Seeing it*, quite another.

And hearing Van Rhys's screams as he was certainly garroted...something else entirely.

When Ben had brought her back to The Barrington, he'd explained the situation to Leo and Tony, while Phaedra had snuck away to soak in a bath. She had stared at the tiles of the bathing room, growing angrier as the water cooled. Not at having been kidnapped, though she wasn't pleased about it. Nor that Morgan might well have died, though she wasn't happy about that either. But because he was going to simply abandon her. Allow her to return to England and wed some bloody dandy. In fact, he'd instructed her to do so.

Phaedra was far more distressed about his abandonment than the unsavory aspects of his nature. And that was why she sought out Olivia today.

"Well, out with it." Olivia set down her trowel, a patient look on her face.

"You know about Ben, don't you?" Phaedra plucked at a leaf, pressing the silky texture between her fingers. "He said you did."

"You're speaking of the coat. I've known since...before we left England. He told me when he came to Halloway Park to dine." Her cheeks pinked.

"I'm sure he did more than admire you over Lord Daring's dinner table."

"Yes." Olivia cleared her throat. "Well. In any case, he admitted to his charade after we—it isn't important." She waved the trowel about, flinging a bit of manure. "I know who Ben was and who he is now, which is vastly more important. Admittedly, having grown up in Five Points has left him with some rather unpleasant tendencies—"

"Is that what you call them?" Phaedra paced back and forth. "It isn't as if Ben just doesn't care for mushrooms, Olivia. Or that he prefers coffee to tea."

Olivia's lips pulled tight. "Ben has a particular way of dealing with specific situations, some of which he learned *after* becoming Jacob Rutherford's nephew. I make no apology for him. Ben told me he would explain it all to you. About Stewart."

"He did. The entire story."

"I wouldn't change Ben, even if I could. His nature is not always polite, but it was bred into him. Like Theseus at Cherry Hill, who must chase down each mouse he sees."

"And then Theseus eats the mouse. Has Ben mentioned how he came to bring me back to The Barrington the other day? After I disappeared from Amberson's?"

Olivia let out a deep breath. "Thank goodness, I don't have to sit here another minute and pretend I don't know what happened to Van Rhys. Of course, he told me. Ben and I have few secrets, and if we do, it is because I've expressed that I would prefer not to learn certain details of his... activities."

"Shouldn't I feel terrible at knowing his fate? Mourn his loss?"

"Van Rhys? Do *you* feel as if you should?" Olivia mixed more manure around the roots of the shrub. "I don't feel the least sad about his disappearance. He was going to shoot you, Phaedra. After luring you away from Amberson's. Lilian and I were panicked. Freddie was crying. So was Daniel. Leo's driver was apoplectic at having to explain your disappearance to Chipplewit." At Phaedra's look, she said, "Apparently Leo's manager is an associate of Mr. Stewart's. Half the staff was out looking for you when Ben arrived. A man named Dibble had gone to Pearl Street with a letter for him."

"Dabble," Phaedra said. "He also works for Stewart. I think he's a valet or a butler. I've never been certain."

"My point is, think of all the fear we experienced at your disappearance. Caused by Van Rhys and his pursuit of a stupid railway," Olivia stated tartly. "Feel badly if you must, but I do not."

"Morgan strangled him with piano wire," Phaedra stated calmly. "Shouldn't I be somewhat distressed about that?"

Olivia tugged at a weed near her knee. "Only if you want to be. This is why I don't ask Ben for details." She made a face.

"You're very calm about all this, Olivia."

"I love Ben, and I do not regret becoming his wife." She looked up at Phaedra. "You do not need my permission to love Morgan. Which you do." She flung a clod of manure at Phaedra's skirts. "You were in love with him before we ever came to New York."

Phaedra considered that for a moment. "I have always felt Morgan knows me in a way no one else ever has. He does not try to convince me to be other than what I am. Doesn't expect me to behave properly. Or cease offering my opinion. He thinks I'm brilliant and admires that I could run a gambling hell if I chose to." She looked down at her feet.

"Not many gentlemen would find a talent for running a hazard table to be appealing, Phaedra. I know Stewart was in London for his own reasons, none of which were probably good, tormenting Ben being one of them, though I don't think he'll be doing that any longer. Nor will Ben be disposed to carve him up like a Christmas goose."

Phaedra thought of the way Ben had casually thrown his knife to end Hurtz's life. How he'd skewered Van Rhys to the wall of the shack without batting an eye. *That* Ben wasn't the charming rogue who adored Olivia.

"They have reached some sort of understanding," Olivia continued. "Morgan is no longer angry about the coat, and Ben is *apologetic* about the coat. A bottle of bourbon was involved. Ben arrived home rather late, horribly intoxicated, after visiting Morgan's home."

"He's seen him, then?" Phaedra hated that she sounded

so...pathetic. "I worried that something had happened." Because *she* hadn't seen Morgan.

Olivia reached up and took her hand, pulling Phaedra down beside her. "He has. I expect you will as well. Soon."

"I don't know if I will, Olivia." Phaedra bit her lip. "He told me he wouldn't be angry if I returned to England and married someone else. As if I could go from him to Emberly, for instance."

A snort came from her sister. "I imagine that was his attempt at being honorable."

"But what if he meant it?"

"You've just spent the last half-hour trying to convince me you shouldn't love a man like Morgan Stewart. Yet, you are desolate at the thought he might not want you." Olivia pulled her close. "I know you were frightened when Van Rhys took you. Not only for yourself, but for Stewart. It is a terrifying prospect to realize that so much of you resides in another human being."

"That's exactly how it feels. As if Morgan has part of my soul and I have part of his." She bit her lip. "Which is why I'm so angry that he assumes I can just traipse back to London and forget him entirely. He was willing to leave me." Phaedra leaned into Olivia. "So that I might flounder about with no one appreciating my knife throwing skills but Ben."

"That is only slightly dramatic," Olivia paused. "I doubt Stewart has any intention of honoring his stupidly noble gesture that you return to England. Nor should you continue to be angry over it."

Phaedra brushed manure from the edge of her skirts. "I suppose you're correct."

"I am." Olivia pressed a kiss to her cheek.

Phaedra nudged Olivia with her shoulder. "The smell is atrocious. I can't believe Ben appreciates you reeking of manure."

"You can get used to anything, given enough time."

They sat in silence for a few moments, with only the bees buzzing about. Olivia cleared her throat. "When Mr. Thomlinson was courting me, he always brought the most enormous bouquets of flowers. Do you recall? They were lovely, of course, but they meant little to me."

"He meant little to you."

Olivia smiled. "I explained to him, repeatedly, my love of growing my own flowers. How I adored gardens." She gestured to the waves of flowers and shrubs surrounding them. "But without asking, barely acquainted with me, Ben somehow knew. The first flower he bestowed upon me was an orchid, to be carefully repotted. Dangerous or not. Barely civilized. Yet he saw me."

Phaedra thought of the knife Morgan had commissioned for her. Carved with her initials. Balanced for her smaller hand. She plucked at another leaf. "Morgan is...more than he appears. The truth is, Olivia, the thought of leaving him tears at my soul. Even if he forced me, I don't think I could. I can't leave him alone in the world. No matter how angry I am that he thinks I would."

"Then don't, Phaedra. You may be all that keeps Stewart tethered. The very thing which tempers his darkness and makes him human. No small feat. I suspect he'll be a better man with you beside him. Here." She tossed an extra trowel at Phaedra's feet. "Push a bit of manure on that plant over there. His name is Harvey."

25

"I am against this in every way imaginable." Leo stomped back and forth across the family's private parlor. "I can't believe it's even up for discussion. Maybe he wants something else."

Phaedra pursed her lips. *Besides her.*

Tony poured a glass of scotch, sniffed at it, and then, satisfied, took a sip. "Thank goodness Olivia isn't lurking about. I miss her, but I confess it is nice to use a saltshaker knowing that actual salt will be dispersed. And that my scotch is not, in fact, watered down tea. Not one of us is happy about this turn of events. What were you thinking, going to his home? Alone. Sending us all into a frenzy that something terrible had befallen you." Tony shot Phaedra a disappointed look.

Very well. Everyone was disappointed.

"Something terrible *did* happen to her," Leo bit out.

Her brother wasn't speaking of being kidnapped by Van Rhys. Leo didn't know. None of them did.

"I had not imagined such a situation. Bad enough to lose

Olivia but this..." Mama waved about her snifter of brandy. "*This*."

This was the word Mama used for Morgan without actually saying his name, as if he might suddenly appear in the parlor, summoned by her accidentally, like some horrible monster from a nightmare. Since Ben's careful recitation of the story he'd concocted of her disappearance, the one which made no mention of Van Rhys but did feature Morgan, the questions had slowly multiplied over the last several days. How had they met? What was the extent of their relationship? These questions were followed by horror at Phaedra's actions, most of which no one had known about until Leo had informed Tony about finding her at Morgan's home.

"He has a name. Morgan Stewart."

Leo made a sound. He was especially distressed. Much more so than Tony. Probably worried about the bloody wager in the Red Book.

"You can't possibly be considering Mr. Stewart, Phaedra." Mama drained her glass of brandy. "He is little more than a street thug."

"That isn't true."

"I think," Georgina said, swirling a glass of bourbon in her hand, "he will ask permission to court her when he arrives. Isn't that the proper thing to do?"

"The cow is already out of the barn, Georgie." Leo stomped about a bit more, that vein in his forehead protruding.

Maggie, Tony's duchess, sat primly at yet another piano Tony had bought for her, because good lord, one couldn't have enough bloody pianos, and banged on the keys before her. "Ruination is not something to toss about, Leo. Or to be announced to the entire room in such a vulgar manner. Having been ruined myself"—she arched a brow at Tony—"I speak from experience."

"Yes, but—" Tony started.

Maggie immediately clicked her nails against the tiny snifter holding her own brandy where it sat atop the piano, giving him a meaningful look.

"I am not a trained cat, madam." Tony swallowed the scotch. "I insist you cease in your efforts to make me one."

"I think it amusing." Georgina winked at Maggie.

Leo chuckled softly.

"I'll never understand your love of bourbon, Georgina." Tony sauntered over to her. "I suppose it helps to block out the fact that you're married to Leo. My understanding is that bourbon will eventually make you blind."

"Amusing, Your Grace. First Cooke, and now Stewart," Leo said, clearly in a foul mood. "Our family will soon be overrun by its seedier members."

"Including you, so utterly respectable with your gambling hell and pleasure palace." Georgina seared her husband with a glare. "Watch your tongue, Leo Murphy."

Mama poured herself another glass of brandy.

Phaedra pressed a hand to her forehead. All in all, this was going about as well as she'd expected.

"And you." Leo turned to point at Torrington, who did nothing more than sigh, plainly resigned to Leo's ire. "None of this would have happened had you not allowed Phaedra to follow you about Hagerty's."

"I don't think anyone *allows* Phaedra to do anything," Torrington said, stroking the edge of Rosalind's cheek. "Have you actually spent any time at all with your sister? The duke took her to Elysium. That's far worse than a boxing establishment."

"I like Mr. Stewart," Rosalind said. "He was lovely to me. Truly a gentleman."

Leo sputtered.

"And you aren't supposed to be going to Hagerty's at all,

Torrington." She tapped her husband on the shoulder. "Are you?"

The room erupted in an uproar, defending Stewart or not. Debating the wisdom of Phaedra wandering about boxing establishments, with Torrington trying to make excuses to Rosalind. The fact she'd been compromised. Halfway through, Rosalind coughed, then went green and had to leave the room, murmuring about breakfast not sitting well when they all knew she was with child.

Maggie pounded on the piano keys to make her point that Tony had once been quite horrible.

Georgina sipped bourbon and reminded Leo of his faults. They were numerous.

Only Mama stayed perfectly calm in the eye of the Barrington hurricane, regarding Phaedra with a thoughtful expression. Not pleased, mind you. But considering.

Far more dangerous, in Phaedra's opinion.

This entire ferocious debate, worse than what anyone had to endure while sitting in Parliament, was the direct result of that carefully scrawled note, barely legible, addressed to the Duke of Averell from Mr. Morgan Stewart asking for a moment of His Grace's time.

That was it. Nothing more. No mention of his intentions or Phaedra.

Which made her quite angry. Was she or was she not his bloody anchor?

A knock at the door and Mr. Chipplewit entered. He leaned forward and whispered something in Leo's ear, which made the vein twitch violently once more in her brother's forehead.

"Stewart has arrived. I've had Chipplewit put him in my office. Hopefully he won't steal anything."

Phaedra gave him a disgusted look.

Tony tossed back the remainder of his drink. "Splendid. Shall we, Leo? Stewart didn't send the note to you, but I'm sure he expects you'll come along."

26

Dear God.

The two of them looked like a pair of stone lions guarding some grand estate, with their matching frowns. They could easily be mistaken for each other except for the expressions on their faces. Averell was carefully ducal, his frown polite. He was more apt to send a cutting remark or insult. But he was the brother who had allowed Phaedra to follow him around Elysium, free to try her hand at managing a gambling hell.

Murphy, on the other hand, seemed about to leap at Morgan and wrestle him to the ground. But then, Morgan had always thought him more of a scrapper, ducal bastard or not. If you took off Murphy's expensive, tailored clothing, Morgan could well imagine him running a pickpocket operation in Five Points.

"Averell. Murphy." He wasn't about to bow and mince to either of these two. Addressing the note to "Your Grace" had been about as far as Morgan was willing to go. In general, he wasn't fond of pedigrees or breeding, considering he had neither.

"Mr. Stewart." Averell greeted him in a crisp, aristocratic tone that spoke of centuries of ducal magnificence. "I'll assume you wish to discuss your intentions towards Lady Phaedra."

"I think I've already made them clear."

Murphy glowered at him. Probably considering how to stab him with the stickpin securing his cravat. He understood the animosity. His reputation wasn't good. Murphy had surely heard the tales of how Morgan had managed to gain control of Eastern Banking after the disappearance of Robert Townsend. His brutal manipulation of the board at the Boston & Albany railroad.

The rumors he'd murdered Gertrude Van Rhys probably hadn't helped. He'd have to live with those. Martin was well past confessing for the crime. His body might actually be in Canada by now.

Honestly, had Phaedra been his sister, Morgan probably wouldn't have wanted to hand her over to him either.

"Your intentions. All dishonorable," Murphy snapped.

Why did Murphy imagine himself to be so much better than Morgan? They were both bastards.

The duke shot his brother a look. "Let Mr. Stewart speak. I would like to ascertain his intentions for myself."

Murphy was a lost cause. But perhaps he could charm Averell. He sincerely hoped that Phaedra would one day appreciate the lengths he was willing to go through to do things properly. Would have been much easier just to take her.

"I met Lady Phaedra at Hagerty's, where she was enjoying the boxing matches. The manner of our introduction isn't important—"

"Phaedra had placed herself in a precarious position and was about to be accosted. It is my understanding you took care of the issue personally." Averell interrupted with an apologetic look at Leo. "Cooke informed me. Care for something from the sideboard, Stewart?"

"Bourbon, if you have it. Thank you."

"Leo, if you will." The duke gestured towards his brother, who glared daggers at him, but nonetheless poured out three glasses of bourbon whiskey and set them on the table.

"I did what I thought necessary to guarantee her safety, both at the time and in the future. Dictating to Phaedra that she simply not return to Hagerty's would have been a wasted effort. Torrington tried. I made sure she could return without encountering future harm." Morgan took a glass and rolled it between his fingers. "I would do so again."

"You must have counted yourself fortunate that you had an opportunity to spin your web so quickly." Murphy drained his glass and slammed it on the table. "You wanted to get Rutherford's attention," he accused.

These comparisons to a spider were rapidly becoming annoying. Cooke's fault, though a bottle shared between them the other night had resolved a great deal of animosity. Morgan would even look on Rutherford with more charity, though he'd left Gertie after finding out she was with child. But he had saved Morgan, making sure he didn't hang for Gertie's murder. At any rate, the more Cooke had to drink, the more he kept comparing Morgan's schemes to webs. Not flattering.

"Are you disappointed, Murphy, that my talents weren't all directed at you?" Morgan held up his hand. "Apologies. I didn't come here to argue."

"You assumed Rutherford murdered Gertrude Van Rhys. You wanted to know what happened to her." There was a thoughtful look in the blue of Averell's gaze. "But he didn't kill her. Nor did you. It is my understanding that the true culprit has been...apprehended." Averell gave him an elegant wave. "As I said, Cooke explained some things to me."

"You were going to bankrupt Elysium," Murphy choked out, "and compromise Phaedra."

"I only accomplished one of those things."

A low sound came from Murphy.

"I'm curious. Did you make the wager before or *after* you met Phaedra?" Averell stroked his elegant fingers along the cut crystal of his glass.

"Before I ever set eyes on her."

"And after. Did you still intend to use her to force the issue at hand? Keep in mind that while I don't care for your methods, or the fact that you were going to use my sister and brother to achieve your aim, I do understand your motivation."

Averell was much more intelligent and less pompous than he let on.

Morgan considered his answer carefully. "I found after a time, I could not. I decided on another way to garner Rutherford's attention."

"By becoming my partner without my knowledge and threatening The Barrington. You were going to hold my hotel hostage by purchasing contracts from all my suppliers. You bought the land in London I planned to use for another Barrington hotel."

That vein in Murphy's forehead was really alarming. If he collapsed during this discussion Averell might never give him Phaedra.

"I do not deny it, just as I did not the night you were in my home. The only way to get to Rutherford was going to be through the people close to him. But Rutherford aside, my proposal is still sound. Generous, even."

"Get out." Murphy slammed a palm on the table.

"I've read through the proposal Mr. Armwood originally presented." Averell ignored his brother's outburst. "Regardless of your original motivations, the terms *are* generous. Your suggestions make sense. Leo will realize it once he calms down, won't you?"

Murphy threw Averell a hateful look.

"Leo, how often have you said that one day we won't be able to depend on income from Cherry Hill and our other estates? How our family must diversify if we are to maintain our wealth while others allow theirs to fade. You wanted that property in London for another hotel, and I suspect"— Averell turned to Morgan once more—"that with a few adjustments to the contract, you'll have it. Then there is the matter of your railways, right Stewart? We want a share of what you currently own in England, which I'm told is substantial."

"How much?" Morgan was surprised by Averell's demand, though it didn't matter in the least. He only wanted Phaedra.

"Twenty percent. If you are going to be a partner of The Barrington and its future enterprises, I think it only fair we share in your good fortune as well." Averell leaned towards him. "I don't just strut around being ducal. I pay attention to what is happening around me. Leo isn't the only one with ambition. You"—he nodded at Murphy—"wanted Armwood's proposal before this entire mess revealed itself. We discussed it at length. You are only dismayed that Stewart is far more manipulative than you are."

Murphy grumbled and poured out another finger of bourbon.

"But let us return to the subject at hand." The duke's eyes, that mysterious blue with the ring of indigo, pierced him. "You ruined her. And just because you did doesn't mean I intend to hand her over. I can easily find her a husband in London. Well." He shrugged. "Not easily. Phaedra is a bit of a challenge. Still, I can't have you bankrupting Elysium."

Morgan's fingers stretched across the table, not appreciating Averell's little threat. "I'll agree to your terms regarding my properties in England. The proposal to become an investor in The Barrington and future enterprises involving the hotel stands. You can have the property in London, I don't care. For the record, I don't want your little pleasure palace."

"More gambling hell," Averell corrected.

"I only want *her*. Let me be clear." Morgan gave them both an icy look, reining in the impulse to just strangle them both. "There is nothing you can do to keep me from Phaedra. This call is a courtesy. I want your blessing for her sake, not my own. If you attempt to marry her off, she'll be widowed almost immediately." He sat back. "I've no desire to estrange Phaedra from her family, whom she loves, despite the poor decision to accept ridiculous wagers placed on her at Elysium."

Murphy flinched. "In hindsight, a poor idea."

"She will want for nothing. Not wealth, attention, and especially not affection. Her happiness means everything to me."

Murphy started to open his mouth, and Averell placed a hand on his sleeve. "My father, the previous duke, stipulated that Phaedra was to have a choice in whom she weds. Ruination or not. Gentleman from the worst part of New York, *or not*. Leo, her affections are fixed on Stewart. If we do not allow her this choice, she will never forgive either of us."

"If you ever so much as cause her a moment of unhappiness," Murphy said in a low voice, "you won't live long enough to regret it, Stewart. You aren't the only one with a bit of muck on his coat."

"Fair enough," Morgan growled. He appreciated a good threat.

"I'll reconsider your proposal, after Armwood makes changes to include the railway and the property in London. The Barrington is to have a discount from any importer of food, spirits, or anything else that you own now or in the future. The hotel receives the best of what is brought to these shores."

The urge to rid the world of Leo Murphy became that much stronger. "Agreed."

"Her dowry—" Averell started to speak.

"I don't want it." Morgan tossed back the bourbon in his glass. "If you must, put it in an account that she can access and I cannot touch. One you control. We will live here, in New York, but she will be free to visit London when she wishes."

Averell calmly sipped his drink. "I'll assume that means you'll be coming as well."

"Set another place at your ducal dinner table, Averell. There is only one other matter we should discuss. A thirty percent share in Elysium."

"I knew it. I suppose if I don't, you'll attempt to bankrupt me." Murphy burst into laughter. "Absolutely not. No."

"You've just said you have no interest in Elysium, Stewart. So why would you want a stake in our gambling hell?" Averell watched him carefully.

Morgan smiled. He was finished with trying to do things properly. Now he was only annoyed and wanted to see Phaedra.

"It's a wedding gift for my bride."

27

"**G**ood evening, *schatje.*"

Phaedra paused at the door of the small parlor that was part of her apartments at The Barrington. Her suite of rooms, which originally had been used by Leo and his family, were on the other side of the massive family parlor and separate from the other Barringtons. Thankfully, considering the unexpected guest seated before the fire.

"You."

"Yes, *me.*" He made a resigned sound. "It will always be me."

She had just come up to her room after dining with her family. A meal that had dragged on with far more courses than necessary as Leo's newly hired chef, this one from Vienna and not Paris, was attempting to impress them all. Her brothers had mentioned not one word about Morgan or their meeting with him, only saying that an agreement had been reached. The only clue to how things had gone was the vein still protruding in Leo's forehead.

Tony had looked far too calm.

"How did you get in here?" She caught a whiff of smoke and apples. Morgan's scent. She wanted to curl into it. Run to him.

"Chipplewit." The lamp cast most of his features in shadow, and he had a book in his lap. The only thing missing was a pot of tea at his elbow. Perhaps a cat. Meanwhile, Phaedra was—

Angry. Hurt. Relieved.

"I didn't want to interrupt your dinner. I think I've done enough damage recently." He seemed strangely unsure of himself. "So I decided to wait for you here."

"You didn't want to interrupt my bloody dinner? You, who have lacked every consideration for me in the past by invading my existence. A man who basically stalked me from London to Cherry Hill, then across the damned ocean. *You* didn't want to keep me from the trout in wine sauce?" Phaedra was suddenly so furious at Morgan. So intensely annoyed, she stomped her feet to make her point. "You've no idea how I feel."

"Phaedra," Morgan said calmly. "I'm—"

"Not prepared for this, are you, scheming spider? Suggesting I go back to England and wed some twit? Emberly, for instance? Or perhaps Lord Ashley."

A blast of frost hit her. "I thought...you might want that after everything you saw. And heard. I wanted you to have the choice if it was too much. If *I* was too much."

"So you would just cheerfully abandon me to some ancient duke? Or a mincing fop."

"I don't believe the word cheerful was ever used or even implied." Ice coated his words. He shook his head and reached for her. "You are incredibly hostile this evening. More so than usual. Come here."

Phaedra slapped at him. "And if Ben hadn't come? Would you have let Van Rhys shoot you?"

Morgan looked away. "Cooke did arrive in time, so the answer is irrelevant."

"Answer the bloody question."

"If it would have saved you, yes," he snapped, turning his chin to take her in once more. "I make no apology for it. There is nothing I would not have done. I've no idea why you are so angry."

"You were willing to abandon me." Her lips trembled. "Whether to death or to some fop in London without even putting up a protest."

"Phaedra."

"Leave me to flounder about with no one else who appreciates my ability to calculate the odds at a hazard table." A tear slipped from one eye, and she wiped it away. "*Me*. Whom you claim to adore."

"I do adore you." He tried to take her hand, and she slapped at him again. "I would never leave you by choice if there was another way. Surely, you realize that."

"Yes, well." She wiped at her tears. "The last person to tell me that is buried at Cherry Hill. And I—" All the crushing loss, the grief which never stopped pricking at her, suddenly crashed over Phaedra in a wave. She pressed the heels of her hands against her eyes before she collapsed in a fit of tears, something she had never done. What if she fainted after sobbing? Morgan would have to fetch the smelling salts.

"*Schatje*." He pulled her, protesting, into his lap. "Marcus Barrington did not leave you because he wanted to."

"I know it isn't the same." She glared at him and thumped her chest with a fist. "But it feels the same, Morgan. *Here*. You aren't even at all alike. I know that." She wiped at her cheeks. "But when you were willing to give me up. Leave me alone in the world. Send me to Emberly..." She looked down at her hands.

"Who is Emberly?" Morgan growled.

"It isn't important. I thought I was being ridiculous, but then you didn't come to get me. And I—"

"I didn't come right away because I thought you would need some time after what happened." Morgan's lips moved over her hair. "I regretted telling you to return to England the moment the words left me. Had you done so, I would only have gone after you."

Phaedra sniffed. "You would have?"

"Yes. We will not be leaving each other to flounder about, as you so aptly put it, Phaedra. I will always come for you."

"I will not abandon you either." She snuggled against him, vastly relieved. "You know that, don't you?"

"Yes." His voice was rough and his eyes the color of mist. "I do."

Phaedra nipped at his throat. "Did you ask for my hand properly? Without threat of piano wire?"

"No violence was required to negotiate terms. Averell has agreed."

Phaedra blew out a sigh of relief. "Well, I'm completely ruined, so I suppose Tony thought he had little option."

A chuckle rumbled in his chest. "You must agree to wed me, of course. That was his stipulation." A blunt finger trailed down her cheek.

"You are my choice," she pressed her lips to his.

"It means living in New York, not London. But we'll visit."

"I assumed as much." She thought of her dream, of Papa eating strawberries and gesturing towards Morgan lurking in the shadows. "The wager was much like the Iliad. Now I understand." Phaedra hiccuped. At Morgan's look she said, "Something my father once told me."

He hugged her into his warmth. "Will you be all right now, ferocious creature? No more tears?" He kissed the wetness of her cheeks. "I cannot bear to have you distressed. After that day with Martin. What Cooke and I—"

"I don't care about Van Rhys," she said firmly. "Or what happened to him. I mean..." She sniffed. "Objectively, I probably should. But he was going to shoot me and—he wasn't a terribly good person."

"*I* am not a terribly good person." Morgan shifted, cupping both sides of her face with his big hands.

"You aren't, Morgan." He could be, though. Morgan had a streak of gentleness in him. A heart, well hidden. Something good that Sister Bridget hadn't been able to destroy. Gertrude Van Rhys had seen it. That's why she'd saved him.

Morgan grabbed her by the back of her head, fingers sinking into her hair, and kissed Phaedra so hard, she couldn't breathe. Couldn't gasp. Certainly, couldn't cry.

"You," he whispered, his voice thick.

"Yes." She pressed her forehead to Morgan's, repeating his earlier words. "Always me."

"I cannot be apart from you, Phaedra. I no longer live well without you. I promise to cherish you until I take my last breath. Protect you. Love you. You may behave, or not." He brushed her lips with his. "My nature will never fully fade, but for you, I will try to be better."

Phaedra pressed her mouth to his. "I love you."

He picked her up, carrying her into the adjoining bedroom, and pushed her down on the bed. Morgan undressed her with agonizing slowness, no matter how she urged him to hurry. At every swath of newly exposed skin, he paused to trail his lips and tongue over the spot, worshipping at the edge of her shoulder and the delicate curve of her collarbone before finding the crest of her nipple. Her fingers shook as she undid each of the buttons on his shirt. Flung his cravat to the side and spread her fingers across the broad stretch of his chest.

A low moan left her as Morgan's body twisted around hers. He'd bedded her several times but never quite like this.

Even though she writhed and begged him for more, to take her hard, Morgan resisted. He adored every part of Phaedra, imprinting himself on her body and heart, leaving no doubt as to the truth of his own feelings.

Phaedra caressed every scar, each horrible wound Morgan bore that had nearly broken his soul, promising with every touch of her lips that no one would ever hurt him again. Phaedra would anchor him firmly. Tether him to her. Temper his darkness. Allow him to be a better man.

MUCH LATER, PHAEDRA LAY ON HER SIDE, BODY SHELTERED in the hollow of Morgan's. The sheets twisted about their hips as she wiggled closer to the heat at her back. He was still buried inside her, his hips moving ever so slightly against her buttocks.

"I'm not a good man, Phaedra," he breathed along the curve of her ear.

"You've said as much. No need to repeat yourself. I believe you." She wiggled back against him suggestively. "I can't believe my brothers actually agreed to let you have me."

"I never said they were pleased." He squeezed her until she let out a squeak.

She pressed a kiss to the arm curled around her. "Ben told me everything, Morgan. I understand why you went to such an extreme over Rutherford. I don't blame you. She was your mother, and you only wanted to know what happened to her." Her fingers laced with his. "I am so sorry for her loss, Morgan."

Morgan nuzzled along her throat.

"In my need to find out the truth, I may have gone farther than I should have. Gertie wouldn't have approved, by the way, though she would have liked you." He nipped at her neck. "I'm going to work on that in the future. But some good has come from it."

"You're speaking to Ben again. And not as enemies." She trailed a finger along his arm. Much of Morgan's bitterness at the world stemmed from what he thought of as Ben's betrayal. "I'm glad, considering that Olivia is wed to him. Would have made things awkward during family gatherings if you tried to kill each other."

A grunt was his response.

"I'll assume Tony took your offer for me better than Leo."

"You are correct. Murphy detests me. He probably always will."

"You'll have to charm my mother. She considers you a thug."

"I am a thug, Phaedra. In a manner of speaking."

"You are a brilliant man of business who tends to be ruthless at times. I think once the initial shock recedes, my mother will like you, or at least become used to you. Haven will be thrilled to make your acquaintance. Truly."

"What does that mean?" His fingers trailed along her stomach.

"Let me just say that Torrington is the only one Leo and Tony like, largely due to his ability with cake, which I believe I've mentioned. Though I'm sure neither is pleased he knew I was visiting Haggerty's and didn't inform them. But in you"—she kissed him—"Leo and Tony have finally found someone they dislike more than Theo's husband, Haven. He's sure to be appreciative."

"Hmm. There are some things I would like to tell you." He held up his hand where the mark lay on the skin above his wrist. "I'll start with this."

Phaedra pressed a kiss to the brand she knew Sister Bridget had given him. "I'm listening."

EPILOGUE

L ondon was never going to be one of Morgan's favorite cities. He felt out of place here, as if the stain of his birth was painted on his back. Or the titled twits who often circled him in such a wary fashion caught the scent of Five Points. He was a source of curiosity, he supposed. The brutal American who had wed *The Disastrous Barrington*.

Morgan and Phaedra had been married in New York barely a week after the negotiation with her brothers, delaying the family's departure for London. The news of the marriage of Lady Phaedra, sister of the Duke of Averell, to the notorious Morgan Stewart had sent Manhattan society into a frenzy. At first, very few had believed it to be true, only a ridiculous rumor.

The rumors had been put to rest by an appearance at the Rutherford Opera house, where Morgan and Phaedra had shared a box with the dowager duchess, Cooke, and Olivia.

They'd left for London the following month, and to say Morgan had been welcomed to the city with open arms would have been an exaggeration. But he'd expected that. The dowager duchess hadn't quite warmed up to him yet. Might take years. Or at least longer than this first visit to London.

And the entire city knew about the wager in Elysium's Red Book.

There was a great deal of speculation over whether Morgan collected on the wager. He did not. But only because Murphy and Averell had granted Phaedra thirty percent ownership in Elysium. Armwood's generous proposal had been signed with the stipulation that Morgan stay a silent partner.

At his core, Murphy was a man of business. He wasn't going to walk away from a deal that would likely make him enormously wealthy no matter how much he hated the new member of the family.

Morgan didn't much care for his new brother-in-law either, he mused, keeping his back to the wall and surveyed the guests crowding the Averell mansion's ballroom.

Both of Phaedra's sisters were in attendance this evening, along with the Duke of Granby and the Marquess of Haven. The Barringtons were all blessed in their appearance, so it was no surprise both of Phaedra's sisters were stunning. The Duchess of Granby was beautiful and still glowing after the recent birth of her husband's heir.

And after meeting Lady Haven, Morgan thought she was more deserving of the title *The Disastrous Barrington*, given she'd painted a nude self-portrait to give to a man *other* than the one she'd wed.

As for Haven? It was hard to dislike the man who had gotten Phaedra interested in swords.

An image of his wife last night in their rooms, clad only in a filmy bit of silk and lace, with her nipples hard as buttons, prancing about and slicing away at his clothing, floated before him. When she'd cut the button off his trousers, waiting for him to flinch, Morgan's cock had nearly shredded the fabric in its desire to get to his lovely *schatje*.

A disgruntled sound came from him as he swallowed the entire flute of champagne clasped in his hand. No bourbon or even a decent Irish whiskey to be found at this gathering. Murphy's doing. Morgan knew for a fact that the ducal bastard kept bourbon on hand at Elysium for Georgina. Phaedra knew nearly everything about the gambling hell, including what sorts of spirits were gathering dust in the basement.

Escorting Phaedra to Elysium upon their arrival in London and announcing that a third of the gambling hell was now hers had led his wife to be incredibly grateful. She'd taken his hand, leading him down the hall to one of the rooms used for pleasure on the second floor. Once inside, Phaedra had knelt before him and—well, at some point he planned to ask her where she'd learned how to use her tongue in such a manner. Then she'd asked him to tie her to the bed.

"Damn." He adjusted his coat. He may have to buy her every gambling hell in London.

He snagged another glass of champagne from a passing servant and wondered what sort of trouble Phaedra might be causing.

"Here." A hand holding what looked like bourbon hovered before him. "Never cared for champagne myself. I doubt you do." Haven, dressed in formal wear but still managing to look disreputable, like some alley cat who'd just been in a brawl, held up his own glass. "Consider it a thank you for improving my standing in the family. I didn't think it was possible for Murphy and Averell to hate anyone more than me."

"Glad I could help."

"The bottle is tucked safely away." Haven took a sip from his own glass and winced. "An acquired taste, I'm guessing.

Your wife had Peckham send it today. Made sure Pith didn't see because that bastard would certainly hide it out of spite."

"Most likely." The Averell butler, Pith, was nothing short of unwelcoming. If Morgan was served cold eggs one more day, he and Pith may need to have a pointed conversation. He looked up just then, catching sight of Phaedra moving confidently about in a mauve silk gown, absent of any decoration but the enormous diamonds swinging from her ears. Another wedding gift. His wife didn't care overmuch for jewels but she wore the diamonds to please him.

Phaedra blew him a kiss, ignoring the disapproving glare of two elderly matrons to her left.

Sassy, marvelous creature.

A deep ache stretched out from his heart, tearing at his insides. He took a deep swallow of the bourbon. Every fiber of his being was in love with Phaedra Barrington. Completely absorbed by her. No one had ever explained how painful the feeling could be.

"Averell refers to you as *the miscreant*, by the way." Haven took another tentative swallow of the bourbon. "Far nicer than you probably deserve, given the things I've heard."

Morgan only raised a brow. "All true."

"I'm *the parasite*," Haven groused. "Granby is *the ice giant*."

He'd met the Duke of Granby and disliked him on sight. Probably the only thing he, Averell, and Murphy would ever agree upon.

"Torrington is welcomed only because he always arrives with the duke's favorite cake in hand. Chocolate toffee, if you're wondering."

"I wasn't." He liked lemon tarts. Lady Torrington was kind enough to send him one every day or so. "Who is that?" Morgan observed some overindulged idiot stalking in the direction of Phaedra.

"Lord Emberly. You can't kill him," Haven said. "Or do what you did to Fairwood."

"Not planning to." But Morgan could *imagine* snapping Emberly's neck all he liked. "Fairwood was an accident."

Lord Fairwood had dared to not only make a wager on Phaedra in Elysium's Red Book but had the audacity to attempt to see it through.

Two hundred pounds to caress the spine of The Disastrous Barrington.

"You broke three of his fingers."

"Weak handshake."

Haven grinned. "Did you enjoy dinner last night? The meal was much improved since my last visit. I have you to thank for that. Pith has never poisoned one of us, but he might risk it with you."

"So there's more to him than cold eggs."

The Averell butler stood just to the right of the main doors of the ballroom. His proper, seething dislike of Morgan was impossible to miss. Cooke had warned him to expect the cold eggs at breakfast, weak coffee, and small portions at every meal, and that was only if the meat wasn't entirely charred or basically raw. He hadn't mentioned poison.

If Phaedra hadn't been so set on staying at the Averell mansion and the dowager duchess determined to throw a lavish ball to celebrate her youngest daughter's nuptials, Morgan would have rented a house a discreet distance away where he could be alone with his wife and not starve.

"Your Grace," Haven bowed.

Taking his cue from Haven, Morgan made a small bow at the approach of the dowager duchess, Phaedra's mother. He'd done everything possible to charm her, and none of it had worked. What she had wanted was him not to wed Phaedra, but that was an impossibility. That she accepted his presence was the nicest thing Morgan could say.

"If you'll excuse me," Haven said. "I believe I'll go look for my wife. Make sure she isn't running into anything or mistaking one of your statues for a servant." He shot Morgan a look, mouthed the words, *small green parlor*, which Morgan assumed was the location of the bottle of bourbon, and wandered off.

"What do you think of the ball?" the dowager duchess asked in her crisp tone, looking down at the glass in his hand.

"Splendid."

"I see you don't appreciate champagne. Unsurprising." Her lips drew together, reminding him of Phaedra. "Phaedra has always known her own mind, which does not mean her opinions are always correct. My husband doted on her. They were exceptionally close. That closeness led him to give her an education and interest in things that are not appropriate for a young lady. Attempts to interest her in things of a more pleasant nature failed."

"The violin," Morgan said. "For instance."

The dowager duchess gave him a sharp look. "A young lady should have talents of her own and an appreciation for music, don't you think, Mr. Stewart?"

"I suppose so. You should probably refer to me as Morgan, Your Grace."

Her lips drew into a tight bud of disapproval. "Phaedra's talent on the violin was...limited. We were all grateful to Haven for suggesting Phaedra take up fencing. She took to it immediately, as she already had a pronounced interest in weaponry. You can imagine that the violin did not stand a chance. My husband"—her voice faltered slightly—"enjoyed military history. Gory, bloody battles. Axes. Spears. Knives. Things most young ladies wouldn't care to read. I suppose that is where her unhealthy interest stems from." She looked down her nose at Morgan, which was amusing since he was a great deal taller.

"Her unhealthy interest?"

"In you, Mr. Stewart." Her discerning gaze ran over Morgan in his dark formal wear. "You clean up well enough, I suppose. Your manners are apparent when you care to use them."

"Thank you."

"It wasn't meant as a compliment, more an observation. None of the gentlemen in London were to Phaedra's taste, though I suppose if I had found a highwayman or an illiterate boxer at Hagerty's, her head might have turned. Tony overindulged her. Took her to Elysium. Allowed her to count markers for him. Manage the ledgers. Terrible breach of etiquette. But Phaedra has never been happy with the conventional. She's far too curious. Intuitive. Manipulative, at times. Marcus was like that. I'm trying to decide what he would have thought of you."

Formidable. That was the word for Her Grace. Much like her daughter, the dowager duchess had little fear of him.

"I hope we would have gotten on." He took another thoughtful sip. She reminded him of Gertie. A spine of absolute steel.

"We'll never know, will we?"

Morgan had promised Phaedra he would try to accommodate her mother, who was terribly upset about Phaedra's defection to New York. And him. He'd vowed during the entire crossing to rein in his chilly manner and be as polite and gracious as possible upon their arrival in London. But the dowager duchess did not make things easy. Her dislike of him was apparent, as was her worry for Phaedra.

"I know what you must think of me, madam. Indeed, my reputation in some instances is justified. But for Phaedra..." Morgan caught sight of her speaking to Emberly across the ballroom.

She looked up, her smile fading at the sight of her mother beside him.

"I am a different man. A better one." He pressed a palm over his heart. "I cannot promise not to overindulge her, because I likely will. She is brilliant and bold. Ferocious. And I will protect her until the end of my days."

She nodded slowly. "I'll hold you to that, Mr. Stewart." But there was a hint of a smile on her lips. "A duchess knows how to remove obstacles as well." She sailed off, having delivered her thinly veiled threat, into the crowd.

Nearly every member of Phaedra's family had threatened him so far. It was becoming rather commonplace.

"I should have gotten here sooner," Phaedra breathed as she rushed to his side and took his hand. "Was she horribly insulting?"

"No, not at all. How is Lord Emberly?" He wanted to sink his nose into her neck and inhale the smell of wild roses.

"Terrified you'd see him congratulating me on our nuptials and possibly strangle him. He's quite harmless, Morgan. Really, I could take him in fisticuffs. Which means you could knock him over with just a flick of your wrist. Did you and the dowager duchess have a pleasant conversation?"

"As pleasant as possible." Morgan laughed softly. "I have been exceptionally charming to her this evening." He handed his empty glass to a passing servant. "May I have this dance, Mrs. Stewart?"

Phaedra took his hand, brushing her slender form against his, enough so that Morgan sucked in a breath at the way his cock stiffened despite being in a room full of people who were all watching them.

"*Lady* Phaedra," she murmured.

"I don't think so." Morgan's hand brushed lightly over her stomach, thinking of his child already growing within. They would spend a few more weeks in London before returning to New York to settle in and await the birth.

Phaedra grinned at him. "You."

"Yes, me. Always me." He leaned over and trailed his mouth along her neck. "Come, my ferocious creature." Morgan swung her into his arms, enjoying her pleased gasp of surprise that he moved so well across the floor. They hadn't yet danced together.

Dozens of eyes followed them as he twirled her about, all waiting for Morgan to make a misstep, but he knew how to dance.

Gertie had taught him.

THANK YOU FOR READING **THE TAMING OF A SCANDAL.** If you loved the story please **Leave a review!**

The Beautiful Barringtons isn't over! Stay tuned! In the meantime, please stay in touch!

Sign up for **my newsletter** and you'll be the first to know what's coming up next! Join my reader group **here** for cover reveals and bonus excerpts.

For a complete list of books and reading order please visit www.kathleenayers.com

AUTHOR NOTES

First, ***schatje,*** the endearment Morgan uses for Phaedra. The modern use of the word can be translated to darling, dear, sweetie, etc. But looking at usage in the 19th century, the more literal translation was "little treasure"...at least according to my research. Apologies to my Dutch readers if I've unintentionally misused.

I've mentioned before in my notes for my previous books (Wager of a Lady, Making of a Gentleman) that the history of New York City fascinates me. The upper class created before 1850 was the starting point for the Gilded Age. The Dutch and English families who first settled Manhattan (such as Martin Van Rhys) were eventually forced to accept men like **Jacob Rutherford**, **Benjamin Cooke** and **Morgan Stewart**. I highly recommend *In Pursuit of Privilege: A History of New York City's Upper Class* by Clifton Hood.

The Barrington is based on the first luxury hotel in New York City, Astor House (originally named the Park Hotel). Built by John Jacob Astor and opened in 1836, Astor House took up an entire city block on Broadway Street (much like The Barrington). Astor House had running water pumped up by steam engines, boasted water closets on every floor and provided guests with French milled soap. The English garden and rooftop garden at The Barrington are both products of my imagination.

Five Points where Morgan Stewart grows up in Sister Bridget's brothel (along with Benjamin Cooke) was one of the worst crime-infested slums in the world during the 19th century rivaling St. Giles in London. Located in Lower Manhattan, the area of Five Points stretched near a large lake known as the Collection Pond (or Collect Pond) which over the years became a dumping ground for slaughterhouses and other refuse.

Mohawk & Hudson was the first railroad built in New York and the first transportation rival of the Erie Canal. Morgan's involvement is of course, my own invention.

The Battery where Van Rhys takes Phaedra for their ill-fated outing was first the site of a fort built by the Dutch and it was there the English demanded the surrender of New Amsterdam (New York). Renamed Fort George in 1714, The Battery housed the Continental Army, then became the site of several forts to repel the British during the War of 1812. By the time of Phaedra's visit, The Battery is a park, complete with amphitheater, amusements, and a visit by the Marquis Lafayette in 1824.

And lastly, this is a work of fiction. I sometimes bend historical facts now and again for the sake of the story.